INNOCENT CORINNA

by

FAITH EDEN

CHIMERA

Innocent Corinna first published in 1998 by
Chimera Publishing Ltd
PO Box 152
Waterlooville
Hants
PO8 9FS

Printed and bound in Great Britain by
Caledonian International Book Manufacturing Ltd
Glasgow

All Characters in this publication are fictitious. Any resemblance to real persons, living or dead, is purely coincidental.

Copyright Faith Eden

The right of Faith Eden to be identified as author of this book has been asserted in accordance with section 77 and 78 of the Copyrights Designs and Patents Act 1988

New authors welcome

INNOCENT CORINNA

Faith Eden

This novel is fiction – in real life practice safe sex

Chapter One

Corinna recognised the girl. It was the mute pantry maid, Kirsta, a dark-haired little thing of no more than eighteen summers, younger by two years, even, than Corinna herself. The man she did not know, though his uniform was the black leather and mail of the palace guards, that humourless, almost faceless body of hulking brutes, whose sworn duty it was to maintain the safety of the royal family of Illeum.

At this present moment, however, Corinna could see his mind was far from that particular duty. He sat himself squarely on the stump of the ancient ash, the one that had been destroyed by a lightning bolt in the year of Corinna's birth, and beckoned to the serving wench. Her face, which in the pale moonlight Corinna could see in three quarter profile, betrayed not the slightest flicker of emotion, and the one eye that was visible to the hidden watcher appeared dull and lifeless.

The man grunted, apparently impatient at the girl's slow progress, but Kirsta made no attempt to walk faster, each step across the small clearing a quite deliberate affair, her feet, just visible beneath the hem of her long woollen skirts, dragging over the rough ground. From the sanctuary of her leafy hiding place, Corinna stared, transfixed, knowing she was about to witness something quite singular, even if she did not yet know what it was.

At last Kirsta stood immediately before the guard, who gestured with a jabbing finger at the crude belt that encircled her slender waist. She appeared to understand and her hands moved to the clumsy clasp. A moment later belt and skirts were sliding to the floor, revealing a pair of well rounded legs, atop which sat a pair of even more well rounded buttocks. Corinna bit her lip and felt certain that, in the still night air, her involuntary intake of breath must have carried to the centre of the clearing.

If it did, however, the pair before her were clearly too engrossed to take note of anything other than what was happening between themselves. The guard grunted again and gestured with a downward movement of his thumb. Kirsta hesitated, but only for the briefest moment and then stepped forward again, lowering herself across his lap, turning to present her naked rump towards Corinna and settling, legs slightly splayed to reveal the dark shadow of her pubic bush, her gaping sex lips and the smaller, puckered hole of her bottom.

The guard's broad, hairy hand spread out to cover one of the fleshy globes, kneading and stroking it, until his fingers suddenly dipped and Corinna saw two of them prising apart Kirsta's pink cleft. A low whinnying sound echoed around the surrounding trees, a peculiar, inhuman noise, and Corinna saw the girl's legs spasm as the two digits penetrated her.

Corinna felt her own sex growing warm and, as she looked down, realised her right hand was pressing into her groin through the flimsy material of her evening gown. With a pang of conscience she tore the hand away, but, as she returned her gaze to the tableau before her, it crept inexorably back to its target.

The guard's movements were becoming more urgent now, the fingers thrusting in and out, Kirsta's bare feet kicking at thin air, but then suddenly he stopped. His arm drew back and then swept down, palm open once again and the sound of flesh upon flesh was like a carter's whipcrack in the night silence. Corinna let out a stifled yelp and tensed, ready to creep away into the undergrowth, but her involuntary utterance appeared to have gone unheeded.

The hand descended again with another whiplash explosion and, as it rose for a third time, Corinna saw the twin scarlet patches on Kirsta's defenceless flesh. Four, five, six times the hand slapped against raw flesh, until Corinna had lost count of the number of blows. With his free hand the guard kept pressing down into the small of the maid's back, yet, though she kicked and threshed, she did not appear to be making any real attempt to break free.

Between her own legs Corinna now felt a trickling damp and closed her eyes, breaths coming more rapidly now, knowing that the flimsy underdrawers were fast becoming soaked with her juices, but past heeding the fact that she would have to be careful to discard them before returning to the bed chamber.

The incessant spanking suddenly ceased and Corinna forced her eyes open again. In the clearing, Kirsta was rising to her feet, though with some considerable difficulty and indeed, she did not remain standing for long. At a nod from the guard she dropped to her knees and he, for his part, began fumbling with the front fastenings of his leather breeches. In the bushes Corinna craned her neck forward, eager for a clearer view, and she was not disappointed.

From the opening in the breeches, a thick, fleshy shaft suddenly sprung into sight, a rigid pole of masculinity that Corinna could scarcely believe was human. The guard spread his knees, reached out and seized Kirsta's mop of dark curls and drew her head forward. Corinna's mouth fell open nearly as wide as did that of the maid as the younger girl bobbed to devour at least half the length of the guard's phallus.

Back and forth, up and down went her head and Corinna saw now that the man's eyes were screwed tightly shut, his grip on Kirsta's hair relaxed, so that now she worked on him unheeded. His breathing was hoarse and rapid, loud enough for Corinna to hear every lungful of air both in and out, and his swarthy features bore a crimson flush.

Innocent though she was, Corinna understood exactly what was happening and, to her horror, she suddenly realised she was jealous of the sluttish maid. To the gods, she thought, whatever is happening to me? Yet still she could not tear herself away from the scene.

As though at a prearranged signal, Kirsta abruptly disengaged her mouth, drawing back her head to reveal the glistening member, veins bulging through stretched flesh, the purplish knob impossibly distended. She rose once more on unsteady limbs, pushed the guard's knees closer together and then straddled his lap. Hands gripping his shoulders for support, she slowly lowered herself, knees flexing.

The huge shaft pressed against her swollen lips and for a few seconds it appeared to Corinna that it must be far too large to enter the girl. But no, to the accompaniment of animal groan and answering squeak, the knob forced entry and then, in one downward lunge, Kirsta had taken the entire shaft within her.

Corinna thrust the knuckles of her right fist between her teeth, the palm of her left hand against her groin, and doubled over in a shattering orgasm of her own...

Chapter Two

The tiny hamlet was almost too insignificant to have a name, but it did. It was called Veris Lee, though few men living more than half a day's ride from it would have known to begin with, let alone remember it. However, to those men who did live and work within that distance, Veris Lee possessed one priceless asset, whose name would be of more significance than that of the village itself.

That asset was called The Wagonmaster, and it was a tavern. And The Wagonmaster, in its turn, possessed its own asset. She was called Moxie, and she was the tavern keeper's eldest daughter.

At first glance, the connoisseurs from among the more wealthy citizens of Illeum might have considered Moxie little to turn the eye, for her clothing was spartan, woven from plain cloth and with little embellishment, and her reddish brown mane was a persistent tangle of unkempt curls and grime. However, for the true connoisseur, there was a singularly latent potential to be considered.

Not yet quite eighteen, Moxie had the broad hips and full bosom of a woman of thirty, yet her face, beneath the smoky smudges which the inn's open hearth daily deposited upon it, was as fresh and virginal as any man could desire. And, curiously, given the times and the circumstances, the rosy cheeked Moxie was indeed still a virgin, her maidenhead held intact firstly by her ability to deliver a telling blow with a right arm made powerful by several years of womanhandling heavy casks in the cellar and, secondly, by her innate distaste for the average male patron at her father's hostelry.

There was also another possibility, but Moxie, despite her enviable command of the vernacular and her ability to comprehend even the most crude nuance from among the most ribald of her customers, would have known nothing of such things. For her part, she was only too well aware of the stirrings her generously fresh figure aroused in the rustic loins of the regular drinkers in The Wagonmaster, and she spent her young working life as much fending off their crude advances, as she did in keeping their pewter pots continually charged.

From his vantage point behind the bar counter, Heskath, her balding father, did little, if anything, to curb the excesses of his clientele. His daughter, he knew only too well, was the house's major attraction – that and the fact that it was the only inn for ten miles in any direction. Certainly the men who crowded nightly into the dimly lit bar were not attracted by the warm, flat ale that was the regular fare.

Regular fare perhaps, though there were alternatives, sought generally only by the odd itinerant who might stumble across the establishment by chance, usually as a much needed break in a long journey. And that description, Heskath considered, fitted admirably the small party occupying the furthest of the three darkened booths which ran along the wall to the far side of the fireplace.

They were wealthy travellers, without doubt, for even without the cut and quality of their clothing to betray their pedigree, there was a bearing about them that came only with money, or power. Or both.

The presence of the four man escort was another obvious pointer. Only two of them had remained inside, lounging with that relaxed assuredness of the professional fighting man against one end of the bar, ostensibly enjoying their own flagons of ale, but all the time poised like massive cats, alert for the first sign of any potential threat to their employers. Doubtless, Heskath thought, their two companions were within earshot of the door and he suspected that there might be even more guards out there with them that they had not yet seen.

It was the woman they were there for, of that Heskath was certain. The two men, apart from appearing capable of taking care of themselves, from time to time allowed sideways glances to stray in the direction of the two inside soldiers. She, on the other hand, maintained a cool detachment, her green eyes never wavering from where her companions sat opposite her, the fabulous mane of deep red hair hardly stirring. Before her, the tall glass of wine remained untouched.

'Everything is set, I presume?' the leaner and older of the two men asked. His nose was shaped like a hawk's and his narrow eyes were deepset and dark-ringed. The woman regarded him with a slightly disdainful air.

'Naturally,' she replied, her voice cool and well modulated.

'And your man knows exactly what he must do?'

The woman's face twitched in a gesture of impatience. 'My man, as you call him, knows *exactly* what is to be done,' she said. 'He will be where he must be and do what needs doing, as I am certain he has done so many times before.'

'He comes well recommended?' the younger fellow said. He was, perhaps, in his late thirties or early forties, though it was clear to anyone who understood these things that he would soon begin to age alarmingly. The florid complexion betrayed more than a slight fondness for intoxicating beverages and it was possibly that fact, rather than the advancing of the calendar years, which was responsible for his thinning hair and receding brow. The woman turned to him in turn.

'My lord,' she said, adopting a sweeter tone than she had employed with the first man, 'this fellow comes upon his own recommendation, for the one quality we need for this task, other than his ability to carry it to a successful conclusion, is confidentiality.'

The younger man leaned forward. 'I'm not sure I follow your meaning, my lady,' he confessed.

She barely managed to keep her amusement out of her voice. 'I'm sure you do, sir,' she replied. 'In as much as we could never recommend this fellow to others ourselves, neither can any of his previous employers recommend him to us. This fellow carries many a dangerous secret in his head, the sort of secrets that could topple dynasties, I'd wager.'

'Then perhaps we should consider, er, disposing of him, when his usefulness to us is at an end?' The suggestion came from the first man and the lady turned back to him. This time there was no mistaking the scorn in her voice.

'You, sir,' she said, 'may try to kill him if you wish, but I warn you, you would not be the first to try to protect himself in such a fashion. There have been at least five such attempts, to my certain knowledge, and only two of the perpetrators still live to regret their actions. From what I know,' she added darkly, 'the two would rather they were as dead as the other three.'

'I see,' the hawk-nose said, though his expression told that he did not believe the challenge to be insurmountable. 'So we have to trust to the integrity of this villain?'

'We do,' the woman confirmed, 'and I, for one, believe

that we can, otherwise I should not have hired him.' She turned back to the second man. 'Everything is in place as far as your part in this is concerned?'

The man nodded. 'Yes, it is all arranged. There is a hunt planned, as you know. That is when it will be simplest.'

'You are certain she will not go with the others?'

The florid man shook his head. 'She will not go, that I can vouchsafe. She is already bored with his company and they are not yet married. Besides, she hates the hunt, for she cannot bear to see living creatures suffer and die.'

'Yet I'll warrant that does not put her off her meat,' the woman laughed. 'Ah, such delicate sensibilities. I fear those will soon be offended.'

The florid man's expression darkened. 'Your man is aware of the conditions – of *my* conditions?'

'He is, but I cannot be as certain of him keeping to them as I am of his discretion.'

The florid man rose and pushed back his chair. 'If he harms her,' he said quietly, leaning across the table, 'I shall kill him myself, confidentiality or no.' His expression had become darkly intense and the colour in his cheeks had risen even higher.

The woman shrugged.

'That, my lord, is your affair,' she said calmly. 'I am interested only in delivering the goods as promised. So long as you are both at the agreed place, at the agreed time and with the agreed sum in gold, that will be my end in this affair.'

'Quite so,' the man said, relaxing slightly. 'Forgive my outburst.' He looked around the inn, which was beginning to grow more crowded. 'And you must further forgive me, for I fear the time is getting on and I must return before anyone misses me.'

When the door had closed behind him, the hawk-nosed man leaned closer to his remaining companion.

'He is an unnecessary complication,' he said. 'A very unnecessary complication.'

'But a necessary pawn in my scheme,' the woman replied. 'When the contract is honoured, I dare say you will find a way of smoothing over unnecessary complications, my lord.'

'Yes, I dare say,' he agreed, sitting back. The woman smiled and her eyes began to roam about the room, coming to rest on the buxom figure of Moxie. Her companion saw the direction of her gaze and gave a low laugh.

'A comely wench,' he commented. The woman nodded.

'Very comely,' she agreed. 'A trifle rustic, perhaps, but nothing that could not be overcome. With a suitable tutor,' she added, her smile widening. 'Who is she?'

The lone horseman reined in his mount at the crest of the ridge and studied the scene below him. It was a small village and it was called Horyx Ford, according to the weathered chart he carried in his pack. It was of no significance to him, other than as a marker point on his overall journey, but what appeared to be happening in the crude square below was certainly of interest.

Like many villages, this one boasted a whipping post. It was not something frequently seen in the larger towns in these so-called enlightened times, but out in the countryside old traditions died hard. Petty criminals met with swift and summary justice at these posts, and there was also a pillory and a set of stocks in this village, normally reserved for the most trifling offenders.

Usually, Savatch knew, these ageing relics of a bygone age remained in place more as a deterrent than anything else, though it was curious how the artefacts were always maintained in a state of excellent repair. On this day in Horyx Ford, however, it seemed that the dedication of the local craftsmen was to be put to good use.

He spurred his horse into a trot and picked his way down the gentle incline. As he approached the knot of villagers one or two heads turned in his direction. He raised an arm in salute and addressed himself to a burly fellow, whose leather apron proclaimed him to be the local blacksmith.

'Hail, friend!' Savatch called out. 'What sport today?' He nodded towards where several stocky village women were holding a younger wench between them. Her hands had been bound behind her and a leather collar buckled about her neck, from which four thick thongs radiated out to the hands of her captors. The girl's dark hair was tangled and matted and there was grime on her face and on her tattered clothes.

'No sport, stranger,' the smithy growled. 'Yon wench is a thieving harlot. She's bedded at least four young men of the village and used the opportunity to steal from their parents' homes.'

'A terrible crime indeed,' Savatch sympathised. 'And what is to be her punishment?'

'Twelve lashes,' the other replied grimly. 'Trouble is, not one man here is prepared to take on the duty, so it'll have to be one of the women. The girl will escape lightly.' Savatch's gaze travelled to where another of the women stood slightly to one side. In her hand she held a loosely coiled drover's whip.

'Not *so* lightly, I think,' he said. His lip curled at one side. 'What about your good self, smithy?' he challenged. 'Aren't you man enough to lash the slut?'

The big man shook his head morosely. 'Not I,' he said.

'My wife would slit my vitals whilst I slept, if I were to lay a finger on any woman.'

Savatch looked about the crowd.

'Your wife isn't here, I presume?'

The blacksmith shook his head. 'No, she's taken herself off to the next village to visit her sister. She doesn't hold with all this. But she'd find out soon enough if I were to take up that whip.'

'Perhaps you should take it to her,' Savatch suggested, with a loud laugh. The blacksmith's expression betrayed that he did not think this such a bad idea, but Savatch new the likelihood of such a thing ever happening was about as remote as he himself becoming a priest. He leaned forward in his saddle and studied the girl more closely.

'I imagine she's quite presentable, 'neath all that dirt,' he said.

The blacksmith shrugged. 'I've seen worse,' he said.

Savatch nodded and stroked his chin. 'I have a suggestion, friend,' he said slowly. 'It could solve all your problems and it might help me with mine.' The blacksmith raised an eyebrow. Savatch continued. 'I'll whip your slut for you,' he offered. 'It won't be the first time, either.'

'And then?' the big man asked, his eyes full of suspicion. 'Then you'll be wanting a fee, I suppose? Well, this is a poor village and there's little enough spare to feed hungry mouths.'

'The girl herself will be my fee,' Savatch said smoothly. 'I'll take her off your hands in lieu of a fee. I need a servant and she will do fine, once her stripes heal. You can make it official, if you like. The village elders need only change her sentence to, say, six lashes and substitute two years labour for the other six. I'll even throw in five crowns in gold, if you like.'

It was an offer, it seemed, far too good for the village to refuse. The girl, an orphan of about nineteen, had been trouble for years and the thought of seeing the back of her, especially a back that had been expertly whipped, was received with delight all round. Very quickly the elders, of whom the smithy, Gurdan, was one, drew up the necessary paperwork. All this while the girl, whose name was Helda, remained sullenly within her circle of escorts, who continued to torment her by jerking her back and forth every now and then.

When the legalities had been completed, Savatch turned to two burly young villagers; lads whose ruddy complexions told of many long hours in the fields already, plus the sort of strength that comes with such arduous labour.

'Put her up on the post,' he said. 'Stand her on a meal sack first and use these on her wrists.' From his saddlebag he produced two wide leather manacles, to each of which was fixed a stout metal ring. 'I don't mind a girl with a striped back,' he explained, 'but hanging with ropes about her wrists could damage her hands for all time. Fat use a servant girl with no hands.'

The whipping post itself was shaped like a letter T, from two thick timber poles, the upright of which had been driven deep into the ground. Someone produced a full meal sack and the girl was led forward. Seeing that the waiting was over, she began to struggle, but the collar made resistance futile and she was dragged up to the sack with little problem. The women kept hold of their lines whilst the two young labourers cut through the thongs that bound Helda's wrists.

Savatch nodded his approval as the leather straps were buckled into place and lengths of rope knotted through the rings. The ropes were then thrown over the ends of the horizontal post and the young men hauled on them until the unfortunate Helda was standing on tiptoe on the meal sack, her arms stretched high and wide.

'Take the sack from under her,' Savatch instructed.

One of the youths stooped and dragged the support clear, leaving the girl hanging with her full weight on her arms and drawing a cry of anguish from her gaping mouth. Savatch turned back to his saddlebag and withdrew another strap, this time much thinner and considerably longer. At its centre a wad of stuffed leather had been affixed.

'Use this,' he said, tossing it to the taller youth. 'It'll save her biting through her tongue, at the same time as stifling the worst of her noise. Make sure you buckle it tight, lad. We don't want her spitting it out.'

As the fellow approached her, Helda kicked back, her bare foot catching him on the inside of his thigh. He gave a cry of alarm and jumped back. Savatch laughed and pointed at another length of rope that lay near the foot of the post.

'Tie her ankles with that, you dolt,' he said. 'Just wind it around the post tight enough to hold her, but don't cut the blood from her feet. She'll need to be fit to walk before nightfall.'

At last the girl hung ready for him, arms straining, feet securely pinioned to the timber, her mouth stretched wide by the cruel gag. Savatch stepped forward, produced a wicked looking knife from its sheath beneath his tunic, and turned to the expectant crowd.

'I'll want a bowl of warm salt water and some fresh clothing for the slut,' he said. 'I'll give a half gold crown for two skirts, two shirts and a pair of sandals.' He turned back to the helpless Helda and, with one swift slash, opened the back of her already ripped blouse, exposing her pale brown skin to the watching eyes. Resheathing the knife, he used his bare hands to tear away the remaining remnants of cloth, revealing a pair of well rounded breasts, pressing one against each side of the upright. There was a low murmur of male voices from among the villagers.

Stepping back, Savatch held out his hand to the girl who held the whip. She passed it to him with a grim smile and he wondered if hers had been one of the families from whom Helda had stolen. Something told him it was.

He examined the whip briefly, paid it out onto the dusty ground in front of him and then, with a deft flick of the wrist and a jerk of the arm, sent the rawhide hissing through the air. The leather landed squarely across the middle of the hanging girl's shoulders and, despite her gag, her scream of agony sent a flock of small birds fluttering skywards from the nearby group of trees.

Again the whip snaked out, this time landing precisely one inch below the red welt that had already sprung up from the first lash. Again Helda shrieked and her whole body convulsed.

'Have some water ready to revive her if she faints,' Savatch called out. Someone had brought a bucket in readiness and a middle-aged woman stepped forward and placed it handily. Savatch nodded grimly and his arm flashed out again. With unerring accuracy the third stripe appeared another inch further down Helda's back, and yet another tortured cry rent the air. Savatch turned to the crowd and reached inside his tunic. This time it was not the knife he took out, but three small gold coins. He tossed them onto the ground at the foot of the whipping post.

'That's in place of the other three lashes,' he said grimly. There was a muttering of disapproval, which quickly subsided when he turned further about, for the fire in his eyes left no room for quibbling. 'She's taken enough,' he said, coiling the whip back into his hand. 'She's passed out already and throwing water on her will bring her round long enough for only one more lash. Take the three crowns and put them to good use for your village.'

He turned to the two fellows who had strung Helda up. 'Cut her down,' he ordered, 'and see to it that one of the women washes her wounds with brine. I don't think I cut the skin deeply, but this place is filthy and I don't want her flesh putrefying on me.' He turned, looking for the blacksmith, who he found standing just a little way to one side of the main body of villagers.

'Smithy,' he said, walking towards the big man, 'I want another horse and a saddle, and I'll pay a fair price for both. It needn't be anything special, but I doubt yonder wench will be up to much walking for the next day or so.'

The blacksmith hesitated, but then as Savatch drew level with him, he nodded.

In the dimly lit back room of The Wagonmaster, the pile of gold coins in the centre of the grimy table sparkled like a beacon. Heskath gazed at the money, more wealth in one place than he had ever dreamed of possessing.

Initially he had been surprised by the red haired lady's offer, and then he had concluded that she was jesting with him, but she had shown him the bag and let him weigh its contents.

'Do oi get to see inside, lady?' he had challenged her. 'Fer all oi know, these could be plumbics.'

The woman nodded. 'Take the bag through to your private rooms,' she had offered. 'Count them if you like, but beware of any trickery. I know exactly how much is there. One hundred ten crown pieces, fellow, not a single one more nor less. And if you should decide to reject my offer, there had best be one hundred still there when you return them to me.' Her eyes had darted to the two guards at the end of the bar and there was no doubting her meaning.

There were indeed one hundred coins in the bag when Heskath counted them. He arranged them into ten neat little equal stacks and sat drooling over them, whilst he considered the implications. Moxie would not be easy to replace, and she was an undoubted attraction at The Wagonmaster. But then the money before him represented more than he could hope to earn in a full good year, and no one was completely irreplacable.

When he returned to the woman's table the money remained behind, hidden with the one hundred and twenty crowns that represented his life savings.

Chapter Three

It was the morning of the third day of her married life, and Corinna Oleana of Illeum lay in her bath, watching the wisps of steam rising lazily towards the ceiling of her bathchamber. She felt extremely discontented, and throughout her young life, for as long as she could remember, Corinna, daughter of Lundt, had had but one remedy for such a situation.

When Corinna was unhappy, she bathed. It was a course of action which had never failed her.

Until now.

She closed her eyes, picturing the cause of her current situation, knowing that even now he would almost certainly be in the refectory hall. For Lazlo, Lazlo Haas of Hafland, Prince of that realm and still not yet twenty-one, had but one burning ambition in life, an ambition which his lanky frame fought hard to deny.

Lazlo Haas, Prince of Hafland, could devour more at one sitting than Corinna could imagine eating for herself in an entire week. Scarcely more than two waking hours seemed to pass before the young princeling would place his gaunt, unsmiling face before yet another dish of some steaming, gravy-ridden bowl of whatever confection the cooks had managed to conjure up on his behalf. Where other men dreamed of sex, Lazlo, Corinna was certain, dreamed of food.

Even on their wedding night he had left the marriage bed in the small hours, descending, so the palace grapevine had it, to devour whatever leftovers he could find in the kitchens. He had at least waited to consummate the marriage, it was true, but even that had been a complete failure, as far as Corinna was concerned.

She had always imagined losing her maidenhead to a real man; a strong, dominant man, who would also be gentle and considerate, kind and loving, yet be her prince in all ways, respecting her, yet commanding her love and devotion, quick to praise and return such devotion, but also quick to punish any girlish misbehaviour. He would even, as Corinna had imagined him, be prepared to take his errant wife across his knee, draw up her skirts, rip away her underdrawers and spank her womanly bottom, should the occasion demand.

She wondered if Lazlo would ever spank her, but decided it was less than likely. During their three days together he had paid her scant attention, either inside or out of the bedchamber. Perhaps, she thought with a sour laugh, she would fare better if she disguised herself as a venison joint. At least a venison joint, in Lazlo's scheme of things, would have fared better than a couple of crude stabs with his erect penis, followed by a groaning collapse as he spent his seed into her womb.

For Corinna's part, the lasting memory had been primarily of the pain as her hymen was ruptured. She had heard that the pain, no matter how intense, would quickly pass as she rose to fulfillment, but sadly there had been little time for that. Even on the second night, still sore from the first, Corinna had been scarcely in the first stages of arousal before her young husband ejaculated again. After which, having performed what he saw as his husbandly duty, sex was replaced on Lazlo's agenda by... food.

She sighed. It wasn't really his fault, she supposed. She

had not been his choice for a bride, nor he hers for a groom. Theirs had been a marriage of convenience – political convenience. As Lord Protector of Illeum, the nearest the realm had to a feudal king, Corinna's father needed allies and, although Illeum was one of the larger countries in the region and Haafland comparatively small, Haafland's coastal cities controlled the important straits through which seventy percent of the region's merchant shipping must pass, and boasted the finest navy in the known world.

In addition, their soldiers were renowned across all civilisation for their bravery and determination, and many countries relied on their Haafish mercenary divisions as the backbone of their army. With the Prince of Haafland as successor to what amounted to the throne of Illeum, no Haafish soldier would raise a sword against the country and many would rally to its banner if it were attacked.

Lord Lundt, her father, was an astute statesman, Corinna knew. Amidst the general unrest and occasional skirmish, he alone stood for peaceful settlements. His own army was strong, well equipped and well trained and now, with the Haafish divisions at his disposal, he could ensure that all the other rulers would see the sense in his approach. Then, in time, as he had gently explained to his daughter, when she and Lazlo ruled both countries jointly, war would become a thing of distant memory and, eventually, of legend alone.

Having been brought up to believe in duty before personal desires, Corinna had willingly acceded to her father's request that she accept Lazlo's proposal of marriage; willingly, that is, until she first saw him, by which time it was too late. The courtiers and courtesans by now had done their work and to change her mind at such a late stage was unthinkable. And so the wedding went ahead, a momentous occasion attended by heads crowned and near-crowned alike, with a state banquet that had lasted, albeit without the bride and groom after the first few hours, well into a second day.

Corinna flicked the soapy water idly and sighed again. There was little she could do, she knew, except prepare herself mentally for the task of bringing babies – heirs – into the world, strong princes and princesses to ensure the succession of the noble line. After that...

She smiled to herself. After that, perhaps things might be different, for a princess might take herself a lover. Such things were never talked about openly, nor openly recognised, but she knew they went on. Princes took themselves mistresses and princesses took attractive men "under their wing", to use a phrase much favoured in court circles. It was not her idea of a perfect solution, perhaps, but at least it was something, something to look forward to in the coming few years of what was doubtless to be unavoidable boredom.

At least, Corinna thought, she did not have to endure Lazlo's dour company throughout most of the daytime. Whether it was simply as a diversion from his unrelenting quest for food, or whether it was because at least he knew he could get to eat whatever he caught, Lazlo did have one other interest, an interest shared by nobility wherever it was to be found. Lazlo, like his peers and forebears, liked to hunt, and it did not seem to matter whatever the quarry might be. The motto seemed to be simple and to the point – if it moves, shoot it; if you hit it, cook it, or at least get some minion to cook it for you.

Which was why Corinna was left to her own devices this fine afternoon; for her father had organised the hunt to end all hunts for the honoured guests who remained behind from the wedding celebrations. They had set off shortly after first light and Corinna, as the new bride, should have gone along with the huge party, even if only to spectate and shout encouragement, but she had feigned a headache and begged to be excused.

For all his boorishness in most matters, Lazlo had been most solicitous, seeming to blame what he saw as his own over zealous attentions to his young wife for her present malady.

'You must forgive me, wife,' he had apologised, 'for I, too, have much to learn in matters of such delicacy. I fear I have taxed your spirit overly.'

Ye gods, Corinna had thought to herself, if he calls that over-taxing, what on earth am I supposed to do when his initial urgings subside? The answer, as she had discovered quite accidently a few years ago, lay, quite literally, in her own hands. And now, alone in her chamber, floating almost without weight in the warm bathwater, she allowed herself one other, quite secret, luxury.

With a sigh she parted her legs, her hand dipping beneath the surface, prising apart her soft lower lips and seeking that little nubbin with all its promise of fulfilment. She sighed again, more deeply this time, and closed her eyes, conjuring up her prince, not Lazlo the prince foisted upon her by diplomacy and necessity, but *her* prince, her strong handsome masterful prince.

Open yourself wider, he said. *Come, my little princess whore, open yourself to me; there are no secrets here.* Corinna moved her legs as far apart as the bathtub would permit, her finger sliding deeper inside herself, the inside of her top knuckle joint rubbing against her steadily engorging clitoris. A low moan escaped her lips as she began to work herself slightly faster.

Show me your devotion, my royal slut. Open your mouth for your prince. Corinna's moist lips peeled apart as she imagined his throbbing member sliding between them. *Suck deep, my slave girl – suck deep. Feel your master's cock in your throat and show me that you are worthy to accept it elsewhere.*

'Aaahhhhhhhh!' Corinna's shriek rent the room as her back arched and her body convulsed. She cried out again, her fingers digging deep into herself, clutching at the flesh as a counterpoint to the tide of sheer ecstasy that flooded over her. She felt herself sliding. With her free hand she grabbed at the side of the bathtub for support and, as she did, strong fingers grasped her wrist. Her eyes flew open, wide with terror, and her bladder involuntarily started emptying itself before she could regain any sort of control.

'My pleasure, my lady, or at least you could easily be.' He loomed over her, a powerful figure of a man, well over six feet tall with powerful shoulders, over which cascaded a shock of black curls. His dark eyes betrayed amusement and Corinna felt her face beginning to burn with humiliation. To the gods, this stranger had been watching her, had seen her pleasuring herself, had been witness to her most private moment!

'Get out!' she shrieked, finally finding her voice. 'Get out, now! My father will have you flogged!'

'Your father?' he said, cocking one eyebrow and releasing his grip on her wrist. 'Not your splendid new husband? Are we still papa's little girl?'

'You are insolent, sir!' Corinna snapped. She hunched forward, trying to restore some modesty by covering her breasts with her arms, drawing her knees up to add extra protection. She glared up at the intruder. 'Now, kindly remove yourself. You have no right to invade the privacy of a lady.'

'Ah, I see,' he replied coolly. 'So that was a lady I was watching just then, was it? I beg pardon, milady. I most certainly had gained the impression that I was watching someone who was most certainly *not* a lady.'

'As I said, sir,' Corinna hissed between clenched teeth, 'you are insolent. These quarters are private. Now go, or I shall summon the guards and have you flogged myself.'

'Is that so?' the man said, apparently unmoved by her threats. 'Well, call your guards, Corinna of Illeum. Go ahead, call them. Only I have just the slightest suspicion that your calls may go unanswered, at least for the next hour or two.'

'You're bluffing,' Corinna accused him, trying to keep her voice steady, though something in his manner told her he seemed too sure of himself to be lying. 'There are guards everywhere in the palace. If I scream they will surely come running.'

'Be my guest. Scream away.' He smiled down at her. 'However, before you damage that pretty throat of yours, I think I should tell you that eight of the guards are asleep, and the potion they have imbibed will ensure they stay that way until we are well away from here. Three more are likewise unconscious, though I cannot guarantee they will revive as easily as their companions. And one more, unfortunately, will not be waking up again at all, at least not in this world.

'I had hoped to accomplish my mission without bloodshed, but the best laid plans are hostage to fortune, I fear. Whoever heard of a soldier who did not drink, eh?'

Corinna felt herself beginning to shiver, and all of a sudden the bathwater seemed to have lost its warmth.

'What do you want?' she asked, her voice scarcely more

than a whisper. 'Why have you come here?'

The wide mouth twitched, humorously. 'I should have thought that a lady of your undoubted intelligence and education would have worked that out for herself by now,' he said. He bent closer, his face only inches from her own. 'I've come for you, Lady Corinna, and I do not intend to leave without you.'

'You're mad!' Corinna gasped. 'Either that or you've been drinking yourself.'

'On the contrary, milady, I assure you I am perfectly sane,' he purred. 'And I *never* drink when working, especially not when the stakes are as high as they are now.'

'So, you are not merely an assassin, you're a hired assassin!' Corinna spat the words out.

The intruder simply shrugged. 'A man must eat,' he said, mockingly. 'And it certainly pays better than being a shepherd, which is what many of my ancestors were. Now, if you will be so good as to stand up and step out of the bath, I do not have all day at my disposal. Your valiant guards will be no problem, but we do have a lengthy journey ahead of us and a rendezvous to keep.'

Corinna gave a derisive snort. 'If you expect my cooperation in my own abduction,' she snarled, 'then you really are insane. I would claw your eyes out first.'

'Then I thank you for the warning,' he retorted. One hand delved inside his pocket and the other snaked out, grasping her wrist again. The leather thong looped about it and was jerked tight, and then he had seized her other wrist and was binding the two painfully together. Corinna let out a yelp of pain and tried to resist, but he had not only taken her by surprise, he was also unbelievably strong.

'Now then,' he said, knotting off the thong. 'Will you stand up, or shall I have to pick you up? I cannot promise exactly where my hands might end up if I do, for that delightful body is very slippery at this moment.'

For several seconds Corinna sat, glaring at the stranger, pulling and twisting at her bonds, though it had become immediately clear to her that there was no escaping the expert cinching. She glared at him in frustrated rage, tears filling her eyes.

'Barbarian!' she screeched. 'Filthy barbarian! Why don't you crawl back to the wastelands from whence you came?!'

His only response, however, was more laughter.

'Lady,' he said, struggling to control his mirth, 'you know as little about barbarians as do I about tapestry work. If you were to meet a real barbarian, it pains me to think how you would react. Now, be a good little girl and get out of that damned bath, else I shall have to teach you a lesson in obedience. And by the way, as I seem to have you at a disadvantage, my name is Savatch and I was actually a guest at your wedding party. Not that I would expect so grand a lady to recall one simple face among such a multitude.'

'Then, if you came here as a guest, you have abused the simplest rules of hospitality, which makes you no better than a barbarian,' Corinna countered. She shook her damp hair and set her jaw squarely. 'And as for getting out of my bath, make me and damn your eyes—!'

Savatch moved, even as she was speaking.

He swooped down, one hand seizing her bound wrists, the other a handful of her pale tresses, and hauled her roughly to her feet. A moment later she was out of the bath and stretched over the back of the heavily carved dressing chair, another thong being knotted about the first and then wound about the front stretcher to keep her bent over the leather padded back, her toes barely touching the floor.

Corinna shrieked and cursed, kicking out in desperation, but Savatch was not only powerful, it seemed he was no stranger to this work. And he had come prepared, too, for now he took from his tunic a thin strap, at the centre of which was fixed a wadded ball of leather. Roughly he prised her jaws open, thrust the ball between her teeth and buckled the strap behind her head, pulling the gag in even more cruelly.

He stepped back and walked slowly around her, apparently admiring his handiwork, as well as her naked flesh. Finally, he stood behind her again and his hand darted between her thighs. Desperately, Corinna fought to press the tops of her legs together, but it was impossible to resist the invasion. She felt one finger slipping inside her still damp slit and heard him give a low chuckle.

'Tender meat,' he growled. 'Very tender. And yet your dear husband prefers to hunt boar. Ah well, he has much to learn – as do you, my pretty princess.'

Corinna heard the chink of a buckle being released and groaned, resigning herself to the worst. Bound and gagged as she was, she had no way of resisting. She bit into the foul tasting leather and steeled herself for the inevitable, now certain the brute was going to penetrate her.

But that was not yet Savatch's intention.

Corinna heard the low whistle of the belt an instant before it struck her wet flesh. A line of fire seared across her upraised buttocks and, despite the gag, her howl of pain filled the chamber. Again he swung and a second scream reverberated in the echoes of the first.

Four, five, six – Corinna lost count, locked in a world of burning pain. He whipped her unhurriedly, with deliberate calculation, allowing the heat of each previous lash to spread itself outwards, before adding the next layer of agony. Tears flowed freely from Corinna's eyes and now she sobbed, rather than screamed. The room seemed to shrink from her and she felt sure she would faint away.

And then, mercifully, he stopped, but only to replace one torture and humiliation with another. She felt the hot knob of flesh pressing between her thighs and his fingers seeking to open her up for his shaft. Instinctively she tensed against him, but a mere flick with the back of his hand across her burning buttock flesh was enough, now, to draw another howl from behind her gag. It was a clear warning and no words were necessary.

Corinna relaxed and allowed him to move her legs wide apart, opening her sex in preparation. Again the hard flesh pressed and this time the soft lips parted for it. She grunted as he entered her, but it was not a grunt of pain, for he slid easily and deeply inside, filling her far further than Lazlo had done. She felt the heat of his hairy belly pressing against her burning buttocks as he pushed home to the hilt, and heard his grunt of satisfaction.

His hands began moving up from her belly, stroking her ribs, pressing and coaxing, until they cupped her dangling breasts. Thumbs and fingers sought and found her nipples and, to her horror, Corinna knew they were swollen beyond anything they had ever achieved so far.

'Princess or pantry maid,' he grunted. 'You're all the same when it comes down to it.' Slowly, he began easing his massive length back, until only the engorged knob was still within her. Corinna tensed, her breath coming in equine snorts through her distended nostrils. He waited, tormenting her, easing in and out a mere inch at a time, but it was a critical inch, for she could feel how hotly his pole was pressing against her clit, something that Lazlo's shaft had not so far achieved.

For a minute or so Savatch continued in this fashion and then, just as Corinna had started to think he was merely playing with her, he thrust deeply home again. This time his right hand deserted her breast, sliding down over her mound, a single finger targeting her now swollen bud. Corinna moaned softly and, before she realised what she was doing, she pressed back against him, as far as her bondage would permit.

'Yes, all the same,' she heard him sigh.

She closed her eyes, her mind reeling in disarray. Damn him to the four hells, her head screamed at her, but there were other voices crying out to be heard, too. Well damn you, too, she thought, her mind suddenly clearing, as Savatch began to pump slowly in and out of her. Perhaps we are all the same, but then so are men.

Hating her body for its treachery, Corinna could not stop it from responding. But then it was not her fault, she told herself, trying desperately to cling on to some last straw of reason. What could she do, tied and beaten as she was? She could not get free from him; she could not even cry out a protest. She was merely a woman, with a woman's body, and who could blame her if that body reacted in the way nature had designed it?

And then, suddenly, he stopped and pulled out of her. He gave her a playful pat across her rump the way a rider might convey affection to his mount, and walked around her, carefully hiding his manhood back inside his breeches.

'Not a bad ride for an untrained filly,' he said. He stooped and began untying the thong that held her bound wrists to the chair. 'But as I said, milady, time is of the essence, and there will be more suitable occasions on which to put you through your paces.'

He helped her to stand, his touch surprisingly gentle,

and then brushed the back of one hand across her engorged teats. Before she could react, he stooped forward, drawing the right nipple into his mouth, his teeth nipping the flesh playfully.

'You are very beautiful, princess,' he whispered, standing upright again, 'but then I suppose you already know this.'

Yes, Corinna supposed she did, for she had heard that men found her so. Taller than average, with a bosom that was generous, yet still held proudly by the musculature of youth, she had long legs and a small waist and her golden hair framed a face that was more than simply pretty.

Her wide eyes were a deep blue, with just a hint of green that betrayed her mood whenever she became annoyed. Her nose was slender and perfectly proportioned, the slightly retroussé tip lending an almost elven quality to her features, and her mouth was full-lipped and generous. Yes, she was beautiful and she could have won the heart – indeed had won the hearts of many already – of any man in the country. And the news that she had married Lazlo had doubtless saddened or broken many of those hearts.

Savatch suddenly seemed to realise where he was and what he was about. He broke the intimate moment, turning away and crossing the room to where a large canvas sack stood against the wall. Corinna supposed he had brought it with him, for she did not recall seeing it before. Indeed, she quickly realised she was right, for, delving inside it, he drew out a curious roll of brown leather and began shaking it out. Her eyes widened in horror as she recognised it for what it was.

'Ah, I see you know all about slave jackets,' he laughed, seeing her expression change. 'Though not intimately, I am sure.'

Yes, Corinna did know, though the jackets were scarcely,

if ever, used about the palace. But she had been in the market at auctions and seen the way the handlers prepared unwilling purchases for the homeward journey with their new masters or mistresses. She had seen the sightless, featureless, anonymous creatures being loaded into wagons, like so many carcasses of beef.

She shook her head, her eyes pleading with him, but Savatch's expression made it plain that there was to be no reprieve.

'I fear, princess, that there is no other way. The guards inside the palace have been dealt with, but there are others within the city walls and a gate through which we must pass. Sadly, that pretty face of yours is too well known to be mistaken for a simple wench, so we must take steps to prevent it from being seen.'

The slave jacket was a simple, but very effective garment. Made of leather, it was sleeveless, but the high neck was attached to a hood which covered the wearer's head and face completely, leaving just two small openings for the nostrils and two more for the eyes, though there was another strip of leather which could be buckled across these apertures, rendering the slave blind. It was a tactic often used to subdue and punish the uncooperative.

'Now,' Savatch said, walking towards her and holding out the jacket, 'we can do this in one of two ways, but do it we will, please believe me, princess, so I suggest you be sensible.' Corinna sighed and her shoulders slumped in resignation. He meant what he said, she knew, and any attempt at resistance would merely be delaying the inevitable. Besides, the heat in her buttocks was an insistant reminder of his capabilities and she did not doubt his willingness to repeat the beating.

She stood passively, whilst he drew the jacket over her

shoulders. It was designed in the fashion of a halberd, front and back joining together at the sides by means of a series of sturdy straps, so that one size fitted all. It was also made to fit slaves of either sex and, to save the need to accommodate the female curves, there were two cutaways at the front through which the breasts protruded.

Savatch drew the front section down between her bound wrists and Corinna shivered at his touch as he eased each breast in turn through its appropriate opening. The hood lay limply against her front as he tightened the buckles in rapid succession, drawing the leather close about her, so that it molded itself to her upper body like a second skin. Satisfied there was no way she could escape from it, he lifted the hood section and drew it over her face and head.

There were laces at the rear to ensure that this part also fitted tightly and, as Savatch drew them in, Corinna felt the supple leather pressing against her cheeks and ears. She peeered out through the narrow eye openings, praying he would not attach the blindfold strap, but her prayers went unanswered, for, no sooner had he tied off the thongs, than he began buckling the broad leather band into place, cinching it so tightly it blocked out every last chink of light.

A whimper of fear escaped her lips and she felt his hand pat her upper arm.

'Easy, my pretty filly,' he said. 'There is nothing to fear from darkness.'

Corinna struggled to subdue the terror that was now welling up inside her. Everything that had happened in these past minutes had happened so fast it was as if it were all just an extension of her daydreaming. Even the whipping had seemed unreal, even if the pain itself had not, but now, as he set about completing her bondage, there could be no denying the truth.

She was about to be kidnapped from her own home, taken to where she did not know, but it was really happening. Fastened inside this cruel jacket she would look like just another ripe female slave, a commodity bought and paid for and off to begin the next stage of a life of unending servitude.

She felt his hands on her wrists, his fingers tugging at the knots that bound them, but she knew there would be no permanent release, for at the back of the jacket was one final refinement, a leather pouch into which her arms were now placed, folded with her forearms parallel to each other, the straps on the pouch then tightened so that her arms were held in an enclosed sling, her breasts thrust forward by the posture that such bondage induced.

Her eyes filled with tears as she imagined how she must look. At the market men gathered to enjoy the sight of female slaves being treated thus, exchanging ribald jokes at the way the women's breasts jutted out of the dark leather so invitingly. There had even been one new owner, anxious to recoup some of his investment, who had offered his new acquisition to all takers in exchange for one crown a time. The poor girl had been led off to a nearby tent, arms bound as Corinna's were now, gagged and blindfolded, to be used by seven or eight rough-looking fellows, who she could not see and would never see again. Corinna had turned away from the spectacle and had expressed her disgust to Lady Esme, who had been her tutor and companion at that time. Lady Esme had dismissed the incident lightly.

'It is the way of these things, my pretty one,' the older woman had said. 'The girl is a common whore, doubtless her mother, too, before her. She would not be here had the courts not decreed it.'

'But whoring is not a crime!' Corinna protested. Lady

Esme smiled, indulgently.

'Indeed not,' she agreed, 'but so many of these wenches are not satisfied with an honest living. That one probably tried to steal a man's purse, or maybe something worse, I don't know. Whores have been known to attack their customers, generally for no reason at all, but then there is little reason among these lower types.'

And that was what she, Corinna, looked like now, she thought. A "lower type", trussed in a slave jacket, breasts thrust out for anyone to see, and still damp between her legs, like a whore between business, like the whore she had acted when Savatch had been pumping in and out of her. Her tears soaked the leather hood and she could not stop them.

Yet still he was not through with her. He lifted her onto the bed and drew her legs wide apart. Corinna thought he was about to ravish her again, but his purpose this time was far more practical. His fingers stroked the triangular bush above her wet slot.

'I fear, milady,' he said, his tone so casual that Corinna could scarce believe it, 'that this fine thatch needs to go. As you may know, all slave wenches are kept clean shaved and my little deception would be in peril if I permitted this to stay.'

Corinna gave a little whimper and made to close her legs, but his grip on her ankles was strong.

'It shall be done, little princess, one way or the other,' he hissed, his mouth close to her ear. 'Now, I can tie you, or you can simply lay there whilst I take the blade to you, the choice is yours. But if I have to waste precious time with more knot work, be sure you will repay me that time when circumstances are more favourable.'

There was, Corinna accepted, no point at all in resisting.

Her rump was still too raw for her not to realise what this creature was capable of, not to mention the fact that her love sheath still oozed its treachery from his attentions to it. She lay limply, trying not to flinch as the sharp blade denuded her mound, glad that she could not see this final testament to her abject subjugation.

He carried her easily, like a sack of meal slung over his shoulder, but it was a terrifying sensation, blind, helpless, swaying about as he walked. Corinna tried to listen out for sounds of other people, but the building sounded deserted. With the leather hood muffling her senses it would have been hard to be sure, but it seemed that Savatch's claim about the guards had not been an idle boast.

He turned right out of her chambers, heading along the wide passage that led towards her fathers rooms, which she found strange, for the only way down to the lower floor was in the opposite direction. The only way, that was, apart from—

It could not be, but yes, he was stopping and she heard the sound of a key being turned in a heavy lock, the lock to her father's private suite. He could not know, surely, for the secret stairway was a family secret, its existence known to only a handful of people! What treachery was this? Who was behind this plot?

The sound of his boots became more muffled as he crossed the thick carpet. He paused and Corinna heard the creak of the old cupboard door opening. There was a rustle as he moved aside the hanging cloaks and a pause as he fumbled for the hidden catch, and then the inner door itself groaned open.

There were four and twenty stone steps leading down to the lower passageway. Corinna knew, for she had counted them as a child when her uncle Willum had first shown her the secret. She counted them now, jolting in time to the harsh ring of Savatch's boots as they descended.

The passage itself was not high, nor was it wide, having been designed and built way back in the mists of time, in an age when a hidden means of escape from the royal chambers had been deemed essential, in an age when kings came and went with the frequency of the vittals carter. It was, however, very long, passing beneath the palace walls, beneath the kitchen garden, beneath the orchard, and emerging in a thick clump of bushes outside the walls of the palace grounds themselves.

Originally, so her father had explained, it had continued even further, emerging beyond the walls of the city itself, at a point on the riverbank well out of sight of the sentinel towers. However, with the passing of the years, that part of the tunnel had become unsafe and her father's grandfather had had it sealed off, the secret of the remaining passage ensured by the fact that the work was carried out by four convicted murderers, under the direct supervision of her own grandfather and two great uncles, who had then taken the miscreants away for immediate execution.

Desperately, Corinna prayed that someone might happen upon them as they emerged at the far end, though she knew it was a forlorn hope, for both original exits had been well chosen to eliminate such a possibility as far as was possible. The bushes that concealed the remaining doorway were in the oldest part of the graveyard used for the burial of executed murderers, other criminals who had died whilst in prison, and for the final interment of those who died too poor to pay for their own funerals.

The prison itself backed onto the northern boundary of the overgrown site, those windows which did overlook it set in the walls of cells, deliberately too high for the inmates to be able to see out to the world beyond their incarceration. The eastern limit of the graveyard was bounded by a small coppice of yew trees, visited only infrequently by the bowmakers to whom it belonged, whilst, at the western side, the sprawling barns of the public stables effectively screened the area from the main town.

It was the stables for which Savatch was headed. As they emerged into the warm sunlight Corinna fought to stay calm, trying to keep her bearings in the enforced darkness, ears pricked for the slightest indication of another human presence. Not that she thought it would help her if they came across anyone. Doubtless, Savatch had answers ready, should anyone question why he should be in the graveyard with a neatly packaged slave girl over his shoulder.

She could imagine what people would assume. She was his, he had just bought her, thus the jacket and hood, and he had decided to give her a quiet taste of what she could expect from him in the future. And what quieter place in which to do that than a deserted graveyard?

She heard his boots crunching on gravel and realised that they had arrived at the rear of the stables, where a narrow path skirted the three paddocks and led around to the main entrance yard. A voice called out something and Savatch returned the salutation.

'Indeed, friend, she turned out to be well worth the money,' he said. 'A little fiery, but then that's how I like 'em.'

'Aye, I see you've had cause to redden her arse already,' the second voice said. He was an older man, his accent that of the countryside, one of many such who were employed to tend the horses and tackles in this busy place.

All around, Corinna could now hear the sounds of considerable activity, and she cringed at the thought of so many eyes feasting upon her nakedness.

'Indeed, friend,' Savatch said, continuing his exchange with the stable hand, 'I gave her a good taste of my belt, but it only stilled her for a while. And the language! Yslandic or not, she knows a few curses that would blanche the faces of even a blacksmith, whatever tongue he held as his mother.'

'Ho! Yslandic, eh? You means she's an Yslandic? No wonder she's a spitfire. By the gods, you've got yourself a handful there!'

'Only half Yslandic,' Savatch said, with a mirthless laugh. Corinna was dumbfounded by his easy and nonchalant manner. The Yslandians were a race which was mostly dominated by their warrior women; tall, fair haired creatures who, it was rumoured, placed their males in permanent chains from the age of puberty, keeping them as helpless slaves until the day they died.

The truth, Corinna realised, was probably less picturesque, but then few ever travelled to that northern wasteland and fewer still were permitted entry via the two high passes that were the only way into or out of that land. But there was no doubting the ferocity of the Yslandian women. Those who ventured south frequently enlisted as mercenaries and were a match for any male warrior who dared try to put their reputations to the test.

And yet here was Savatch, openly boasting that his new slave was part Yslandian! Where most men, having got this far, would have been satisfied with slipping away as quietly and discreetly as possible, he was standing there bragging of his conquest. The sheer effrontery of the man was unbelievable!

'Is my wagon stood ready, as I asked?' he said, suddenly turning back to business. The stable man confirmed that it was.

'I've regreased that back axle, too,' he said. 'She was wearing a bit dry and you'd 'ave had troubles there before you'd gotten too far along the way. I trust I did right?'

'You did,' Savatch confirmed. 'Everything else all right?'

'Well, the tack's seen better days, but it'll serve a while yet. I just hope you didn't give too much for the rig. Whole lot ain't worth more than ten crowns, and that's being generous.'

'Ah well, my six crowns was well spent,' Savatch laughed. 'And here's two more for your good self.' There was a chink of coins changing hands and then they were on the move again, Savatch following the other man inside a building.

The back of the wagon had been piled with rough sacking, onto which Savatch lowered Corinna. She heard a low whistle.

'Big titted wench, ain't she?' the older man joked. 'You can see which half of her is Yslandic and no mistaking. I don't suppose...?' Corinna heard the sound of the coins being jingled in his hand and tensed. No, please by all the gods, she thought. Please, not that! To be hired out for the gratification of a crude stable hand. The blood froze in her veins and her heart seemed to stop.

'I think not, friend,' Savatch replied, after what seemed an eternity. 'This one I keep for myself. I don't like to think of another man's sword being sheathed in my scabbard.' Corinna let out a long, silent sigh.

'As you wish, friend.' The older man laughed, but there was a note of disappointment in his voice. Corinna heard the rustle of the canvas being closed over the back of the wagon and struggled to ease herself onto her side, for her weight on her pinioned arms was rapidly becoming very uncomfortable. She felt the cart dip on its springs as Savatch climbed up into the driver's position and then the vehicle lurched forward, tumbling her over onto her stomach, her breasts crushed painfully under her.

They were soon out into the main street, the familiar sounds and cries of the street vendors penetrating the leather padding over Corinna's ears. The steady clip-clopping suggested there were two horses pulling the cart, though there were other horses about, for it was a busy time of the day. She heard Savatch crying out to their animals to halt and realised they had arrived at the main gate.

'Halt, friend!' It was the customary greeting of the duty guard. 'Identify yourself.'

'Savatch of Andrium. My papers.' There was a pause. 'And you'll want to see this bill of sale.' There was another pause.

'She's in the wagon, is she?' Clearly, Savatch had come well prepared and had shown the guard some paper purporting to legalise the purchasing of a slave. 'Any good, this Soniska woman?'

'Not bad,' Savatch replied easily. 'Take a look if you like, but watch out for yourself. She kicks as well as bites, and if you heard the filth that comes out of such a pretty mouth, well, it would curl your hair, friend. But then, she's half Yslandic, so they told me, so it's to be expected.'

There was another pause, followed by the rustling of the canvas, and Corinna realised the guard was accepting Savatch's invitation. The cart creaked as the man pulled himself over the tailboard, and then a rough hand grasped her shoulder and rolled her onto her back. Fingers squeezed her breasts and she kicked out, her shin making solid contact and bringing a satisfying grunt from her tormentor. She tensed herself for his retaliation, but he simply guffawed.

'Waste of time kicking a guard there, girlie,' he sneered. 'Say, friend, fancy making a quick crown before you go? I've seldom seen such juicy melons on a wench.' Once again, Savatch gave his sword and scabbard routine and the man climbed back down again.

'Well, can't fault a fellow for asking,' he laughed, closing the canvas once again. 'Mind you, you'd do well to get yourself one of our cod protectors, or tie her ankles down well. A man could suffer damage, elsewise.'

'Aye, well, I'll teach the wench what's expected of a decent slave,' Savatch parried. 'A few hours in that slave jacket will sap the spunk from her. I'll wager she's a more tolerable bed warmer by nightfall.'

Despite her terrible predicament, Corinna had to admit that the man was something special. Where a lesser mortal might have betrayed himself with nervousness or indecision, Savatch seemed to relish the entire thing as a challenge – and a challenge, it seemed, that he was more than a match for.

The wagon swayed and creaked along at that pace which all waggoners know will keep their team in action for the maximum number of hours in each day. The roads of Illeum were little different from those that were to be found anywhere else in the world; quagmires in the wet season, mile upon mile of boneshaking ruts at all other times. Corinna scrabbled around in her dark confinement and tried to ease enough of the sacking against one side of the wagon so that she could prop herself against it with at least some small degree of comfort.

As the torturous miles passed beneath the groaning wheels, Corinna tried to clear her mind and think properly.

In truth, there was little else for her to do. She turned her thoughts to everything that had happened since the morning, knowing that her only hope of escaping from her present, desperate predicament lay in understanding whatever was behind it all.

She considered what she knew, which was little enough. Firstly, she had been kidnapped, which was obvious enough, she thought grimly, otherwise she would not be lying here, strapped inside the cruel leather sheath, being tossed around in the back of a rickety wagon. Secondly, her abductor was no amateur. He was well organised, confident, and had a panache that bordered on the arrogant. No, it was arrogance, Corinna corrected herself. He had had the gall to stroll into the palace – her home, by the gods – and simply help himself to her and help himself in every way imaginable. He had also said that his motivation was money. A lot of money.

Therefore – and so far the deduction process required no great feats of brainpower – someone was very determined to have her in their power. The burning question was *who*? Another question, Corinna reasoned, was why? Find the answer to one, she told herself, and you were half way towards discovering the answer to two.

Ransom? She considered the possibilities. It seemed unlikely. The Lord Protector of Illeum was not a poor man, but then he was also not a man without power and influence. A common brigand, the sort of man who might kidnap the equivalent of royalty, simply for money, would almost certainly not have the gall to attempt such an enterprise. If it was simply gold he craved, it would be far less risk laden to abduct the daughters of a few wealthy merchants, not the only offspring of a man who commanded armies.

So, it was not a matter of money. Ergo, it had to be

political. In fact, Corinna thought with a desperate sigh of realisation, *everything* had to be political, when it came to it. Her marriage to Lazlo was a prime example.

Political.

But to what ends?

Corinna knew there were several treaty negotiations in the air at present. Maravania and Dasnia had spent many years squabbling over the sovereignty of Darcht, a small and largely barren island in the straits of Arros. The patch of rock had no value at all, neither pecuniary, nor strategic, though its one small harbour had been a foul weather sanctuary for hundreds of small fishing vessels over the centuries.

Even that fact had never been enough to convince either protagonist that the bleak island was worth fighting a proper war over. However, there was also the matter of the Vorsan states, seven individually insignificant little dukedoms that had recently come under the mantle of one ruling power, the Barendi family of Erndst, not the largest of the states, but the one most favourably situated in regard to access to the rest of the continent.

Lal Barendi, with grandparents whose ancestry could be traced easily to the ruling families of three other Vorsan territories, had emerged as the great unifier. In five years, he had drawn the separate states into a federation that potentially had the power to rule a huge area of the civilised world.

Barendi, with a bloodline that also had roots in Dasnia, had been quietly fuelling the fires of discontent between that country and Maravania and courting the ambassadors of Yslandia in a bid to persuade them to bring pressure to bear, Maravania being one of the two countries that bordered the land of the legendary amazons.

However, with Yslandia being snowbound for so great a part of the year, she relied upon the seas for the trade she needed in order to survive. Which was where Haafland came in. As long as Haafland remained in Lundt's camp, Yslandia would remain ostensibly neutral.

And, whilst Lazlo remained as Corinna's husband and, thus, heir apparent to what amounted to the throne of Illeum, Haafland would most certainly remain in Corinna's father's camp, thus ensuring, if not quite the balance of power that Lundt sought, at least a stalemate, which would prevent any real chance of escalation to full-scale warfare.

So, Corinna reasoned, her abduction had something to do with the balance of power. Illeum, with its large population and considerable natural resources, was the main – no, *only*, buffer against what could so easily become a worldwide conflict. Illeum, Haafland, and a handful of other minor, though not insignificant allies, stood between certain powers and their ability to expand beyond their existing borders.

And, as Corinna was only too well aware, the alliance between Illeum, Haafland and the others was founded upon one person and one person only. Lundt. Lord protector Lundt, her father.

Which made her, Corinna, an invaluable property and, potentially, a crucial negotiating tool. She grunted, biting into her gag, the irony of the situation not escaping her. She, Corinna of Illeum, daughter of the one man who was capable of maintaining peace and equilibrium throughout the entire, so-called civilised world, was currently lying in the back of a filthy wagon, trussed in a slave jacket, having been ravished by her kidnapper as though she were some common harlot.

She shifted her position yet again as the wagon bounced

over a particularly deep rut, and wondered whether she had been missed yet. Time was beginning to lose its meaning for her. The all smothering darkness leant an air of total unreality to everything and she had no way of judging whether they had been on the road for one hour, three hours, or even ten, though she doubted it had been anywhere near the latter time.

In her mind she pictured the world map that had been on her dayroom wall as a child, when all the Vorsan states had been independent, internally feuding little principalities. Names of countries and cities floated before her closed eyes, succession lines of kings, princes and electors rolled down over those countries, a legacy of the thoroughness of her tutors, yet still she could make no real sense of all this.

Yes, there was little doubt that several countries could make good use of her as a bargaining tool, but which one was actually behind this audacity was beyond Corinna. And what their immediate goal was it was difficult to say. Politics, she had been brought up to understand, ran by its own rules and those rules could be rewritten, almost daily, to suit the purpose of those actually politicking. Meanwhile, she was now in the hands of a man who seemed perfectly capable of rewriting *whatever* rules he chose.

He had already killed at least one man and that by his own admission, if not boast. He had managed to walk past a squadron of palace guards, not to mention the various domestic staff, who at times seemed too numerous to count, and then walk out again with one princess, trussed like a slave girl, draped over his shoulder like so much baggage. But then, Corinna thought, he had had the advantage of the passageway.

It was the secret passageway that bothered her most, for she had always been brought up to believe that only the immediate family, plus a few of their most trusted retainers, knew of its existence, let alone where to find its entrances. True, the secret was no longer as vital as it had been in the days of her ancestors, for it was many years since Illeum needed to fear invasion, let alone a siege of its ruling family's home, but still very few people knew of that secret tunnel.

Which meant, without a doubt, that Savatch had had help from within the palace itself and not just from some lackey. Yes, it would be easy enough for any one of a number of the palace servants to drug the wine given to the guards, but there were too many other things that would need the cooperation of more than just a servant. His timing had been too perfect; he knew his way about the palace, he had picked his moment to coincide with that time of the day when there would be nobody, servant or otherwise, in that area of the upper floor that was the family living accommodation, and he knew about the passage.

The list of potential collaborators was not overly long. Vice Chancellor Menndt, her father's Chief Minister, would have known about the passage and he was also a frequent visitor to the palace, to the extent that Lord Lundt had set aside a private chamber for the old man's use. But Menndt was as loyal a man as one could wish, and had held his office since before Corinna had been born.

Then there were the family themselves. Her father, of course, but that was out of the question. Uncle Willum. He wasn't her real uncle. He had been orphaned as a child when his parents had been slain in the forest by the hands of vile bandits, and her grandparents, their friends, had taken him into their home and raised him as one of their own and their sons' brother. His shrew of a wife, Benita, though Corinna doubted she would know about the tunnel.

And her father's real brother, Rufus. There was also her aunt from her late mother's side, who had lived at the palace for some years until her illness had grown so acute that she had been moved to the hospital run by the Priestesses of Gar. It was possible that aunt Elisor knew of the passage from her late sister, but it was unlikely that she still retained enough control over her shrinking brain to remember it. Most days, she had enough trouble remembering her own name.

Willum was too close to even consider and he had been there ever since Corinna could remember. He had taught her to shoot a bow at the age of five, had taken her fishing, both in the rivers and lakes and in the shallow offshore waters at Bragliod. Slightly overweight and now balding, his florid, cheerful face and cuddly presence had been a part of Corinna's very life.

The waspish Benita was a different prospect. Corinna had never liked her from the time she had first come to the palace for the betrothal party. Corinna had been nine then, but even then she was old enough and astute enough to realise that this was no love match. Benita was the youngest daughter of the Elector of Thass-Orman, a small and relatively unimportant border country, set mostly in the mountains, but the oldest democracy in the south and, more importantly, set atop a wealth of mineral deposits. Like her own, Willum and Benita's marriage had been a political expediency, but Benita, for all her temper tantrums and dark moods, was not a political animal, of that Corinna was certain.

Uncle Rufus was a curious man. He had been, until Corinna's marriage to Lazlo, the nominal Regent of Illeum, should anything have happened to Lundt, but it was unlikely that he would ever have taken an active part in government had that contingency arisen. Very much a loner, he was a dedicated scholar and lived most of his life in a small palace high in the hills, emerging into society only infrequently. He had been at the wedding, a tall, gaunt figure, with hollow eyes and a raggedy beard, his clothes looking very dark and drab against the festival of colour elsewhere.

He spoke little and barely acknowledged anyone, though he had spoken to Corinna and had given her a beautifully bound text of his treatise of Vorsan history. For all his apparent aloofness, he was a kindly man and Corinna could not see him as a traitor. Which left her no nearer to the truth than when she had started this exercise. She sighed, swallowed the spittle that the awful gag kept generating in her mouth, and eased her position for the hundredth time.

Chapter Four

Moxie was far from happy with her new situation. At first, when the Lady Dorothea had offered to buy her services from her father, Moxie had seen it as a great opportunity, a chance to be free of the smoky, smelly atmosphere of the inn, a chance to escape the drudgery of constant cooking and cleaning, a chance to be free of the groping hands and leering faces.

However, it had not been long before she discovered that she had jumped from one frying pan straight into another. Not that she was expected to slave over pots and pails as she had been at The Wagonmaster, but she was left in no doubt as to why the austere redheaded woman had bought her. Lady Dorothea preferred the intimate company of women to that of any man and she, Moxie, was to be little more than a bed companion, for want of a better description.

Not that Lady Dorothea confined her sexual exercises merely to the bed, or even the bedchamber. On their journey back from the inn, her ladyship had suddenly turned her steed off the main roadway and led Moxie's mount into the trees. She had then dismounted, spoken quietly to the leader of her escort, and two of the men had then lifted Moxie from the saddle, stripped her naked despite her frenzied attempts to resist, and tied her with her back to a slender larch tree, before riding off back to wait at the roadside.

Lady Dorothea had walked casually over to her and hefted Moxie's breasts in her leather gloved hands. Moxie had been too frightened to speak, but Dorothea had done all the talking necessary.

'These fine melons are for my appreciation only, in the future,' she had said, levelly. Her hand had gone down over Moxie's belly and settled on the narrow cleft between her legs. Moxie had shivered, as much from fright as from the cold evening air.

'And this little slot, also, is mine,' Dorothea continued. She leaned forward and kissed Moxie gently on the lips. 'This mouth, too,' she said and her fingers pressed harder into Moxie's sex. 'From now on, my little country peach, you will learn what it takes to please and to enjoy another woman. Those barbarians at your father's inn are so typical of the male species. They are not for you, my precious.'

At last, Moxie had found her tongue and screamed out a denial, but the Lady Dorothea had merely smiled down at her.

'In a short while, missy, you will come to think differently.'

'Never!' Moxie had shrieked, and then made her first big mistake. 'Never, you filthy bitch!' she had screamed. Lady Dorothea's leather covered palm had crashed into Moxie's cheek so hard she was knocked almost senseless. She barely heard Dorothea's parting words.

'You will learn your lessons the hard way, evidently,' she had sneered. 'And you will also understand that I do not pay out good money to have a simple bumpkin call me names.'

She had sent her guards back to release Moxie, but the unfortunate girl was not given her clothes back. Instead, they slung her naked across her saddle and tied her there, so that the remainder of the journey had been an uncomfortable ordeal in the extreme. But it was nothing on what was to come.

The following day Dorothea entered the spartan room where Moxie had been locked overnight. She had two guards with her and they quickly cuffed Moxie's arms behind her back, and then connected the chain to a thick leather collar that they buckled about her neck, shortening the chain so her hands were pulled up cruelly between her shoulderblades. They were then dismissed, leaving the two females alone.

'I trust you enjoyed a good sleep, young lady,' Dorothea said, knowing full well that naked, on a bare floor, Moxie most certainly had not. 'And this morning you will learn your first lessons in obedience. Your father tells me you are still a virgin.' Dumbly, Moxie nodded. 'Well, we shall have to attend to that first, I think.'

She seized Moxie's arm and, with astonishing strength for a woman, dragged her out of the room and into the small walled courtyard that stood at this side of the building. Arriving in darkness, Moxie had not been able to tell much about her new home, but now she saw it was a large house, with three floors and turrets at either corner. In fact, she realised, it was almost a castle.

In the yard was set up something that reminded Moxie of a carpenter's sawhorse, though it was considerably higher and its top padded with dark leather. She saw there were straps attached to each of the four supporting legs and another strap hung open at either side. Naïve as she was in many things, Moxie was in no doubt as to the purpose of the bench. She was about to be whipped over it.

She considered resisting, but the futility of it was all too obvious. Even had she not been so cruelly bound, Moxie would have been no match for Lady Dorothea. The woman was far taller and, despite her otherwise slim build, was possessed of broad shoulders and wide hips, which the leather riding breeches and silk blouse did little to conceal. When they drew up to the horse she lifted Moxie easily, straddling her across one end with her back to the horse itself.

With a speed and precision obviously born of practise, she rapidly secured Moxie's ankles and added extra straps about her thighs. She then moved around behind the helpless girl and forced her back until she was lying almost horizontal, her bound arms between her back and the leather padding. She buckled the wide strap across her stomach to prevent Moxie rising up again.

She placed one hand on Moxie's left breast and squeezed the succulent flesh with evident relish. To her horror, Moxie saw her nipples beginning to rise and closed her eyes, trying to conjure up pictures of everyday, mundane things in an effort to distract her body from what was being done to it.

'Of course, your insolence should really warrant a sound whipping,' Lady Dorothea said, her voice little more than a whisper. 'But I have other ways of teaching obedience.' Her hand left Moxie's breast and slid slowly down over her stomach, until it rested upon the distended lips of her virgin sex. She inserted one finger and probed carefully, pausing when she came to the hymen, which was still obviously as intact as the girl's father had claimed. Not that physical virginity itself held any value for Dorothea, but she found it easier to ply a girl who had yet to know a man within her.

Moxie let out a small moan and Dorothea leaned over and licked across the girl's lower belly, just above the little forest of pubic curls. Again Moxie groaned and Dorothea smiled to herself. She was going to enjoy this.

'What's it to be, girl?' she asked softly. 'A whipping, or

do you beg me to deflower you?' Moxie whimpered and there were tears beneath her closed eyelids. Dorothea moved her finger slightly, coming back to press against the girl's swollen bud. 'Well, speak up,' she demanded, her tone more urgent. 'Whipped or fucked, you graceless little cow, it's all the same to me.'

Moxie forced her eyes open. 'Please, mistress,' she begged, confusion making her voice tremble, 'please don't whip me. I'll – I'll do anything you want, and I'm so sorry for what I said to you. Please believe me. Please forgive me.'

'So, if it's not to be the whip...?' Dorothea waited, determined to make the girl say it herself. The inference was not lost on the innkeeper's daughter.

'The – the other,' she stammered. 'The other thing, please, mistress.'

'What "other thing" would that be, my precious country rose?'

'The other... what you said. About—' She caught her breath, trying to remember the expression Dorothea had used. 'Something about flowers, mistress.'

'Deflowering you, you mean, you silly girl,' Dorothea said with a chuckle. 'So, you want me to deflower you?' Her finger moved slightly again and Moxie shuddered, nodding her head as she lay there.

'Yes, mistress. I want you to deflower me, if that's what it is?'

'And do you know what is meant by that?'

Again Moxie nodded. 'I think so, mistress. It's what happens to a girl the first time she goes with her man and he—' She closed her eyes in shame. 'When he puts his manhood inside you,' she finished, with a great effort of willpower. 'But mistress, you don't have a man's thing, do you?'

'Silly girl,' Dorothea chided. 'Of course I do. See here.' She reached into the compartment beneath the horse and drew out a long, leather covered dildo. To Moxie, who had never seen a man naked before, it looked horrendous. She gasped.

'But it's so big!' she wailed. 'I couldn't possibly!'

'Oh, I think you could possibly,' Dorothea taunted her. 'But first we must give it every assistance. Here, take it in your mouth and make it nice and wet.' She thrust the phallus between Moxie's lips. 'Suck, my little dove, and don't let it go until I tell you, else I'll take the whip to you anyway.' Terrified at the prospect of being whipped by anyone, let alone this heartless creature, Moxie sucked for all she was worth.

Dorothea, meanwhile, moved back around in front of her and took up a stance between her widespread knees. Slowly, her eyes sparkling with anticipation, she lowered her head and placed her mouth over Moxie's warm slit, probing between her outer lips with her long tongue. Moxie groaned again, this time much louder, and her back arched as far as the strap across her would allow.

Steadily, unhurriedly, Dorothea began to lick the helpless girl's clitoris, revelling in the musky aroma that filled her nostrils, sensing it growing stronger and stronger as the girl's excitement and arousal increased. From behind the leather penis, Moxie's cries were becoming more urgent now and her head was lolling from side to side. She was near to orgasm and Dorothea knew it. Judging her moment to perfection, she suddenly straightened up, reached along Moxie's prone form and snatched the penis from her mouth.

Before Moxie had time to understand what was happening, Dorothea had introduced the slightly tapered tip between her outer labia, the combination of spittle and love juices joining together to prepare a well lubricated passage for the long phallus. She pressed slightly, embedding the first inch inside the girl, feeling the resistance from the virgin membrane. She looked down at Moxie, whose eyes were open now.

'Kiss your innocence goodbye, little rose,' she said, and thrust against the base of the shaft. Moxie's tender flesh was no match for the hard leather and yielded as easily as Dorothea had anticipated, though still tearing a small yelp of pain from Moxie herself.

'Ah, no! Mistress, please!' the girl squeaked, but the initial pain was rapidly being engulfed by the other sensations that were washing over her. 'No, pleeease!' she cried again. 'Pleeeaa-ooohhhh!' Her shrieks became totally incoherent now and only the strictures of her bondage kept her from completely convulsing. Stepping back and releasing her grip on the dildo, Dorothea grimaced with pleasure. She had seldom seen such a violent climax, let alone an innocent country virgin. Whoa, but that thousand crowns had been money well invested!

It was only after Moxie had finally subsided, lying there with her delicious breasts rising and falling as she gasped for breath, that Dorothea prepared to show the unfortunate girl the true extent of the punishment she had planned for her. She turned and walked across the courtyard, opening the small gate in the farthest corner. Beyond stood a young groom, his hand entwined in the lead rein of a beautiful black stallion. She nodded to him and turned back to Moxie, and the lad followed, the impressive beast at his heels.

Hearing the sound of hooves and the snorts from the big animal, Moxie turned her head and opened her eyes. At first she seemed bewildered, but when she saw the saddle and understood what was intended for her, she started to struggle and scream for mercy.

'No, mistress!' she shrilled. 'No-ooo, you promised!'

'I promised you would be spared the whip in exchange for your maidenhead,' Dorothea said. 'Well, your maidenhead's gone, but we need to give your slot some preparation for the future. You need to learn control and how to pace yourself, else you'll be useless to me, my girl.' She unbuckled the widest strap and eased Moxie into a sitting position, from where she had a much clearer view of the huge shaft that rose from the centre of the saddle.

'Oh, mistress, please,' she sobbed. 'I can't possibly. I already feel I've been torn in two.'

'It won't harm you,' she said derisively. Moxie whimpered still more and tried to back away, but there was no means of retreat. 'Time for you to ride a different horse, my little wanton rose,' Dorothea said. She quickly released the girl's legs and lifted her down, dragging her across to the horse. She lifted Moxie's right foot and placed it in the stirrup. 'You've ridden before, I suppose?' she said. Glumly, tears smearing her cheeks, Moxie nodded. 'Good. Well, up you go. I'll steady you.'

'I can't, mistress,' Moxie wailed again, realising she was expected to impale herself on this phallus. Dorothea's reply was uncompromising.

'If you don't, it's the whip for you and then I'll let the duty guards have you for the day. They'll fuck some obedience into you, I can assure you.'

Sobbing bitterly now, Moxie, with Dorothea steadying her and giving assistance to her lift, swung up into the saddle. Her right foot scrambled for the other stirrup and the groom swiftly reached out to help her gain some purchase. His face said everything, his eyes shining at the sight of the buxom girl's sopping sex above his face.

He wished he could stretch up and use his tongue on the enticing pink meat, but he knew Dorothea would have him flogged if she suspected he was even considering such a foolish move. No, time for the wench later, when she tired of the mistress's toys and games and was ready for some genuine male meat. He kept his features impassive as Moxie slowly lowered herself, Dorothea reaching out to steady the shaft on which she was to be splayed.

It entered her easily, but it was longer than the device Dorothea had used on her earlier and she felt her stomach lurch as its full length slid home.

'A neat seat, as they say,' Dorothea quipped. 'And now we must make sure you don't slip from it.' There were straps attached at either side of the saddle and these were now buckled tightly about Moxie's thighs, clamping her immovably in position, after which her feet were removed from the stirrups and the stirrups themselves removed altogether. Now Moxie's full weight was upon her naked bottom and upon the thick phallus. The horse took a half step forward and she rocked on it, the unyielding leather pressing hard against her most vulnerable spot. She let out a gasp.

'Fine,' Dorothea said, noting her reaction. 'A couple of hours on Midnight should make you think twice before opening your mouth to me in the future. Ventor,' she said, addressing the youth, 'I presume you have been properly prepared for your duties?' The groom nodded. Beneath his tunic he had been locked into a cunningly designed chastity device, a concoction of leather straps and steel mesh that would prevent him being able to take any advantage of Moxie in her present helpless state.

'Would you like to see, mistress?' he offered. Dorothea

shook her head with an expression of obvious distaste.

'I don't think so, Ventor,' she said. 'The sight of male genitalia, even suitably chained up where it should be permanently, in my opinion, fills me with disgust. As long as Mistress Agana has seen to you, you may take Moxie for a little trot in the woods. And I do mean a trot, not some easy walk.

'By the time I see the wretched creature again I want to be able to see that she's suffered properly. You may from time to time massage her breasts and nipples, if you can find a stump or fallen tree to stand upon. Make sure she stays aroused at all times and have her back here in time for lunch. Satisfying one appetite generally increases another, I find.'

As the lad wheeled the horse round and headed back towards the gate, Moxie was definitely not happy in her new situation.

Chapter Five

Corinna came awake with a start, hardly able to believe she had fallen asleep at all. The wagon had stopped and everything was silent, save for the occasional snuffling of the horses. She tried to sit up and cried out through her gag when she moved, for her trussed arms had become numb and the slightest movement sent daggers of fire through her shoulders. Whimpering with agony, she scarcely heard the rustle of the wagon canvas.

'Time for some exercise, princess.' The wagon creaked on its springs as Savatch hauled himself up alongside her. She could smell his sweat as he put his arm beneath her and raised her into a sitting position. He leaned her forward and she felt his fingers fumbling with the laces at the back of her head. After what seemed an eternity the hateful hood was pulled off and Corinna winced at the sudden intrusion of light after so long in complete darkness.

He reached behind her again, undid the gag strap, and pulled the sodden leather wad from her mouth. Corinna gasped, swallowed, and ran her tongue around her sore lips.

'My arms,' she managed to gasp, at length. 'I can't feel my arms.' Savatch did not reply, but he did turn his attention to the straps that secured the arm pouch. When he finally pulled it from her and her arms fell to her sides, Corinna cried out in pain and bit her lip to fight back the tears that were so close. Savatch grasped her right arm and began massaging the muscles.

'I fear I may have left you a little overly long, princess,' he said. 'However, this should serve as a salutary lesson to you. From now on we have no further need of this thing, just so long as you behave yourself and don't try anything stupid.'

'Wh-where are we?' It seemed, to Corinna, that it was a stupid question, but she needed to get the man talking, weaken his guard and find out as much as she could as quickly as possible. Savatch grunted as he fumbled with the straps holding the two sections of the slave jacket together.

'About thirty miles from the city, but on a little used country road. I'm surprised the extra bouncing about didn't wake you.'

'I'm surprised I slept at all,' Corinna retorted. 'I suppose it was being in the dark for so long. What time of day is it?' The light from outside the wagon was still bright, which meant they could have been on the road for no more than five or six hours, which would agree with Savatch's estimate of the distance they had come.

'There's about an hour or so of daylight left, milady, but we have already reached the place I have prepared for our overnight refuge.' He pulled the leather halberd over Corinna's head and tossed it into the sacking. 'Give me your hands.' His tone brooked no argument and Corinna dutifully presented her hands to him.

From beneath the sacking Savatch drew a set of steel manacles, which he snapped tightly into place about her wrists. The two locking fetters were connected with five links of chain, a distance equal in length to the span of Corinna's hand. It was not much, but it was a great improvement on the bondage she had endured thus far.

'We are stopped for the night, then?' she said. 'Are we

to eat?'

'Indeed, we shall eat shortly, princess. But first we must prepare our lodgings. Come, or would you like me to lift you down?'

'Now that you have returned me some use of my hands, I think I prefer to get down myself,' Corinna said, primly. She scrambled over the tailboard with as much dignity as she could muster, determined not to let him think his humiliation of her had fractured her spirit, yet all the while only too aware of her nakedness and the hairless slave girl mound between her thighs.

Standing on the rough ground, Corinna looked about her. They were deep in woodlands, but the wagon was halted in a small clearing, alongside a rustic, single storeyed building that had seen far better days, though the door seemed stout enough and the windows had been boarded over with heavy planks.

'Where is this?' she demanded, as Savatch indicated for her to walk towards the cottage. He shrugged.

'Does it matter?' he said. 'It's just somewhere sheltered to stay for a day or so, until I hand you over to the people who are paying for you.'

'And who are they?' Corinna said. 'Or am I not permitted to know?'

'You'll know soon enough, lady, but it's not for me to tell you. Now, get your pretty arse inside. It'll be dark before long and it gets cold out here at night.'

'Then perhaps you might consider letting me have some clothes,' Corinna snapped. Savatch grinned.

'I think I prefer you just the way you are,' he said. 'It would be a crime to cover up such lovely flesh.'

'The crime, sir, has already been committed. Have you any idea what they will do to you when they catch up with you?'

'First they have to catch me,' Savatch laughed. 'And there have been many who have tried and failed, believe me.' Somehow, Corinna did not find it difficult to believe him. With a grimace, her bare feet scraping on the stony ground, she led the way into the building.

With the windows covered as they were, it was very dark inside, only the smallest chinks of light penetrating between the rough planks. Savatch ordered her to stand still and moved past her and, a moment later, there were several sparks from a flint and the wick of his tinder box flared into life. He reached down, lifted an old oil lantern and lit it, stretching up to hang it from one of the overhead beams.

By its light Corinna made out a table and two chairs, a bench along one wall and a rough palette in one corner. On the table stood a sack from which had spilled several packages, which she guessed contained provisions.

'Am I expected to sleep there?' she said, pointing towards the palette and wrinkling her nose in disgust. 'It's filthy. In fact, the entire place is disgusting.'

'There are no palaces this deep in the forest, I'm afraid,' Savatch said. 'Be thankful to have shelter at all. And no, your ladyship, you will not be sleeping there. I have made other arrangements for you.' Corinna's fettered hands instinctively moved closer to her denuded sex as he spoke, for something in his tone told her that those plans did not all involve sleeping. She thought back to the way he had taken her in her chambers, using her as carelessly as a man might use a whore. Her spine tingled at the thought he would almost certainly use her similarly again.

Savatch pointed to an inner door, deep in the shadows of one corner.

'You will be staying in there,' he said. He grasped the short chain between her wrists and pulled her across to the door. Corinna saw it was firmly bolted, with a lock through the bolt. Savatch pulled out a key, removed the lock and slid the bolt back, pushing the door open with his foot.

'Oh yes,' he said, drawing her into the room, 'I forgot to tell you that you would have company other than my own. This is Helda.'

Corinna peered into the gloom, unable to penetrate the near total darkness. The only light was what little came through the open door, provided by the lantern. It was not much, but Savatch quickly remedied the situation, lighting a second lamp and hanging that overhead.

The girl squatting in the straw which covered half the floor was small-boned and very pretty, despite her dishevelled state. Her dark hair had not seen brush or comb for some time and there were smudges of dirt on her face and body, the latter being completely naked. Corinna saw that she, like herself, was cuffed, but that there was another chain locked about her slim ankle, stretching across to a ring set in the stone wall.

'You're inhuman!' Corinna cried, rounding on her captor. 'How can you keep a woman in these conditions? I would not treat a dog so!'

'I dare say there are many things I do that you would not, princess,' Savatch replied, easily. 'The girl was in that state when I found her and would have been in a far worse state, but for me.' The girl shifted her position and now Corinna saw the dark welts across her shoulders.

'I suppose you're going to deny it was you who marked her thus?' she hissed, accusingly.

Savatch gave his contemptuous shrug. 'Not at all,' he said. 'However, had I not intervened those three stripes would have been a dozen, maybe even more, and they would not have been so expertly delivered. I fear the woman who was going to wield the whip would have committed a butchery, for the punishment would have been meted out as an act of revenge, not an act of justice.' Corinna stared at him, scarcely able to believe what she was hearing, nor the fact that he genuinely seemed to believe he had done this poor creature a favour.

'You seem to relish beating women,' she said derisively.

Yet again he shrugged. 'When they need it, yes,' he agreed. 'And some need it more than others. Now, if you would like to make yourself comfortable, I will do something about food. I left Helda with sufficient food and water until our return, but she seems to have the appetite of a horse, as well as the manners of a pig.'

Reluctantly, Corinna lowered herself onto the straw. It felt harsh and tickly against her naked flesh, but at least it seemed fresh. She kept as great a distance between herself and Helda as the width of the room would permit, and lay back against the wall as Savatch locked a chain about her right ankle in the manner in which he had secured the peasant girl.

Savatch stood back, surveying his two captives, particularly Helda, who averted her eyes and stared at her feet. After a few seconds consideration, he seemed to come to a decision.

'You are right, princess,' he said, nodding and turning back to Corinna. 'She is a filthy wench and no mistake.' He bent down again and released Helda's ankle fetter. 'There's a small stream a little way into the trees, which is probably why this place was built here in the first place. I think a renewed acquaintance with water will do you the world of good. Plus, you need a good shaving. I prefer my women smooth.'

As Helda rose, Corinna saw the thick thatch of dark curls between her legs. She looked back at Savatch and then down at the straw. The man was truly monstrous, she thought. He treated women like mere chattels that existed purely for his personal distraction, and regarded their bodies as mere ornaments and playthings. And yet, in a strange way, there was something almost hypnotically attractive about him. Corinna shook herself mentally and closed her eyes as he led Helda from the room.

It was a very different creature who returned to their cell less than an hour later. With the layers of grime washed away and her hair cleaned and brushed, Helda was every bit as pretty as Corinna had presumed and now she also kept her chained hands close over her newly depilated sex. When Savatch had rechained her and left the room, Corinna was the first to speak.

'Was it true what he said?' she asked gently. 'About the whipping?'

The girl gave a curt nod. 'Yes, lady, it were,' she said, in an accent that was thick with the countryside. 'Those bitches always hated me 'cos I were prettier than they, and then they fixed it so everyone believed I were a damned thief. The elders might all 'ave been men, but they was beholden to their womenfolk in every way.

'The cow with the whip would've stripped my back to the bone, if the way she treats her horse and oxen is owt to go by. What Master Savatch did was painful, true enough, but he got my punishment cut from twelve to six and then paid a crown each in place of the last three stripes.'

'How long ago was this?' Corinna asked.

Helda made a wry face. 'Dunno, lady,' she said. 'Few

days back. I sort of lost time a bit, if you know what I mean. I've been sat in this room for at least two days now, whilst he's been getting all sorts of things ready for something he's got planned.' She paused and screwed up her face.

'He called you "princess" just then,' she said, her brows furrowing together. 'You ain't a real princess, are you?'

Corinna smiled. 'That's not my title, no,' she said, 'though I am of the nobility. In fact, the highest nobility in the land. My father is Lord Lundt Oleana.'

Helda's mouth fell open.

'Then you are a princess, sort of,' she gasped. She stared at Corinna and her eyes fell upon the naked patch that Savatch had shaved that morning. 'Did he shave you, too? And you a royalty,' she said when Corinna nodded affirmation. 'Your pa'll likely chop off his bollocks when he catches up with him!'

'If he catches up with him,' Corinna said. 'Master Savatch seems to think he won't. Tell me, what do you know about him?'

'Little enough, highness,' Helda said. 'I think he might be a minor noble himself. He speaks like gentry, as you probably noticed, though he ruts like a ploughboy and is equipped like a donkey.'

'Yes, so I discovered for myself,' Corinna replied grimly.

Helda's eyes grew even wider.

'You mean he tupped you, too?'

'In my own chambers, to add insult to injury. He trussed me like a slave girl, beat me, and then mounted me like I was a common whore.'

'Well, I'll be—!' Helda gasped, and then burst into a fit of giggles, which she managed to suppress only after several seconds. She looked up at Corinna, her expression sheepish.

Chapter Six

After her ordeal on the stallion, Midnight, Moxie was not eager to incur her new mistress's displeasure again too readily, and quickly became adept in her new role. In truth, she was also rapidly beginning to enjoy it and the pleasures she received in turn were far more enjoyable than the succession of enforced orgasms she had suffered during her ride through the woods.

She was given her own room, adjoining Lady Dorothea's private suite. Adjoining Moxie's room, in its turn, was her own bathroom, the tiled bath sunk into the floor, with a drain plug to allow the water out and no need for bailing with buckets, as she had grown accustomed to at home. She did not even have to fetch the hot water for her bath, for Dorothea kept a retinue of young pages for the menial tasks.

The red haired aristocrat, it seemed, did not just spurn men sexually, she actively delighted in humiliating them in every way possible. The page boys, for example, all wore sheer silk hose, dainty feminine slippers and velvet doublets, their hair kept long and curled each day with heated tongs. They had also, as Moxie discovered when eavesdropping on a conversation in the kitchens, been castrated.

Moxie wondered if Lady Dorothea might not be an Yslander, for she had heard the many legends concerning their treatment of their menfolk, but she also knew that the Yslandic women were very pale skinned, with hair that was so fair as to be almost white. No, she decided, Lady Dorothea might be many things, but an Yslandic amazon she was not.

It was not only the young eunuchs who were led a hard life, either, for Dorothea's housekeeper-come-major-domo, Agana, was a tyrant where the female staff were concerned and the only people who escaped her wrath were Moxie herself and Mistress Doxoff, the elderly cook, who, it was rumoured, had been here before the house itself had been built and who, in the manner of cooks all over the world and down through the ages, held a position that demanded respect and not a little awe, due entirely to her ability with food dishes.

Most of the maids and scullions tried to keep clear of Doxoff, for she was possessed of a quick tongue and evil temper at times. Moxie, however, found her to be a warm old lady and Doxoff, in her turn, seemed to take to the young country girl, though she frequently teased her over her position in the household.

'Good day, my little warming pan,' she would say, when Moxie appeared mid-morning in search of something to eat. 'I see the milk of kindness is still not enough to sustain you through the day.' And Moxie would inevitably blush, for there was truth in what the woman said. She was no more than a plaything for their mistress, and not a particularly expensive one either.

She had, however, been given many new clothes and been introduced to the magic of tight corseting, which had reduced her waistline considerably and given an added emphasis to the generous curves above and below it, which pleased Dorothea greatly. She now wore silk stockings and was gradually learning to walk in the elegantly crafted high-heeled slippers that were the fashion for ladies of and associated with, the nobility.

Quite what Dorothea's rank was, or her position in society, Moxie had not yet been able to determine, but the lady was not short of wealth, that much was in evidence from the fabulous furniture and draperies that adorned the vast house. And her own wardrobe put even Moxie's new outfits to shame. She had more than two hundred specially made gowns in the chests and cupboards of her dressing room.

Despite this, during the daytime she often preferred clothing that was pointedly masculine in its conception. She had several pairs of full length leather boots, into which she would tuck leather, or suede, riding breeches. And her blouses were cut like shirts, worn low at the front and with huge sleeves. About her throat she would complete the effect with a choker of either velvet, or still more leather, decorated with anything from a single cameo to a row of wickedly gleaming metal studs.

Agana also favoured breeches and shorter boots, wearing sleeveless leather jerkins above the waist, which displayed her powerful arms and shoulders. She also carried a short crop, which she hooked onto one side of her ever present wide leather belt, and she frequently employed this to hurry up any maid or page that she happened to decide was not putting enough effort into whatever task they were employed upon when she saw them.

For what she decided were more serious offences, there would be proper floggings, staged with a theatricality that was designed to instil the fear of the gods into her minions. Dorothea occasionally punished the young male miscreants personally, but generally she was content to leave the household discipline in the capable hands of her trusted lieutenant, and the girls were Agana's prerogative at all times.

She delighted in bringing out her own whipping horse, setting it up in the main hall and gathering the other staff to witness their unfortunate colleague's chastisement. The victim would be stripped and strapped down, face down in the case of the girls and face up, more often, in the case of the boys. She would then whip them slowly, creating a crimson pattern wherever there was exposed flesh, yet never breaking the skin.

Her final refinement, before delivering a last volley of strokes with a long, whippy cane, was designed to complete the debasement of the punishee without inflicting actual pain. For the girls she would employ a large dildo, similar to the one with which Dorothea had first ruptured Moxie's hymen, and work it in and out of them, frequently using both available orifices until the poor creature orgasmed.

For the males she used a slightly thinner shaft, plugging them with it, before turning her attention to their own rods. To Moxie's surprise, although the young men had no testicles, they could still achieve an erection, though their final spasmings did not yield any fluid, of course. Agana did not manipulate them herself, but delegated that task to one of the prettier female staff, choosing a different girl every time, so that she might also share in the helpless fellow's humiliation.

The chosen girl was required to strip to the waist and employ both hand and mouth, and woe betide her if she was too long in drawing the business to the required conclusion, for she would be next astride the horse and all present knew this.

Agana was a handsome figure of a woman, slightly taller even than Dorothea, but she was not exactly beautiful. Her features were too square, her jaw too mannish, and her hips too narrow for conventional beauty, and she was almost flat chested, where Lady Dorothea was as well-endowed in that feminine department as the buxom Moxie. It seemed she was determined to exact a spiteful revenge on the rest of her sex for having been born without prettiness, for the more comely the maid, the more often she seemed to attract Agana's wrath.

It was, Moxie rapidly concluded, a singularly odd household, but curiously, she was beginning to feel at home in it.

Many miles away, Corinna was decidedly less happy, for Savatch had taken exception to a comment she had made to him when he had brought the two girls their frugal supper. It had been an innocuous enough insult, she thought, especially in the light of what he had done to her that day, but her captor had seized upon it, apparently as an excuse to have more sport with her.

'We shall see who is truly the animal here, milady,' he had said to her. 'And this time we have no need for undue haste. I fancy another sample of those regal delights, but I'll have you beg me for it first.'

'Never!' Corinna spat back, but she already had the awful feeling that he would have her submit in the manner he decided. Savatch lost no time in getting down to work. From his pack he produced two sturdy looking leather cuffs, each with rings attached, and buckled them tightly about her wrists. He then knotted two long lengths of cord through the rings, threw the free ends over the beam above, and quickly hauled Corinna up until she was standing on tiptoe, arms held high and wide, the strain on her shoulders terrible.

Now he took a wide collar, also with several rings

stitched into the leather, and fastened this about her throat, which forced her to stand with head held erect, the thick leather pressing into the soft flesh beneath her jaw. He tied more cords to either side of the collar and then hitched them over the beam, dragging the table over to stand on whilst he worked. From a corner of the room he produced a long pole and lashed her ankles, one at either end, so that she was forced to stand with her legs splayed and her sex stretched blatantly wide.

Still he was not finished with her. Next came three more broad straps, the longest of which was cinched tightly about Corinna's waist, the other two buckled about the tops of her thighs. There were more rings set in these, and Savatch set about putting them to effective use. He lowered the cord holding her left arm aloft and added two more shorter cords to the ring. One he tied off to the waist belt, the other to the ring on the outside of the thigh strap on that side, leaving about twelve inches of slack in each case.

He then hauled on the overhead cord until Corinna's arm was drawn out from her body. When he repeated the process with her other arm she was left standing with her arms held out to either side, in the manner of a mother who is about to scoop up her child running towards her. It might also have been seen as a position of supplication.

It was more comfortable than being stretched out on tiptoe, but now her arms were held even more rigidly. The overhead cords prevented her from lowering her arms, the waist and thigh cords prevented her from raising them. She was effectively frozen into the one position, in the manner of a statue. Corinna sfared at Savatch, trying hard to hide the fear she felt.

'Does it please you to see a woman like this?' she asked quietly. Savatch's mouth twitched.

'It does indeed, princess,' he replied, studying her carefully.

'Then why do you continue to address me as "princess", which you know I am not, and yet still continue to treat me in such abominable fashion. You insult me, sir, by word and by deed. Have your way with me as it pleases you, for I plainly am in no position to resist, but spare me the sound of your insolent tongue.'

As she spoke, Corinna realised she was taking a dreadful risk, for the man was obviously of uncertain temper. In her present position she was helpless to defend herself, and she had already seen enough evidence of what he was willing to inflict on a woman. Savatch, however, seemed quite amused by her defiance.

'If my tongue irks you so much,' he said, 'then perhaps we should try you with another. Helda!' He turned to the peasant girl, who had remained squatting in the corner of the room throughout, watching Corinna's growing plight with wide eyes. She crawled forward at Savatch's command and looked up at him, like a dog awaiting her master's next instruction.

'You know what to do?' He patted her on the head, reinforcing the master-dog image. Helda nodded and began crawling towards Corinna. She stopped before her and raised her head, and Corinna could feel her warm breath against her denuded crotch. A moment later she felt the little tongue as it flicked upwards along the length of her labia. She barely suppressed a little grunt, though whether it was caused by pleasure, or surprise, she did not want to ask herself.

'Corinna gritted her teeth as Helda licked again. 'The gods must have hated mankind, the day they created you,' she hissed. Savatch smiled broadly.

'I should say rather that he hated womankind, wouldn't you, proud lady. Ah, but that I were an artist, to capture so much beauty in so fine a state of readiness.'

'May all the imps of Hasroth share your soul in an eternal supper!' Corinna cried out, but her voice caught in mid-sentence as Helda's tongue found her clitoris and the girl's lips suddenly sucked on it. 'Foul devil!' she shrieked, as Savatch laughed at her attempts to fight off the growing desire that was mounting within her.

'Relax, little princess,' Savatch said, his voice surprisingly gentle. 'As you say yourself, you can do nothing to the contrary, so enjoy Helda's ministrations. I have learned she is very skilled with that mouth of hers, and not just with men. That, methinks, had something to do with the feelings running so high among certain of her former village's womenfolk.

'And when she is finished with you, I shall enjoy her myself, especially now she has been cleaned up somewhat. Think on, princess, for your little nymph lover there shall be the one who prepares my pole for your tight little slot.'

Despite Corinna's best efforts at resistance, it was not very long before Helda's wicked mouth and tongue were having the effect Savatch so obviously required. She stood there, transfixed in her bonds, head held high and proud, yet panted and writhed in her straps, her every muscle twitching, her every nerve tingling. And, from between her legs, now came a whole series of particularly crude sounds as Helda greedily lapped and sucked the juices her efforts had brought forth.

'Enough!' Savatch cried out and kicked Helda's rump lightly with his booted foot, to emphasise the instruction. The dark haired girl sat back on her haunches, leaving Corinna poised on the brink of orgasm, teetering on the very precipice of lust, her sex now wide open and dripping with its eagerness.

'Are you ready for me now, princess?' Savatch asked, nonchalantly.

'Damn you!' Corinna screeched through clenched teeth. 'Damn you to the seven hells! Do what you want and have done with it!' She closed her eyes and tried to shake the stray strands of hair clear of her face, but the high collar restricted any movement to a minimum. When she opened her eyes again Savatch was holding something in his right hand. He shook it out and Corinna saw it was a miniature whip of the multi-thonged variety sometimes used to punish criminals.

However, unlike the larger version, there were no barbed weights woven into the tips of the thongs. Instead, the leather had been knotted. Savatch flicked it towards her and Corinna cringed.

'For every pleasure there must be a pain, princess,' he whispered. 'And every pain, in its turn, brings its own pleasure.' He flicked his wrist again and this time the thongs struck across her breasts. Corinna jumped, twitching helplessly in her bondage, and her love tunnel contracted as the tiny fire needles in her chest transferred their heat to somewhere deep within her.

'Please!' she gasped. 'You cannot be so cruel!' For it was, she knew, the ultimate cruelty he was inflicting upon her now. As the tiny whip descended upon her naked body, time and again, the pain it brought also brought forth a new burning – the burning of desire. In her head, Corinna knew it was wrong, but in her gut, her basest womanhood screamed out for the growing pressure to be released.

At a signal from Savatch, Helda resumed her own assault upon Corinna's senses, but Savatch was not about to grant her early release. Judging each moment to perfection, he kept stopping himself and drawing Helda back, holding Corinna at the very edge of the chasm, but not yet permitting her to tumble.

He stooped, removed his boots, and then quickly divested himself of his shirt and breeches. Corinna saw, once again, his impressive equipment, tumescent now, but already beginning to display signs of interest. He tapped Helda's back with the whip handle and she turned to him. Without further instruction she knelt up, cupped his testicles in her hands, and sucked his flaccid length into her mouth.

It took her less than thirty seconds to complete her task, drawing back her soft lips, finally, to reveal Savatch's glistening shaft in all its attentive glory. Corinna stared at the sight through half closed eyes, and finally surrendered to the inevitable.

'Please, my lord,' she gasped. 'Please release me from this hell on earth.'

Savatch grinned and stroked his shaft with one hand. 'What is it you require of me, princess?' he asked, trying to sound innocent. Corinna breathed hard, unable to take her eyes off him now, knowing she would have to say the words, to beg for what she should have hated him for doing, yet feeling she must die if she remained unfulfilled in this way.

'Please sir, don't make me beg of you,' she whimpered, but Savatch was unmoved. He continued to work his shaft with one hand and stretched out the fingers of the other, placing them gently against her lips. Without conscious thought, Corinna drew the fingers into her mouth and sucked lightly on them. He allowed her to continue for a few seconds and then withdrew them again.

'Well, princess?' he asked, one eyebrow cocked. Corinna

let out a long sigh, acknowledging defeat. She closed her eyes.

'Please, my lord,' she gasped, 'your princess begs you to fuck her.'

'My lady has only to command in such a fashion and her every wish shall be granted,' Savatch said. He stepped forward between her splayed legs, bent slightly at the knees, and pressed the tip of his massive rod against her eager lips. He straightened up slowly, his length easing into her an inch at a time, until, finally, she was forced onto tiptoe again and he was filling her completely.

Corinna opened her eyes and stared up into his.

'You evil bastard!' she hissed, but the vacant smile on her lips belied the sting intended by the insult.

Some thirty miles away, in Illeum City itself, deep in the dungeons beneath the palace, Kirsta, the mute pantry maid, hung naked from a hook in the ceiling, held upside down by the chains which bound her ankles, her back a mass of red welts.

Lord Lundt turned to his younger brother, Willum, and shook his head sadly.

'It's no use, I fear, Willum,' he said resignedly. 'They can beat her till she dies, but she isn't going to tell us anything other than what we already know, dear boy.'

'I agree, brother,' Willum nodded. 'Pity no one thought to tell us the wench could neither read nor write. With her tongue as useless as it is, she can't say, whether she wishes to or not. What'll you do with her now? Give her to the executioner?'

Lundt shook his head. 'No, not yet, brother,' he said. 'Maybe not at all. After all, the girl's a simpleton as well as a mute and she was led into it by others, in particular that knave Sorbart.'

'Who is also saying nothing,' Willum reminded the Protector.

'Indeed, there isn't much he can say, either. All he knows is what he *has* said, I'm sure of it. He received a message to meet with this stranger outside the city limits and was offered ten thousand crowns there and then, with the promise of another ten thousand when the abduction was successfully completed.

'He was due for retirement in another year or two and was resentful of the fact that he never rose above corporal in the palace guard. He was also promised that Corinna would not be harmed and that the people behind this monstrous scheme were only interested in the ransom money.'

'Has there yet been any ransom message?' Willum asked. His florid face was still even more flushed than usual, from his exertions with the whip on the unfortunate Kirsta. His elder brother shook his head.

'Not yet,' he confirmed, 'but I dare say it will not be long in coming. But I swear to you, brother, if any harm comes to our daughter, I will sack the entire continent to find the perpetrators, whoever or whatever they might be.' He paused, gathering his composure again.

'Sorbart did say one interesting thing,' he continued. 'He said that the stranger who gave him the gold was also at Corinna's wedding. He swears he saw him in the main hall, though he was dressed more finely than on the first occasion.'

'I take it he has furnished a description of this wretch?'

'He has, and my secretaries are going through the guest list as we speak, eliminating the obvious. Then we shall have to take a closer look at those who are left. Most of them will still be in the city. If necessary I shall arrest and detain them all until we get to the bottom of this matter.'

He turned and looked back at the semi-conscious maid, who was moaning softly.

'Further punishment of this stupid girl will gain us nothing. Apparently, Sorbart told her that the sleeping draught idea was a big joke, to get his own back on the duty guard commander. Sorbart admits he has been tupping the wench on the side for several months and she was besotted with him.'

'Then you wish her set free?'

'In time, yes, but not for a little while yet. She must be made an example of in some fashion. Perhaps the jailers can shave her head and put her on display in the main square, strapped tight in a slave jacket and available to any man who might take the fancy. She will also be present to watch Sorbart's execution.'

'A wise decision, brother,' Willum said. 'And, as ever, a just one. I will see that your instructions are carried out, if you wish it so.'

'I wish it so,' Lundt confirmed. 'Get the silly creature down and give her to the jailers to prepare. And I want a placard fixed above her head in the square, together with a warning and an offer. If any citizen knows anything about this nefarious audacity, let him come forward within the next six hours and his life shall be spared in return for information.

'After that, anyone discovered to have *any* involvement in the plot, no matter how insignificant, will die the most horrible death the executioners can conceive.'

Corinna thought she must have died a thousand deaths that night, though none of them were in any way horrible. Still suspended upright by Savatch's ingenious bondage, she swayed unsteadily, only half conscious, but aware of the heat still raging throughout her body.

Between her splayed thighs, Helda crouched with her tongue hard at work yet again, ensuring that the helpless Corinna remained just below fever pitch, whilst at the table, Savatch poured himself another glass of wine and allowed himself a short while in which to recover from his exertions.

He was still naked and his flaccid penis lay slumped in his lap, but Corinna was only too well aware, even in her bemused condition, that that state of affairs could be altered very rapidly. Only the high collar prevented her head from lolling from side to side now, for she no longer retained anything but the most rudimentary control over her reflexes. Dimly, she was aware of what had been done to her and knew she ought to have been repulsed and deeply ashamed, but the innocent Corinna of that morning had been corrupted and depraved in a way that she would never have believed possible, had it not been done already.

Oblivious to the strain of her bonds, she moaned and grunted like a bitch in heat, desperate for Savatch to fill her aching void again, craving above all else to be returned to that world of sensuous abandon to which he had taken her three times already, not caring any longer that he was her captor, just happy to be his captive and freed, by his ropes and straps, of the need to cling on to any inhibitions.

She opened her eyes and gazed across to where he sat. Her mouth was slack and her throat dry, but somehow she managed to form the words. Savatch looked back at her and smiled.

'Certainly, my little princess,' he said affably, raising his glass in a mock toast. 'But give a man a few minutes to regain his strength.'

Lord Willum Oleana regarded the crumpled form of the pantry maid, Kirsta, and grunted, though not with any distaste at the sight of her ravaged back and buttocks, for in truth he had gained much satisfaction from his whipping of the girl. His only dissatisfaction over the affair was that it could not have been his shrewish wife, Benita, hung by the ankles at his mercy and, as the lash had ripped through air and flesh alike, he had tried to imagine that it was she and not the mute servant he was thrashing.

One day, he told himself. One day I will make her pay for the hellish life she has inflicted upon me. On the floor at his feet, Kirsta stirred, moaning softly. Willum extended one foot, placed the toe of his boot under her armpit and levered her over onto her side. Kirsta opened her eyes, but there was little sign of recognition there. He stared at the rounded body for a full minute and then turned back to the door of the cell.

The fire was already dying in his belly and there would be little joy in ravishing the girl whilst she was so senseless and, in any case, there were far better looking wenches among his brother's palace staff. The senior bedroom maid, Petra, was a handsome filly and she also seemed to respond well to a sound spanking during foreplay. There was something eminently satisfying, Willum had always thought, about the sound of palm or lash slapping against lush female flesh.

The evening was already growing late and the bedroom maids would be finishing their duties for the day at this time. He smiled to himself, stepped out into the passageway and closed the cell door behind him, dropping the heavy securing bolt into its housing before he set off towards the stairs to the palace above.

Corporal Baadik had seen action on battlefields the length and breadth of the continent, had faced drunken rioters outnumbering his guard patrol by at least ten to one, and had fought and won three duels, yet never had he felt so afraid as he did now.

Captain Mossarian, his tall and angular section commander, stood a little to one side of Baadik, but it was Lord Lundt, the Protector himself, who was the source of Baadik's apprehension. The Lord Protector's features were a mask of rage as he studied the lists on his desk before him. There was a heavy silence for several minutes, save for the occasional rustling. At last, Lord Lundt set down all the folios except one. He looked at it again and then finally raised his eyes to fix Baadik with a steady gaze.

'Savatch, you say?' he asked, simply. Baadik swallowed and nodded.

'Yes, sire,' he confirmed. 'And he had all the correct paperwork, complete with genuine seals. I took a close look at them.'

'And you say he had a girl with him?'

'A slave, sire, yes. I had a good look at her.'

'And yet you say you could not describe her?'

'No, sire.' Baadik swallowed again. 'He had her in a slave jacket, one of those with a hood and mask that covers the face completely. He said she was a bit spirited and he'd had a bit of trouble with her. But she was a slave all right, I'd swear. She was shaved in the manner of a slave girl, anyway.'

'You mean the wench was naked, apart from the slave jacket?'

'Yes, sire, she was.'

'Which means you probably wouldn't remember her face,

even if she hadn't been hooded,' Lundt said, grimacing. 'Anything else about the man, anything unusual?'

'No, sire, nothing at all.' Baadik gave the Protector a brief description of Savatch and Lundt nodded.

'I think I recall the fellow,' he said, half turning to Captain Mossarian as he spoke. 'He was a guest at Corinna's wedding, as I remember. Did he act at all strangely?' he asked, turning back to Baadik. The stout corporal shook his head.

'Not at all, sire,' he said. 'He was well at ease and was even laughing and joking. He didn't even seem to be in that much of a hurry.'

'I see,' Lundt mused. His eyes flicked back to the paper in his hand for a brief moment. 'So, if this Savatch is our man, it would seem he is a very audacious fellow indeed. Always assuming it is him, of course.' He tapped the sheaf of paper on the desk with one long finger.

'These are all the gatehouse records for the day?' Mossarian nodded.

'Right up to half an hour ago,' he said. 'Of course, there is the possibility that whoever abducted Lady Corinna is still holding her somewhere in the city.'

'Yes, captain, that possibility had not eluded me. Give orders to double all sentries and search every wagon in and out thoroughly. And no slaves leave the city until the guards have seen their faces, even if the bitches bite their hands off.'

'Understood, sire.' Mossarian looked thoughtful. Lundt looked at him keenly.

'Something troubling you, Captain Mossarian?'

'Only that it is very early yet. There's no possibility of this being a mistake. The lady couldn't be somewhere, all safe and sound, not realising that everyone's looking for her?'

'No possibility at all, I'm afraid. Her personal maid confirms that none of her clothes are missing. And then there's the small matter of several drugged guards and one man dead, plus the confession of the guard Sorbart, together with his description of the man who bribed him, a description, incidentally, which tallies closely with the corporal's description of this Savatch.'

Mossarian glared at Baadik and then turned back to the Protector. 'What shall I do with Corporal Baadik, sire?' Baadik felt a cold fist knotting itself into the wall of his stomach. Lundt sat back and spread his hands on the desk before him.

'I don't really think there *is* much you can do, captain. I fear even the extra gate checks are shutting the stable door far too late. Baadik was not really guilty of any dereliction of duty, not as I see it. He did check the man's papers and his wagon and he saw what he was meant to see, a naked, hooded, and even shaven slave girl.' He paused, considering the implications of this last statement, and Mossarian could tell he was picturing his daughter being handled so intimately by the man Savatch.

Mossarian knew how the Protector must be feeling, for he had two daughters of his own, one of whom was about the same age as the Lady Corinna, though not, he was honest enough to admit, anywhere near as pretty. Lundt took a deep breath and let out a long sigh.

'Return to your duties, Corporal Baadik. Any punishment I decreed for you would be unjustified and simply an anguished father hitting out at those nearest to him.' Baadik snapped his heels to attention, hardly able to believe his ears.

'Thank you sire,' he barked, raising his right fist in the

regulation guard salute. 'I shall remain forever in your debt.' Lundt's face eased and he almost smiled.

'You have an excellent record, Baadik,' he told the grizzled veteran. 'Perhaps one day I shall have need of you to discharge that debt.'

Chapter Seven

Corinna awoke from a deep, dreamless sleep and opened her eyes warily. Helda still slumbered heavily in the straw a few feet from her, and the door to their room stood ajar, a bare minimum of pale yellow light filtering in from the lantern in the outer room. Quietly, taking care not to jangle the chain that was once again locked about her ankle, Corinna sat up.

There was no sound to be heard, save for Helda's soft breathing, but she sensed that Savatch was not far away. Gently, she reached over with her manacled hands and tested the chain that held her to the wall. As she had suspected, it had been locked on expertly, not tightly enough to cut into her skin, but with insufficient slack to make it worthwhile even trying to slip it over her foot. She sighed and sat back, and her hands went automatically to her crotch.

Ye gods, she thought, I'm still wet. And she could smell the odour of her own musk, intermingled with *his* smells. Corinna closed her eyes again and her shoulders slumped. Memories of the previous night came flooding back, memories she wished she could forget. But they were too vivid, everything seeming clearer now than it had at the time.

She remembered how she had hung in her bondage, wantonly displayed, helpless and pleading, but not pleading for release, at least, not for a release from the straps that held her. She had begged Savatch over and over again and, time and again he had obliged her. She groaned as she thought of how abandoned she had been, how she had allowed herself to be brought down from the level of lady to whore, and shuddered at the thought that her father should ever get to hear about her unforgivable weakness.

She should, she reasoned, also be worried that Lazlo never found out, but strangely, when she thought of her husband it induced no emotion whatsoever. She thought she understood why, and hated herself for it. Savatch was little more than a barbarian, despite his show of courtly manners – at least, he mocked her with his courtesy when he wasn't rutting with her. To her disgust, she realised she was smiling.

'I trust you slept well, Lady Corinna.' She opened her eyes with a start, for there had been no sound of his approach. Savatch stood in the doorway, arms folded across his naked chest, but he had at least put on a pair of breeches since she had last seen him.

'This is hardly a comfortable bedroom,' Corinna pouted, but she made no attempt at covering her nakedness with her arms. Savatch shrugged.

'Needs must when the devils drive,' he said, simply. 'Had there been the opportunity, I should have provided a mattress for you, but sadly, my schedule was a tight one.'

'I noticed that *you* had a mattress in the other room,' she pointed out.

Savatch laughed. 'But not one on which you would have fancied sleeping, no more than did I myself,' he replied. 'You will see the filthy thing is outside, behind the hut, for I found it to be infested when I examined it, otherwise I should have brought it in here last night. I wish you no unnecessary discomfort, I assure you.'

'No unnecessary discomfort?' Corinna echoed, her eyes

widening. 'You chain me, beat me and then ravish me continually whilst your ropework forces me to stand lewdly before you, and you have the gall to say you wish me no discomfort.'

'I vouch you seemed comfortable enough at times last evening, my girl,' he laughed. 'And you seemed content with the resting place I did furnish for you.' Corinna lowered her eyes at his painful reminder.

'Meantime, my lady,' he continued, 'there is breakfast to be had and you need a wash. Come, the stream will refresh you and there is a place where you can attend to your other needs. You will have some little time back in here later, for I have a small journey to undertake in order to bring this business to a satisfactory conclusion.'

The early morning air was cold and there was a sharp edge to the breeze and Kirsta shivered violently as she was led out into the execution yard, for the jailers had stripped her of everything but a wide leather belt about her waist, to which her wrists were cuffed at either side.

Heavy steel fetters had been riveted about her ankles and the thick chain that linked them dragged heavily in the dust as she shuffled forward between the two grim faced guards. She looked up at the scaffold and her knees almost gave way under her, but to her surprise the men grasped her elbows and guided her across to the far wall. She turned from one to the other, her eyes questioning.

The guard on her left smiled, but sourly. 'It's not your neck this morning,' he grunted. 'But the Protector wants to make sure you understand what happens to traitors.'

There were about fifty other people present to witness the execution, standing around in small knots, shoulders hunched against the post dawn chill. Kirsta looked about her, watching the grim faces. She saw Lord Lundt standing with his brother, Willum, the man who had whipped her so savagely the day before. Her flesh still screamed at any sudden movement, despite the salve that the physician had applied to her wounds back in her small cell.

Lord Willum's hatchet-faced wife, Benita, stood with two other ladies, the only females apart from Kirsta herself, who were present. There were other faces familiar about the palace, too. Kirsta recognised Vice Chancellor Menndt and several of his officers, two senior colonels from the guard and at least six captains. Up on the scaffold, standing patiently beneath the massive crossbeam, the hooded executioner and his two assistants stood waiting, their black leather breeches gleaming as brightly as did their oiled chests.

The door to the prison section opened and Sorbart shuffled out, fettered and flanked in a manner similar to Kirsta. He too was naked and a steel collar had been locked around his scrotum, to which a hefty weight had been attached. Kirsta swallowed hard, seeing how her former lover grimaced with every step. They were evidently intent on inflicting the maximum pain and humiliation on the treacherous guard, right up to the very moment of his death.

He climbed the wooden steps only with difficulty, and one of his guards had to help him make the last few. When he at last stood on the staging, he turned and looked down at the waiting witnesses. For a few seconds Kirsta thought he was going to speak, but if the thought had occurred to him he had dismissed it immediately, for he turned back to face the sinister trio who were charged with carrying out his sentence.

He made no attempt to resist when the nearer assistant grasped his arm and pulled him into the centre of the platform, but his eyes flickered downwards to the outline of the trap on which he now stood. A thin leather collar was quickly buckled about his throat and to this was clipped a long wooden pole, at either end of which dangled a leather manacle.

The assistants released Sorbart's wrists from his belt one at a time, and quickly resecured them to the pole, so that he was forced to stand with his arms held wide. The executioner took the dangling noose and adjusted it about the condemned man's neck, so it nestled snugly above the collar, and tightened the rope so it just slightly compressed the flesh, the heavy knot positioned under the back of his right jaw.

Sorbart stared up at the rope, noting the slack loop with the thin thread holding it. Even the slightest jerk would break the thread, so that when he dropped he would fall several feet before the slack was used up. At least, Kirsta thought, they had spared him the slow death of strangulation. However, as she quickly saw, the executioner had added a twist of his own.

The burly man now threw a thin cord over the beam and pulled it taut. The free end terminated in a wooden handle, fashioned like the handle of a child's skipping rope, and this he now gave to Sorbart who gripped it tightly in his right hand. The executioner said something to him and he nodded, his face expressionless. The guard on Kirsta's right grunted.

'What's he doing?' he whispered to his companion. The guard on her left snorted.

'You obviously haven't seen many of Xargos's executions, lad,' he replied, speaking from the side of his mouth. 'This is one of his own little specialities. As long as Sorbart keeps that line taut, it holds a spring-loaded device back. Once Xargos draws the bolt lever, the only thing keeping the trap up is a special catch attached to that device. If the line goes slack, the spring knocks the catch out and bang, down goes Sorbart.'

'You mean he actually executes himself, in a manner of speaking?'

'Correct. He has to stand there and receive the flogging that was ordered and try to remain conscious. But I've seen men deliberately loose their grip long before that time. Xargos's whip is laced with metal barbs and he's a powerful fellow, as you can see.'

The two assistants now hurried to complete their preparations. A stout pole was fixed to the back of Sorbart's belt and another belt passed around beneath his armpits to secure it upright, its lower end an inch or so above the wooden trap. A second pole was clipped onto this and either end secured to Sorbart's ankle fetters, holding his feet a fair distance apart. Yet another line was thrown over the beam and attached to the upper belt, drawn tightly so it would prevent the prisoner from falling.

'Surely that'll stop him before his neck goes,' the younger guard observed. The other guard shook his head.

'When the spring goes for the trap it also frees the other end of that rope,' he said. 'All very clever, don't you think?'

Xargos now took up the leather hood and, with a final look at his prisoner's face, drew it over Sorbart's head, masking his features from the small crowd. One of his assistants handed him his whip, coiled and oiled, and stood well back. Xargos paid out the whip and Kirsta saw Sorbart's body flinch as he heard the sound of the thick leather hitting the boards behind him. Kirsta screwed her eyes shut, not wanting to see any more, but the guard to her left jabbed his elbow savagely into her ribs.

'Watch, girl,' he snarled. 'The Protector's orders, otherwise we'll be taking you up next.' Reluctantly, Kirsta obeyed, just in time to see the first lash descending across Sorbart's naked back, cutting open the flesh which was already swollen from the whippings he had received the previous day and evening. An animal-like howl rent the air from beneath the leather hood and Sorbart's knuckles whitened as he gripped the cord handle ever tighter.

With a deliberate lack of urgency Xargos shook the whip out again. After several seconds his arm flashed again. A second shriek split the morning stillness, echoing around the stone walls like a wailing wind. Sorbart staggered forward a few inches despite his bonds, and would surely have fallen had it not been for the line which held him upright.

Twice more the whip slashed into him, the tiny barbs ripping flesh to the bone. How much more he could take, Kirsta dreaded to think, for there was every chance he might die of blood loss before his grip loosened. However, the torturous affair was not to last much longer.

A fifth stroke brought forth little more than a low groan and then, as Xargos gathered himself for the sixth, the crowd heard the voice of the doomed man from beneath the muffling of the leather hood.

'Damn you all!' he screamed. 'Damn you all to the lowest of the hells. Bastards – all of you!' His right arm jerked once and he threw the handle into the air. Kirsta saw the line fly upwards, heard the harsh clank of a metallic mechanism and then the floor beneath Sorbart disappeared and he was sent plunging downwards, until the hangman's rope halted his descent and, with it, the last agonising moments of his life.

Chapter Eight

The woman sat easily in the saddle in the shadows beneath the low hanging branches, her face hidden by the hood of her long black cloak. But to Savatch there could be no mistaking her for another. He reined in his horse and wheeled it off the track towards her.

'You are late, Savatch Bannaradis.' Her voice was cool, with a slightly musical accent. Savatch grinned as he drew alongside her.

'My apologies, Vala Valkyr Kirislanna Friggisdottir,' he saluted, using her full name as he always did when first meeting her. 'There were patrols on the roads and I had to make several detours to avoid them.'

'I saw some of them myself,' the woman conceded. 'However, once they saw my face they lost interest in me.'

'I cannot believe that, my beautiful Alanna,' Savatch said. 'Such a face would command the interest of any red-blooded male, to be sure.'

The woman threw back her hood, revealing the long, pure white hair that marked her unmistakably as an Yslander. The piercing blue eyes fixed Savatch with a challenging stare, but the corners of her wide, full mouth, twitched good humouredly at the compliment.

'And I vouchsafe the little princess had commanded more than a fair share of your attention these past hours,' she said. Savatch shrugged easily.

'She has her attractions,' he conceded, 'but they pale before such beauty as yours.'

'Flatterer,' Alanna snapped and swung easily from her saddle. Savatch dismounted likewise and moved towards her. He was a tall man himself, but his head scarcely topped hers. As ever, he found himself wondering what she would look like suspended in chains, but even he had never had the temerity to consider translating his imaginings into reality.

Vala Valkyr Kirislanna Friggitsdottir was as deadly as she was beautiful, a princess herself among a nation of women famed for their fierceness and strength. Her title, Vala, signified that in addition to her warrior qualities she was also believed to be possessed of a second sight, though if she ever saw what images filtered through Savatch's mind whenever he was near her, she never gave any hint of it.

She leaned towards him and they kissed, a brief touching of lips. At other times, in other places, their greeting might have been far more intimate, but this was business, as they both knew only too well.

'You have the girl safe?' Alanna asked, though she knew the answer even before Savatch spoke.

'She's safely kennelled,' he said, 'with another little bitch for company. I'm making good use of a place I discovered by accident some years ago.'

'What you discovered, so others might too,' Alanna pointed out.

'I think not, my pale goddess. The building is deep in woodland that has not been forested for many decades, for the area has become flooded and there are dangerous mires among the trees. A man needs be totally certain of his route before venturing there.'

'Lundt's net will be cast wider and wider, and don't forget it. You have flitched the jewel from his crown, and I doubt he'll rest until he has her back again.'

'Then his will be a tired life, I fear,' Savatch retorted. 'The Lady Corinna will not be going home in any great haste, from what I understand. Her custody is the only sure way of keeping Lundt to any bargain.'

'Do these people really think he will agree to their demands without getting his beloved daughter back?'

'I believe they do, my swan lady. And they may well be right. Lundt will not risk his daughter's life. He will do almost anything to ensure her safe survival, even if it is in some far-off place.'

'Survival it may be, but safety is a matter of opinion,' Alanna said. 'I would rather be dead than fall helpless into Fulgrim's hands. Lal Barendi's dirt-raker is no woman's friend, I hear.'

'Fulgrim may not be the worst of her problems. There are other interested parties tied in with this thing. I'll wager there may soon be a very unpretty falling out among thieves, but as long as I get my gold, that is another man's problems. I hate politicking, as you well know.'

'The scourge of humanity,' Alanna agreed. 'When do you meet with them?'

'I meet Fulgrim and the lush an hour from now. There is a disused watermill about three miles over yonder.' He waved an arm in the general direction of north. 'They are expecting me to deliver the girl to them there.'

'But you do not trust them?'

'Would you?' Savatch laughed harshly. 'At least my villainy is honest work, at least compared with their chicanery. I'll stake my horse they've already positioned bowmen and footsoldiers all around the place. My last breath would be drawn the moment they saw Corinna.'

'I think you are correct in that assumption,' Alanna

nodded. She shrugged her cloak back over one shoulder, revealing her superbly athletic figure clad in the close fitting leathers of a warrior. 'We shall wait and watch for your return and deal with anything that follows.'

'How many do you have with you?'

'Six. They wait a little way back in the woods. We have had to gather here separately to avoid arousing too much interest. The sight of seven Yslandic women riding together would certainly not pass unnoticed.'

'The sight of seven such separately will cause scarcely less suspicion, surely?' Savatch said.

Alanna laughed, a very musical sound indeed. 'It might, if they still resembled Yslandians,' she said. 'Whoever has heard of an Yslandic warrior woman with red or black hair? And what Yslandic fighting woman would be seen driving a potato cart?'

'You have been thorough, I see,' Savatch admitted, grudgingly.

'As I always am,' she returned. Her expression softened. 'As you are, also,' she added. Savatch looked up through the foliage, gauging the position of the sun and cursed, mentally. Had he arrived at his intended time there would have been easily a half hour to spare, and it was several very long days since he had last been alone with the seeress warrior.

Sensing his frustration, Alanna laid a gentle hand upon his shoulder and kissed him lightly again.

'Patience, my horny brigand,' she teased. 'There will be time aplenty when this business is safely settled, that I can promise you. And you had best conserve some of that barbarian strength, for I have doubtless remained far more celibate than you since we last parted.'

Now Savatch laughed. 'As far as men are concerned,

yes,' he quipped. Alanna smiled and turned back to her horse.

'You do not have the prerogative on comely wenches, you cunt-struck devil,' she said. 'In fact, were there time, I'd fancy a closer inspection of this princess of yours myself.'

'Yes,' Savatch muttered under his breath, turning back to his own mount, 'I'll bet you would, my beautiful ice maiden.'

Corinna picked the wedge of meat from the bowl beside her and chewed half-heartedly on it. Against the far wall Helda sat picking at her food likewise. The peasant girl had said little since Savatch's departure. She seemed to be in awe of Corinna, or at least her rank, despite the fact that they were both naked, chained prisoners.

Corinna, who had earlier spent some time examining the iron ring to which her ankle chain was fastened, could stand the silence no longer.

'We need something like a knife,' she said. 'It needn't be a knife. An old nail, a baling hook, anything made of metal. I don't know how long these walls have stood here, but the mortar between the stones is soft.'

'He wouldn't leave a knife lying around for us, lady,' Helda said, speaking with a mouthful of venison. 'He ain't that silly, believe me. I gets the impression he's quite used to chaining women up.'

'Quite so,' Corinna agreed, 'but the best of us can make mistakes. We should search beneath the straw and see if we can find anything. Even a piece of flint might do. If we can chip away enough, with two of us pulling together, me might shift these stanchions before he comes back.'

'We should try to free you first, lady,' Helda said quietly.

'I'm just a village girl, so I don't mean more to him than just a warm pillow and a good fuck, if you'll pardon me. But you need to get away, I reckon, else something terrible is going to happen to you. I can feel it.' The girl put aside her bowl and began scrabbling beneath the carpet of straw. Corinna did likewise, but after ten minutes of methodical searching they had found nothing.

Corinna sat back. 'It's no good, I'm afraid,' she said. 'He put this straw here himself, I think, so he would have noticed anything on the floor and removed it. I'm sorry, Helda, I wasn't thinking clearly.' She let her eyes wander around the room. They stopped when she reached the boarded up window.

'On the other hand,' she said, speaking as much to herself as to her fellow captive, 'as I was saying just a few minutes ago, the best of us can make mistakes. Those planks have been there a few years, or else my eyes deceive me.'

She stood up and walked across the small room, her ankle chain dragging heavily at her leg. There was just enough slack for her to reach the window, though she had to stand with the chained foot awkwardly stretched out. She probed around the bottom of the lowest board and her fingers found rotted timber.

'Ah!' she exclaimed. 'Yes, I think I might have just the thing.' She dug slowly, using her fingernails to crumble away the soft wood, a tiny piece at a time. Helda, meanwhile, sunk her teeth back into the meat, ripping it away.

'This might help, mistress,' she said, holding up the glistening bone. 'It ain't going to be any use on the mortar, but that wood looks like it's nigh had its time.' Corinna grinned and took the proffered implement, turning it over and examining the sharper end. Helda might have been a peasant, but the girl had a sharp brain.

'Excellent,' she said, and redoubled her efforts, the bone making far greater inroads than her nails could ever have hoped to achieve. Fifteen minutes later Corinna had created a hole big enough to admit her hand and, as she scraped away the last vestiges from around the framework, which was also badly damaged, she had exposed several inches of one of the crude nails that had been used to fix the wood in the first place.

She grasped the end and pulled, but the rusted iron refused to budge.

'Try bending it, lady,' Helda said. She stood and hobbled across to where she could see what Corinna was trying to do. 'You may loosen it, but if not, the iron will fatigue. I seen the men breaking off old fixings in the village like that. Trouble is, they had pliers to help.'

'We may have something nearly as good,' Corinna replied. 'But first we need to make this hole just a bit bigger.' It took another ten minutes of digging and pulling, but finally the whole end of the plank had been removed and a hard shove against the remainder bent it outwards at least a foot.

With a grunt of satisfaction Corinna reached down and hooked the staple on her right wrist cuff over the head of the nail. Planting her left foot firmly for leverage, she pulled back and sideways. The nail bent, though not very far.

'Now push it back again, lady,' Helda urged. 'It'll get easier as you go, you'll see.' Corinna unhooked the cuff and placed the iron wrist band itself against the nail head, pushing this time, instead of pulling. Again, to her delight, the nail yielded in the opposite direction.

Savatch rode with deliberate slowness from the moment he came in sight of the old mill, following the river bank trail and letting his gaze roam from side to side in a manner which seemed casual, but which missed nothing. There was no sign of the men he was to meet, but his trained eye three times spotted movement among the bushes on the far embankment.

It was impossible to be sure of numbers, but he estimated at least a dozen men so far, and he was still a hundred yards short of his target. Doubtless there would be others hidden away inside the building itself, and more in the undergrowth which stopped just short of it. There would also be others, mounted men, not far off, ready to respond to any signal from their masters.

'Treacherous fools,' he said, half under his breath, though it was no more than he had expected. In fact, he regarded their crude attempts to set a trap for him as an insult to his intelligence. He reined his horse in a few yards from the mill and sat back in the saddle.

'Fulgrim!' he called, cupping his hands to his mouth. 'Show yourself, my lord!' There was a moment's pause and then the gaunt figure of Fulgrim appeared in the doorless entrance on the veranda that ran around the first floor level of the building. The Vorsan's face wore a sour expression.

'Master Savatch, I presume?' he called back. 'But why are you alone?'

'For the same reason that you are not, my lord,' Savatch countered. 'My being here alone is my only insurance against riding out alive, I think.'

'I fear you have an overly suspicious nature, Master Savatch,' Fulgrim replied. Savatch laughed and swung his leg over the saddle.

'It's helped me keep a healthy hide these many years,' he said, dropping lightly to the ground. 'Have you brought my gold?'

'I have half here and half a little distance away. I too have a suspicious nature.'

'And a squadron of troopers, I warrant,' Savatch retorted. he walked to the precarious looking steps which led up to Fulgrim's perch. 'So, we appear to have a delicate stalemate on our hands, my lord,' he said, placing one foot on the first step. 'You have my gold and I have your baggage, and neither of us appears to have much faith in the other.'

'Do you have a solution to suggest?'

'That I do, my lord. You, myself and two of your men – you can select whichever you like – may ride back with me, bringing the half of the gold you have here. We will collect the remainder on our way. I will then take you to the Lady Corinna.

'You may still, of course, consider it worth trying to cheat me of my commission, but I am prepared to take my chances on that score. You may think odds of three to one are favourable, but I would advise you that they may not be.'

'But how can I be sure that you, in your turn, do not have men laying in wait?'

'You cannot, sir, but I will give you my word that I do not. Upon my mother's soul, there are no men with me, nor are there any where I shall be taking you.' He smiled inwardly as he spoke, not having mentioned the small matter of seven fully armed and very highly motivated Yslandic warrior women. But then his oath had specified men, not women.

The pile of yellow dust was growing larger by the minute. Corinna paused, the bent nail clutched in her hand like the lifeline it was. She looked over her shoulder to where Helda was crouched, her gaze intent.

'It's working,' she said, 'but I shall need a bigger gap at the window. Use the bone and start freeing the end of the next plank. And I will come back for you, I swear.'

'As you wish, lady,' Helda replied. Corinna stared at her, suddenly realising that she had not fully understood the peasant girl.

'You don't want me to, do you?' she said, accusingly. 'You actually want to stay with that monster.'

Helda lowered her eyes. 'It's so hard to explain, lady,' she said. 'Legally, he now owns me. I am his slave and he is permitted to do as he wishes with me.'

'But he's a criminal,' Corinna insisted. 'My father will hang him for what he has done.'

'I know, lady,' Helda said, 'but would you really want that any more than I?' She looked up again and there was something about her expression that made Corinna feel as though there were ice cold feet walking up her spine. 'Remember, lady,' the peasant girl continued, 'I was there last night. It was my tongue that was commanded and my tongue that did his bidding. It was also my ears that heard.'

Corinna turned away from her, unable to meet her stare. She looked at the cavity she had created around the iron ring.

'Helda,' she said, her voice unsteady, 'I remember last night only too clearly and the recollection brings me only shame. I do not presume to judge you, nor the life which has made you what you are, but my whole being is ashamed of what it became.'

'As is mine, lady,' Helda replied. She hesitated, her lower lip quivering. 'And yet,' she said, 'I fear you have been captured by his spell.'

Corinna twisted the bent nail in her fingers and could not look up when she replied.

'Savatch's spell is based upon evil,' she said. 'It twists and corrupts and it will bring nothing with it but evil and sorrow. The man is a corrupt abomination and his magic, for what it is, is a selfish and wicked thing.' She stopped, shaking her head.

'But then,' she continued, 'perhaps we are all selfish and wicked things.' She paused again, before going on. 'However,' she added, 'some of us have the strength that comes from duty to a cause greater than our own base desires.'

Jekka Riiork Haagasdottir dropped to her knees and listened. The cutaways over her ears in the dark green leather helmet that covered her head completely allowed full rein to her acute sense of hearing. She peered out through the narrow eye slits, watching for any signs of movement in the dense undergrowth to either side, and then half rose into a crouch and glided across the open space ahead of her until the next patch of greenery swallowed her green clad figure invisibly.

She knelt again, ever alert, and drew the long assassin's knife from its scabbard at her belt, wiping the edge gently on her tight leather leggings. There was only one of them coming, of that she was sure, but he was undoubtedly riding point as a vanguard for the main body, trailing the small party of four back to wherever Savatch was leading them. She removed a green glove from her right hand, placed a finger and thumb between her lips, and trilled a signal call.

From the woods on the far side of the trail an answering call came back a few seconds later. Jekka smiled, crept a few feet nearer to the edge of her cover and waited, coiled like a green serpent ready to strike, the colour of her fighting leathers ensuring that her quarry would not see her until it was too late.

'You take me for a fool!' Fulgrim's hand hovered over the hilt of his sword, but he did not yet attempt to draw it. Experienced and skilled as he was, there was something about Savatch that told him it might be a foolish move to face him head on. However, he controlled his fury only with the greatest of efforts. He looked down at the cowering girl and spat on the straw before her.

'You surely cannot think that I have staged this as some sort of pantomime trick, my lord?' Savatch said. He pointed to the gaping hole where the two planks had been pushed out of the window frame, and then at the cavity in the wall and the little pile of mortar dust immediately beneath it. 'Your princess is a resourceful young woman,' he said. He stooped and picked up the bent and rusted nail.

'Very resourceful,' he muttered, grimly. 'However,' he continued, turning back towards the outer room, 'she cannot have gone too far yet. Her wrists are still chained and she has a long chain still locked to her ankle, which she will have to carry. She is also barefoot, for Helda's sandals are still in the other room, so she cannot travel at any speed without tearing her feet to shreds.'

'But she could have gone anywhere in these woods,' Fulgrim pointed out. 'There are only four of us to search and we could easily miss her.'

'There are only four of us, true,' Savatch said, pushing past him, 'but I have help close at hand.'

Fulgrim's expression darkened even further. 'Help?' he echoed. 'What treachery is this? You swore an oath that you had no men here.'

Savatch smiled. 'So I did, my lord,' he agreed, 'but as you will shortly see, I have remained true to it. And you may take your hand away from your weapon. If I wished you dead you would be so by now. I could kill you and your remaining men, take the gold and forget about Lady Corinna, could I not. However, there is an honour among thieves which I have always upheld. I will get your little princess back for you, take my gold, and you may go in peace.'

'And if you don't get her back?' Savatch flashed him a look of pure contempt.

'Well then, my Lord Fulgrim, you will take your gold and I shall leave in peace.'

The ground underfoot was rapidly becoming softer and softer and now Corinna's bare feet left small puddles of water wherever they landed. She stopped, backed up against a broad tree trunk, and listened for sounds of pursuit, but the forest yielded nothing more than its routine noises.

The initial elation of her escape had faded now and reality was returning with a heavy tread. She was alone, still chained and naked, miles from civilisation and help and without even the first idea in which direction she should be travelling. From what Savatch had said she was at least thirty miles from Illeum City and, assuming that he would have sought temporary sanctuary in a place he considered unlikely to be happened upon by chance, a good many miles from anywhere else inhabited.

The woods were thick in most places, and where the undergrowth thinned at all it seemed that the ground was becoming waterlogged. For the past ten minutes conditions had been worsening with every yard of flight, and Corinna realised she would have to turn back and seek a different route. She looked up to the sky, trying to give herself some sort of clue from the position of the sun, but what little she had learned from her tutors concerning navigation refused to be recalled to her aid, now that she had use of it.

It would have to be, she thought, a matter of chance. Straight back led to the hut and, by now, probably to Savatch, who would waste little time in trying to recapture her. And he was quite possibly no longer alone, which meant she had no time to lose.

Corinna made up her mind. Gripping the loose chain tightly between her hands she turned to the left, took seven or eight steps and sunk up to her knees in soft, cloying mud.

Fulgrim was still in a state of mild shock. His gaze travelled over the semicircular line of Yslanders, who made a stunning sight in their gleaming fighting leathers, their long legs and wide hips displayed by their practical outfits in a manner that would ensure a man's thoughts would turn from fighting at the first glimpse of them.

'You are seriously telling me, Master Savatch,' Fulgrim said, finding his voice again, 'that all my remaining men are now dead?'

'Every one, I'm afraid, my lord,' Savatch said, with a hint of amusement in his voice. 'These ladies do not play children's games when it comes to such matters. I truly wish it had not been necessary, but it was your decision that things have had to take such a turn.'

'I merely brought those men along as a precaution,' Fulgrim protested. Savatch stifled a laugh.

'As did I with these ladies,' he retorted. 'Perhaps now we can stop the games and concentrate on the more serious matters. Unlike your blundering soldiers, these Yslanders are skilled in all manner of ways and are trained to fight under any conditions. They will find the Lady Corinna, I assure you.'

'But these are not all Yslanders, surely?' Fulgrim pointed at the girl on the left of the line. Her hair was a deep auburn. Next to her was another girl with jet black hair. Only one of the women had the distinctive white blonde mane of the Yslandic warrior woman, though another had corn yellow locks.

'A necessary deception, my lord,' Savatch explained. 'However, whilst we are standing here wasting our precious time with idle chatter, our quarry is getting ever further from us. I suggest, my Lord Fulgrim, that you and your remaining men remain here with your gold. I doubt that any of you are possessed of the necessary woodcrafting skills for this hunt.'

'What about the other girl?' Fulgrim asked, jerking a thumb in the direction of the hut.

Savatch raised an eyebrow. 'What about her? She isn't going anywhere. You will have noticed that her chain remains intact.'

'But she assisted Corinna in her escape, did she not?' Fulgrim persisted. 'Surely she is to be punished?'

Savatch's eyes narrowed. 'Whether she is, or whether she is not,' he replied pointedly, 'is not a matter for your concern. The girl is mine, as is the princess until you pay over the gold. Be warned, my lord, that Helda is not to be touched – in *any* way,' he added darkly.

She was going to die, Corinna knew that now. The mud was up to her breasts already and she was still sinking steadily. Desperately, she tried to stretch her arms out before her in an attempt to create some buoyancy, but what little effect that move had was countered by the weight of the fetters and chains that bound her wrists. Additionally, the ankle chain was contributing its own share to the impossibility of her situation.

The tears that welled up in her eyes were born more of frustration than terror, for she knew it was a waste to end her life in such a fashion. She had been so near to freedom and, after such an effort to break clear of Savatch's improvised prison, to have wandered into this treacherous bog had been plain carelessness.

She was not afraid to die, she told herself, but as the cloying goo crept over her chest, she knew that that was not true. It was not death itself she feared, so much as the manner in which she was going to go. She could already picture herself, being sucked ever deeper into the darkness below, her mouth, throat and nose filling with the foul smelling bog. The tears came faster now and she wished she had a knife, or some other way of giving herself a kinder death.

'By the teeth of Freya Moggstromm, what the hell have we here?!' The melodic feminine voice jerked Corinna from the trancelike state into which she had been rapidly descending. She craned her neck to find its source and her eyes shot wide open, for not ten feet from her stood one of the most incredible sights she had ever seen.

The two women were Yslanders, she was certain, though neither of them had the usual translucent white hair associated with that race. The taller had a mass of flaming red tresses, whilst her companion was a mousy brown colour. Both were clad in tight fitting leathers of a dark green and their lithe bodies reminded Corinna of twin serpents.

'Please!' she cried out. 'Please help me. There will be a

great reward for you if you get me out of here.' The redhead turned to her companion and laughed.

'We know,' she said, turning back to Corinna. 'By the Halls of Athgaard, we know, milady.'

Chapter Nine

Lord Lundt pounded the table with his fist and his eyes looked as though they were about to pop out of his skull, such was the depth of his rage. He stared at his younger brother and pounded the table again.

'When did this happen?' he demanded.

Willum paced nervously up and down in distraught fashion, wringing his hands together. 'Some hours ago, brother,' he said. 'On the road to Garassotta.'

'What on earth compelled you to send your wife from the city whilst the situation remains as it is?' Lundt demanded.

Willum shrugged his shoulders. 'I thought she would be safer out of here altogether,' he whined. 'And she had a heavy escort. Once back at my palace I knew she would be safe.'

'And you did not think she would be so here?' Lundt snapped. 'We do not have that many traitors, Willum, you fool. And as for her escort, it was clearly not heavy enough. Did any survive?'

'None, brother. They were cut down to a man. A group of travelling minstrels found the bodies, recognised the uniforms and sent a rider straight here to find me.'

'Damn!' Lundt struck the table again. 'These people, whoever they are, leave nothing to chance, but at least we know it is not money they are after. They now have not only Corinna, with whom they can exert pressure upon myself, but they also have your wife. Should anything then happen to me and the title fall to you, they have a power over you, too.'

'That is how I see the situation, too, brother,' Willum agreed. 'And yet we have still received no demands.'

Lundt sat down heavily behind the table and idly riffled through the pile of documents which sat upon it. he looked up again and his face was the colour of ruis clay, from which the fine white palace porcelain was made.

'We will, though,' he said. 'We will.'

'I'm afraid she doesn't look much like a princess at the moment,' Savatch laughed, 'but I think, my Lord Fulgrim, that once you wash off the grime you will discover the Lady Corinna underneath.'

Fulgrim looked down at the mud-caked figure at his feet and laughed. 'Even as she is I would recognise her from any distance.' He looked up at the two green garbed amazons. 'It would appear you reached her only just in time.'

Jekka nodded, her red tresses shimmering with the movement.

'Only just, my lord,' she replied, her piercing blue eyes twinkling. 'Another few minutes and she would have been gone. Would you like us to take her and wash her in the stream. We would have done so on the way here, but I decided you would rather have the good news earlier than later.'

'Indeed, that's a good idea,' Savatch interrupted. 'But keep a tight hold on her chain. The little minx is a slippery one, it would appear.' He turned back to Fulgrim.

'Meanwhile, your lordship, if we return inside I believe we have some accounting to do and then you shall have your princess, all freshly scrubbed and shining.' He made to turn away, but stopped, speaking quietly over his shoulder.

'And I should warn you, my devious friend, that if you harbour any thoughts of sending a pursuit party to retrieve *my* gold, no amount of rank, power, influence, or military protection will keep you from my revenge. Thief I may be, villain I undoubtedly am, but I *am* a man of my word, else we could cut you down now and have both gold and girl.'

Chapter Ten

Benita Oleanna was more terrified than she had ever believed it possible for any mortal to be. It was some hours since she had watched her escort cut down before her very eyes, yet still she could not fathom what was happening.

The assailants had not only worn her husband's household livery, some of them she had recognised as actually being members of his own small army, including the ringleader, Captain Nestard. However, neither Nestard, nor any of the other murderous crew would answer her questions. She had simply been stripped naked, a slave jacket buckled about her and the blinding hood laced over her head, before being tossed back into the carriage.

They had been travelling now for what seemed an eternity. There were at least three men inside the vehicle with her, from what Benita could tell, but so far not one of them had tried to take advantage of her condition, though she did not doubt that the sight of her breasts protruding through the leather front was inducing certain thoughts in them.

She pressed her thighs together in an effort to conceal the thick bush of pubic hair she knew would act as further enticement to them, and wondered again what they wanted of her. It had to be Willum, she thought, trying to get her mind back into something akin to its usual orderly state. Yes, that was it. They wanted her in order to exert pressure on Willum.

First it had been Corinna, who would give them leverage

against Lundt. And now herself, so that whoever it was had both brothers in the palm of his hand. Except that they almost certainly did not know Willum, nor would they know of the loveless marriage into which he and Benita were locked.

If they really thought Willum would give in to any pressure using her, they were almost certainly in for a disappointment, she thought grimly.

The carriage rattled on, its occupants travelling in total silence.

Corinna was lifted into the saddle behind one of Fulgrim's men and her arms manacled about his waist. This not only prevented her from slipping off the horse, it also ensured that there was no possibility of her escaping.

'It will not be a long ride, my lady,' Fulgrim said. 'We will be rendezvousing with a carriage only a few miles from here and you will be made somewhat more comfortable. For the time being,' he added.

Corinna said nothing, but then the leather gag that had been strapped tightly into her mouth would have made speech impossible, even had she been able to think of a suitable retort.

Savatch finished arranging the coins into piles and pushed several across the table to Alanna. The white haired Yslandian picked up a single coin and bit into the side of it. Savatch smiled indulgently at her.

'I don't think even Fulgrim would bother trying to pass us off with dud gold,' he laughed. 'Besides, he never intended to part with it in the first place. He was cunning enough to suspect I might first arrive without the girl, so he brought it along in order to allay my suspicions, but he was relying on his cutthroats to ensure I never lived to take it from him.'

'I cannot believe he took you at your word when you said you were alone,' Alanna said, replacing the coin on its pile. 'I know you to be a man of your word, whatever other fiendish traits you possess, but how could he have been so stupid?'

'Lady Dorothea doubtless convinced him of my honesty in certain directions,' Savatch replied, slowly transferring the piles of coin on his side of the table into one of the leather sacks in which they had first arrived. 'But I was very careful in the oath I swore. I did not claim to be alone at all. I merely swore that I had no men waiting to pounce on him.'

Alanna shook her head, trying not to laugh. She looked up from her coin stacks.

'You,' she said, pointing a long finger accusingly across the table, 'are an incorrigible rogue.'

Savatch nodded contentedly. 'I know,' he said, tapping the next pile of coins and jingling the bag. 'And right now, a very rich one.' He swept another pile of coins into the sack.

'Not only that,' he added, as yet another pile disappeared, 'but as our business now seems to have been satisfactorily concluded, I am also a very hungry villain, with an appetite for the sort of meat that only you can furnish, my beautiful ice queen.' He turned and looked meaningfully at the door to the inner room where Helda still lay a prisoner.

'And I've even got a little present for you,' he said, smirking.

Chapter Eleven

The sight of Willum's livery on both the outriders and the coach sent Corinna's hopes soaring, only for them to be dashed again when she understood the reality of the situation. If there was one way in which her captors could avoid being apprehended with her by the patrols that would doubtless now be scouring the countryside, this was it. No trooper would dare challenge the coach of the brother of the Lord Protector.

The sight of the bound and hooded woman already inside the coach brought memories of her own abduction flooding back. She shivered despite the heat of the afternoon, as she recalled the way in which Savatch had brazenly shaved her and then taken her as though she were no more than a brood mare and he a stallion.

Stallion, she mused, as she settled against the leather seat. Yes, that was a good description of the wretch. Hung like a stallion. Corinna remembered conversations among the palace women, servants and dignitaries alike, conversations that were not meant for the ears of a young lady, but conversations she had nevertheless overheard. Hung like a stallion.

Having seen plenty of real stallions in her short time, Corinna had thought it just a phrase. But now, having seen and serviced Savatch's equipment, she was not so sure. Serviced? She jammed her teeth hard into the gag, angry with herself for using such an expression, even mentally. But in reality that was exactly what she had done. She had simply serviced his needs and slaked his lust.

But then, she thought closing her eyes, he had also serviced *her*. Yes, she had been bound and helpless and there had been no way for her to stop him, but she remembered everything now with total clarity and she could not hide from the simple fact that she had ended up begging the wretch to do what he did. And yet, as the coach swayed onwards and she began to drift into a light sleep, Corinna knew that she did not feel one single ounce of remorse. Guilt perhaps, but not remorse, and only the gag in her mouth prevented her from smiling.

Willum reined in his grey stallion, having ridden harder and for longer than he could remember having done in many years, and the effort had taxed him considerably. Behind him the four men of his personal escort came likewise to a halt in a clatter of hooves and jingling of harnesses. He turned and addressed the lean looking young captain who commanded them.

'You know your instructions, captain?' he wheezed.

The officer nodded. 'Yes, my lord,' he replied stiffly. 'You are going in response to a message which said you should be alone and would receive the kidnappers' demands. We are to turn back and three of us are to await your return at the inn we passed just a way back. Do you know how long you will be, my lord?'

Willum shook his head. 'It is impossible to say,' he replied. 'I have no idea what lies ahead of me, nor how long this matter will take.'

The captain's face displayed his concern. 'Are you sure it is wise to go, especially alone?'

'I have been assured of my personal safety,' Willum told him. 'These people have nothing to gain from harming me, for that would surely harden my brother's resolve. No, captain, I am to act only as their emissary, I think. They have Corinna and my wife – they do not need another hostage.'

'Will you not at least tell me the meeting place?' the officer persisted.

'The message warned against it,' Willum replied, evenly. 'Besides, I doubt that any of the main perpetrators will be there. I suspect I shall be taken on to another place before they show their faces.'

The guard captain saw that his continued argument was pointless. He watched as Lord Willum spurred his horse forward and broke into a canter that soon reduced him to little more than a speck on the distant trail. He turned to his men with a shake of his head.

'There,' he said with grave sincerity, 'goes a very brave nobleman.'

Corinna recognised the house as soon as she saw it come into view. She had never visited the near castle mansion, but she had seen pictures of it, for it was a very famous building with a long history and its present owner, the Lady Dorothea of Varragol, was distantly related to the ruling family, the Oleanna's. Surely, Corinna thought, this treachery has cut deep.

She was lifted bodily from the carriage and hustled into the building through a side entrance, from where she was led, still naked and still chained, the gag still strapped tightly in place, down to the subterranean level which housed the dungeons with which every major house in the land had been built. Behind her, she heard the muffled protests of her anonymous travelling companion, as she too was dragged unwillingly down the wide stairway.

The two captives were bundled into separate cells and the door banged shut on Corinna without anyone bothering to remove her gag, which now was surely superfluous, she thought. She looked around the small room, which was sparsely furnished indeed. There was a narrow cot, on which sat a thin and threadbare mattress, a single metal stool, bolted into the stone floor, and an iron bucket with a heavy wooden lid, set in the furthest corner, which was, in truth, not very far away at all.

There was no lantern in the cell, the only light filtering down from a narrow, barred slit, which was set just below the ceiling in the wall opposite the door, and consequently was too high to afford Corinna a view to the outside.

She raised her hands, forcing her wrists behind her neck, and fumbled for the buckle of the gag strap, but to her annoyance and frustration her fingers encountered a small lock there. She would have to remain with the gag in place until someone came along to release it. Thinking a very ignoble curse, Corinna slumped down onto the side of the cot and waited.

It seemed an age before the door finally opened again. Corinna looked up, to be confronted by the sight of Fulgrim standing in the narrow entrance, hands planted firmly on hips. He said nothing for several long seconds, but studied his captive with hooded eyes. His features, Corinna thought, reminded her of a hawk and there was little doubt in her mind that he was just as dangerous.

A Vorsan, and high in Lal Barendi's power structure, he was in his own right the Duke of Jerod, the most northerly country in the Vorsan alliance. He, like Savatch, had been a guest at Corinna's wedding to Lazlo, but then just about every member of the world's nobility who could travel had been at the great state celebration. The Vorsans had timed their move well, for that wedding had been the excuse for so many strangers to come into Illeum that the presence of so powerful a Vorsan leader would raise not the slightest suspicion.

Lal Barendi himself had not attended, sending apologies, a lavish gift, and the excuse that he was confined to his bed with a mild bout of fever. Corinna returned Fulgrim's stare and wondered if he was working on his own initiative, or whether, as she now thought likely, the Vorsan head of state was also in on the plot, or indeed, even its main instigator.

'I trust you will not make it necessary for me to bit and bridle you again, young woman,' he said.

Corinna licked the spittle from her lips and fought back the urge to spit it at him. 'I hardly see that it was necessary in the first place,' she retorted, with as much dignity as she could muster. 'Is this the way you Vorsans treat ladies and repay their country's hospitality?'

'Sometimes the end justifies the means,' Fulgrim replied. 'I serve one country and one flag and am loyal to both. To me you are just a bargaining tool, a commodity with which to trade.'

'But if you return me to my father as damaged goods, he will surely make you pay dearly,' Corinna warned. Fulgrim gave a loud, derisive snort. He stooped slightly, bringing his face close to hers.

'You had better dismiss any thoughts of being returned to you father right now,' he sneered. 'Not soon, not ever. Once we relinquish custody of you we shall doubtless find ourselves at war with Illeum, which is the one consequence we seek to avoid by this enterprise. No, lady, you will remain our prisoner for the foreseeable future.'

'Then why not just kill me?' Corinna suggested,

wondering what on earth possessed her to put such thoughts into his head, supposing that they were not there already.

'My father would never know the difference.'

'I think he might, little princess,' Fulgrim said. 'He will seek assurances that you are well and witnesses will have to see you. Besides,' he added, 'it would be a great pity to waste such a succulent morsel. You will provide many a welcome diversion, I am sure.'

'And just exactly what do you mean by that?' Corinna demanded. Fulgrim straightened up and paced back and forth, as far as the confined space would permit.

'I mean precisely what I said, Corinna Oleanna,' he said. 'Every man present at your wedding doubtless harboured thoughts of what he might do if you were his. Well, now you are mine, in a manner of speaking, though there are others with claims who will no doubt wish to share in your charms.

'You are ours forever, my lady, to do with as we choose, and I choose what any red-blooded male would choose. Afore long, wench, I intend to have you skewered on my cock!' Corinna recoiled in horror.

'You are disgusting, sir!' she cried. 'What man of nobility would address a lady of breeding in such coarse fashion?' Fulgrim laughed again. It was a harsh, sinister sound.

'I suggest, Corinna, that you forget your breeding, else I'll have your dainty notions thrashed out of you. From now on you are nothing but a whore and you shall be treated as such. You will be presented on occasions for inspection by neutral ambassadors, in order to satisfy your father's anxieties, but you will never be permitted to speak to them.

'Meanwhile, my royal beauty, you shall earn your corn. It will not only provide pleasure for others, but it will prevent you from growing bored in your captivity. In fact,' he said, turning to the door again, 'I have arranged a very amusing and ingenious reception for you this very evening. I must change for dinner now, but we shall be meeting again soon... very soon.'

The door clanged shut and he was gone, leaving Corinna alone again in the half darkness, shocked to a state of numbness by his revelations.

In another, much larger chamber, scant yards along the same corridor from Corinna's cell, the Lady Benita now found herself in an even worse predicament than before. The leather slave jacket had been stripped from her, but in its place an even more fiendish device had been employed.

The hefty guards had sheathed both her arms in tightly laced gloves, except that these gloves were quite unlike any Willum's wife had seen before. Instead of fingers, they tapered into mittens, at the end of which were stitched thick iron rings. These rings, in turn, had been clipped to hanging chains, which were then winched in until the helpless woman was hauled up onto tiptoe.

Now long leather boots were laced onto the length of her legs. These too tapered to rings at the toes and these rings were fixed to more chains, that held her legs obscenely wide and kept her toes just clear of the flagstones beneath them. A high collar had then been added, forcing her to keep her head high, for fear of the soft skin beneath her chin being pierced by the sharp prong which rose from the front of the device there. Then a harness of thinner straps had been buckled about her torso and the circular straps at the front drawn tightly about the base of each breast, forcing the dark skinned globes into distended shapes that stood out from her chest in a bizarre fashion.

Finally another harness was buckled about her head,

which at present held in place a thick, cylindrical leather gag that resembled an equine bit, and could also be employed to hold a thick blindfold which currently lay on the bench to one side of her, alongside a coiled whip and a long riding crop. The chain of events since the ambush and her subsequent treatment for the course of the journey to this place had left Benita stunned and only now, as she hung like a grotesque marionette, did her senses start to properly register what had been done to her.

But if the shock of her treatment had been extreme, even worse was to come. When the door opened and her husband, Willum, stepped into the room, for an instant her heart leapt. She hated and despised the man, but surely she was now saved. One look at the fire that now burned in his eyes was enough to convince her of her mistake.

She tried to scream at him, but the bit gag muffled most of the sound and what did escape was nothing more than a series of incoherent squawks. Willum folded his arms across his chest and grinned maliciously.

'Excellent, my dear wife,' he said. 'You have always been a nag and now, at last, you have been bridled like one.' He stepped forward and his hand plunged to her gaping and unprotected cleft. He gave a little grunt and stepped back.

'Dry as ever,' he sneered. 'Well, you'll soon get to change your ways, you malevolent witch. Oh yes,' he continued, seeing how her eyes grew steadily wider. 'You have refused me my rights as a husband for the last time, but from now on it'll not be only me you have to satisfy. I shall give you over to any of the guards who is desperate enough to crave a shrivelled hag like you.'

In truth this last insult was unjustified, for Benita, who was several years younger than Willum, was still a handsome figure of a woman. She did not have the well-endowed breasts of a Corinna, a Moxie, or a Dorothea, but what she did have were firm and well-muscled and stayed proudly erect without much underpinning. Her dark skin, proof of her southern ancestry, was smooth and flawless and her face, if a little narrow featured for some tastes, was elegant and refined.

Willum, however, was just getting into his stride.

'Shrivelled and dry, that's what you are, my dear wife,' he went on. 'And so full of your own superiority. Most women would have been glad to marry the brother of the head of a state as powerful as Illeum, but not you. When Lundt's own wife died you even tried to court him, and I know you visited at least one apothecary to try to acquire a potion that would rid you of me without arousing suspicion.

'Oh yes,' he crowed, seeing the expression in her eyes change dramatically, 'I know that was several years back now and it took a great effort on my part not to unmask you for the traitress you are back then. But I have bided my time and now my revenge will be all the sweeter.

'The whole world believes that you have been taken prisoner in order to exert pressure on your poor distraught husband, in the same way that Corinna will be used to influence Lundt's policies. I think that is so very amusing, don't you?

'Meanwhile, you will remain here until the chase cools, and then both of you will be moved to a place I have prepared in Jerod, there to amuse not only myself, but hundreds of others with whom I will share you. Not that I shall share young Corinna, of course. That tender morsel is for me alone. But you, you conniving bitch, will be put to as many cocks as I can bring to you.'

He turned to the bench and picked up the whip, but quickly discarded it in favour of the crop. He swished it harmlessly through the air between them and Benita cringed, but there was no way she could take avoiding action, held immovably as she was.

'Later, my dear, murderous wife, you shall have the dubious pleasure of watching me take my cock to our sweet Corinna, which will be revenge on Lundt for ever having been tasteless enough to take you to his bed. First, however, I shall take my cock to you, but not until you beg me for it.' He swished the crop again and Benita squealed into the gag, although the braided leather missed her by several inches.

'Oh yes, my withering angel, I shall have great delight in hearing you beg. However, for that, unfortunately, I shall have to remove your bit. Never mind, for it will go back in before I climb into your saddle.' He reached out and unbuckled the two fastenings, snatching the gag from her mouth with a vicious jerk. Benita immediately let forth a stream of abuse.

'Snivelling, filthy, perverted coward of a half man!' she shrieked. 'I'll never beg you for anything, you apology for a – aaaaggghhhhhhhhhhhhhh!' Her voice rose an octave as Willum slashed the crop across her breasts, drawing huge welts from each and sending a white fire searing through Benita's entire body.

'Silence, you whore!' he roared. 'You no longer have an opinion. From now on you are just a collection of orifices and they all exist for one purpose only.' Willum stepped forward, thrusting his face close to hers. 'And that purpose is not talking, understand?'

'You have lost your reason!' Benita gasped through sobs of agony. Willum roared with laughter.

'Far from it,' he chuckled maliciously. 'Rather I must have lost my sanity to endure your machinations and whinging complaints all these years. I should have taken a whip to you a long time since, but at least I now have the chance to make amends for that oversight.'

'Willum, I beg of you!' Benita whined. 'Please let me down and don't continue with this madness. Whatever plans you have for Corinna I will help you in them, for there is certainly no love between myself and that toity bitch, much less between her father and I.'

'That may be true now, but it was not always so, was it?' Willum snarled. 'As I said, you were quick enough to insinuate yourself between his sheets after Helena died.'

'I did it only as a comfort for the poor man,' Benita wailed. 'It was just a kindness, for he was so beside himself at his loss.'

'His "loss" was quite convenient for you, was it not?' Willum snapped. Benita stared at him, her lip quivering. 'Helena's riding accident was never completely explained, as I recall.'

'How dare you, Willum!' Benita shrilled. 'How dare you suggest that I – yaagghhhh!' Again Willum cut her short, this with a back-handed flick of the crop that slashed across her tautly stretched stomach muscles. He stepped back and waited for the first shock of the pain to recede.

'I dare anything I wish, now,' he hissed. 'Anything at all and yes, I can see now that I misjudged you when I called you shrivelled. All these years you've kept these charms from me and now I intend to enjoy them, but not so greatly as I shall enjoy the young Corinna.'

'Then take me if you will,' Benita sobbed. 'After all, I am so lewdly available to you I can hardly prevent it.'

'Not until you beg me for it, woman,' Willum taunted.

He was thoroughly enjoying his power now, savouring every moment. Benita shut her eyes and made to shake her head, but the cruel spike beneath her chin jabbed into her and brought another gasp of pain to her lips.

'Never!' she groaned. 'I will never beg you. You can kill me first.'

'Killing,' Willum said, very quietly, 'would be far too easy a release for you. Your cunt has a sentence to serve and serve it it will, though not before I have savoured its heat.' His arm swung again and a second red line appeared across Benita's stretched breasts. She shook and spasmed in her bondage and another shriek of agony echoed around the unsympathetic stone walls.

'You will beg me yet!' Willum growled. 'I guarantee it. So why not spare yourself and forget that haughty pride. You're in for a heavy ravaging, either way.'

Despite the thick walls and door, Corinna could hear the sporadic screams from within her cell and the sounds reminded her, only too clearly, of her own surrender, though she did not yet know the identity of the sufferer. In between, the stone and iron between them blocked out the sound of conversation, so she had no way of knowing what was going on, save that it was obvious that some poor female was being made to suffer abominably.

She shivered, but not because the cell was cold. Indeed, the heat of the summer had penetrated through the unglazed window and the place was tolerably warm, despite her nakedness. But Corinna knew only too well that, before much longer, it could be her screaming in terrible agony. She closed her eyes, huddled herself into a ball on the narrow cot and pressed one ear hard into the thin mattress, the other blocked with her finger, desperate to shut out the sounds.

Savatch had been bad enough, but something told her that these people here were a hundred times worse. She wondered where her abductor was now, and whether he had truly realised what he was delivering her into.

Savatch, in fact, was drawing near to the end of a long afternoon's diversions with Alanna, who needed no whip to spur her to greater efforts. In fact, of all the woman Savatch had bedded, she was the only one who had ever come close to exhausting his prodigious stamina, and yet he still craved to take her in the way he had taken Corinna.

The tall Yslander sat up and picked several blades of grass from her white tresses. She looked over her shoulder at the prone Savatch, and could not suppress a smile.

'What will you do now, my villainous friend?' she asked. Savatch opened his eyes and stared up at the pale blue early evening sky.

'I fear, my lanky lovely, that we need go our separate ways, at least for a while. We must leave Illeum, that much is certain. Perhaps we could meet up in your homeland, for Romaskaand forms a neutral buffer between this land and that.'

Alanna shook her head. 'I think not,' she said. 'Soon the real snows start again and I have grown too fond of the climate in the south to want to return for a winter, much as I miss the mountains at times. No, I should prefer somewhere like Dovania. The seas off its shores are clear and calm and the breeze from the southern ocean is warming.'

'I can live with Dovania,' Savatch agreed. He raised his left hand and idly traced a line down Alanna's long spine. She quivered slightly at his touch and her own hand went between his thighs, cupping his limp penis. She felt the flesh stir and grinned.

'That will die of overwork ere long,' she warned, but she continued to coax it as it slowly began to rise once more. 'I suppose you will be taking your little peasant tart along to occupy the nights on your travels,' she said.

Savatch sighed. 'I suppose I will,' he said. 'I had thought of giving her to you as a present, but I don't doubt you will be travelling with Jekka, or one of your other girls, so your own nights are scarce likely to be idle.'

'Scarce likely, I agree,' Alanna said. She saw that his staff was now almost fully risen and she rolled over onto him, sucking it into her wide mouth. Savatch groaned and vowed that he really would have to get the beautiful giantess under better control. He thought of white leather straps and made a mental note to invest a few crowns of his new fortune in having some specially crafted before he got to Dovania.

Chapter Twelve

Dorothea dismissed Moxie and waited until the buxom little former bar wench had closed the door behind her, before turning to Fulgrim.

'Where is the noble lord at present?' she asked.

Fulgrim raised his eyes to the ceiling. 'Where do you think?' he asked. 'Amusing himself in your dungeons with his unfortunate spouse. I would not care to be in her shoes at this moment. Cruelty has many faces, but the release of so much pent up hatred after so long will not be a sight that even I would relish.'

'He will want to turn his attentions to the younger one soon,' Dorothea pointed out. 'What will you do then?'

Fulgrim laughed. 'I shall let him have his head,' he said. 'I have no personal desire for the wench, other than the normal, and I shall savour her personally in good time. However, for now I shall allow Willum to believe that Corinna is his personal domain. I shall even have her prepared for him in suitable fashion. I have given very precise instructions to your head woman and she seems only too willing to oblige.'

'Oh yes, Agana most certainly will oblige in such matters. I sometimes think she is even more cruel than even your reputation has of you, sir, though it would be a close run race, I'll wager. However, you do realise that the time will come when we have to deal with Willum on a more permanent basis? He will soon change his mind concerning the removal of the women to Jerod. He will not be able to come himself, not immediately, and the thought of being separated from his precious little Corinna will not appeal to him.'

'It most certainly will not,' Fulgrim agreed. 'He will probably hatch some foolish alternative plan, something which is like to put our main enterprise in serious jeopardy, and we cannot tolerate that.'

'So, you will kill him?'

'Probably. Unless you fancy an extra slave in your retinue?'

'Willum Oleanna?' Dorothea laughed. 'I somehow think not, my good lord. The prospect does not appeal to me at all, though I might find some way to amuse myself with him before he is finally disposed of.'

Benita finally and inevitably capitulated. Through tear-filled eyes and in a haze of pain-ridden delirium she begged her husband to take her, but Willum was determined to draw out his revenge to the utmost. He left the cell, returning a few minutes later in the company of a stunning brunette, whose magnificently athletic body was sheathed in tight leather, her powerful arms left bare and her feet shod in the most incredibly heeled boots. In her hands she carried a silver tray, the contents of which were hidden by a velvet cloth.

'I should like to introduce Mistress Agana to you, wife,' Willum sneered. 'She will prepare you as a slave should be prepared for the beginning of her new life of debauchery.' He stepped back and made room for Agana to set about her work.

She set the tray down on the bench and drew the red cloth aside, revealing a series of metal rings and a long, wickedly pointed needle. Already beyond true sensibility,

Benita scarcely flinched as the needle was passed through her right nipple, and she hardly felt the heavy gold plated ring which Agana threaded through the piercing afterwards.

The woman was highly skilled at her craft and, very soon, Benita was adorned as Willum had requested. Her own, delicate earrings were replaced by heavy, gold plated lead pendants which dragged grotesquely at her lobes. Both nipples sported the heavier gold rings and a similar adornment was threaded through the septum between her nostrils. Agana then took up two much finer rings and, piercing each of Benita's labial lips in turn, threaded the rings into place and fastened them.

Her needle was then turned to the tender folds of flesh on Benita's inner thighs and two more rings were added to the growing collection. These, in their turn, were used to anchor the labia rings, which were drawn to the side and attached with tiny clips, thus ensuring that Benita's sex was held open like a hungry mouth. Her spread-eagled pose was thus made even more obscene, much to Willum's evident satisfaction.

'You are a true artist, Mistress Agana,' he complimented the tall brunette. Agana smiled, cat-like.

'I have one more refinement, if you would like me to add it,' she suggested. Willum shrugged.

'Be my guest,' he offered, making an open-handed gesture towards the comatose Benita. 'I am sure your ingenuity will not disappoint me.'

And ingenious Agana's final touch most certainly was. She crossed the chamber to another bench and rummaged among the collection of dubious looking implements that were piled there. Finding what she sought, she returned and took up a stance immediately in front of Benita.

'Open your mouth!' she snarled. Hardly conscious of

what was happening to her now, Benita obliged automatically and Agana immediately seized her tongue between the jaws of a wicked looking pair of pincers. She drew the pink flesh out and her needle sunk though it, drawing a gurgle of protest and further pain from her victim. Agana, however, ignored this and, by the time she released the pierced tongue, it boasted a large, circular cameo across its centre.

'That will make it difficult for her to speak,' Agana said, 'and it also produces some very interesting sensations, though I recommend you let me fit a jaw clamp before you avail yourself of her mouth. Those teeth could ruin a man for life.'

'I thank you for the advice, mistress,' Willum said. 'Perhaps you could carry out the necessary adjustments now?' Agana nodded and returned to the equipment bench. This time she fetched two small double clamps, which she inserted at either side of the unresisting Benita's mouth. The clamps were then screwed to the sides of the back teeth at top and bottom, preventing the helpless victim from closing her mouth, holding it wide open for whatever purpose Willum might like to devise for it.

Agana, as she replaced her piercing needle on the tray and careful folded the velvet cloth, doubted he needed any advice on that account. She paused at the door, examining the effect of her handiwork and nodded. Yes, the bitch was ready for real humiliation now. She wondered if she would get the same chance with the other one, the Protector's daughter. She had seen the young wench being brought in and knew she would get even more enjoyment from introducing that particular noble filly to her own peculiar arts.

However, for the present, she had been given very precise

instructions concerning the girl. She lifted the needle, placed it to her lips and smiled. Plenty of time for you, my precious, she said to herself.

Corinna feared the worst when the stunning, leather-clad brunette entered her cell. The woman carried a thick sack, which clinked ominously when she placed it on the floor. Corinna looked up at the powerful woman, her face betraying the trepidation she felt. Agana stared down at her, her face impassive.

'I am to prepare you to meet your new owner,' she said, simply. Corinna struggled into a sitting position.

'My new owner?' she repeated. 'What foolishness is this? I am a lady of noble birth, not a common slave. If I am to be held hostage, for whatever devious purposes, then so be it, but I must protest at my treatment. I should like some clothes, to begin with.'

'Oh, I shall dress you, milady,' Agana said, with a mock bow. 'Though I doubt your new suit will be overly to your liking. Now, you can resist, or at least attempt to resist, in which case I am authorised to use whatever force this requires. I doubt you will be much of a match for me, but you are welcome to try.' As if to emphasise her point she reached out, seized Corinna's arm in one hand and hauled her easily to her feet. Corinna recognised defeat when she saw it and decided to remain passive.

'A wise decision,' Agana said, recognising the signs of submission. 'A pity in many ways, but no matter.' She stooped and opened the sack and drew out a tangle of leather straps, buckles and chains, which she began to wrap about Corinna's body, cinching it tightly into place.

By the time she had finished Corinna was already helpless, her waist compressed by a leather corset, straps encircling her breasts, with chains running up from the top of the corset to the high, studded collar which Agana locked about her neck, and her arms encased in fingerless glove sleeves, which were in turn attached to the sides of the corset by single links, forcing the unfortunate girl to remain with her arms held stiffly at attention.

The breast straps were now tightened, squeezing Corinna's impressive melons into an even more striking shape, and small circular clamps snapped about her prominent nipples, forcing her to wince with pain as the tiny serrated teeth bit into the tender flesh. Knee length boots followed, joined to each other with lengths of chain that permitted steps of no more than a few inches and, like Benita before her, her own dainty earrings were replaced with larger, heavier versions.

'Yes, you make an excellent slave girl,' Agana said, turning her prisoner around before her. She patted Corinna's full rump appreciatively. 'And I dare say that will provide as good a sheath as anything else you possess,' she added with a grim smile. 'We'll leave the mouth for the present, but we shall meet again quite shortly, I think. Your new master is rapidly acquiring some very different tastes. He is indeed an excellent scholar.' She chuckled as she picked up the now empty sack. 'I don't think it will be too long before he requests me to adorn you in the same fashion as Benita now wears,' she added, turning towards the door. Corinna stared after her.

'Benita?' she cried. 'Whatever are you talking about?'
Agana paused in the doorway, turning her head back with a vicious smile.

'Of course,' she said silkily, 'you did not know, did you? The hooded slave who shared the carriage ride here with you was the esteemed Lady Benita; only she is not so esteemed any more, I fear. Now she is just another pierced slave, cock fodder for the commonest soldier, if your master has his way... which he will,' she added, closing the door behind her with a heavy crash.

Benita lay in an exhausted heap, her arms and legs still laced into their leather sheaths, though she was no longer suspended by the rings at their extremities. The vicious clamp still held her mouth agape and she could not rid herself of the taste of Willum's spendings. She could not even muster the strength to try to expel the cruel leather dildo he had buried in her rear passage, before finally sinking his seemingly inexhaustible shaft into her burning vagina.

He had turned her onto all fours and, as promised, had thrust the bit back between her jaws and ridden her as a stallion might ride a mare, snatching at the leather bridle he had attached to the bit and spurring her on with repeated slashes of the crop against either flank. Now, abandoned and spent, Benita's entire being felt like it was on fire. She groaned and lifted one useless hand to her mouth, but the thick leather rendered her fingers unusable and the bit would have to remain in place until someone took pity upon her.

Easing onto her stomach, her head resting on her sheathed arms, Benita understood that pity was a commodity that was likely to be in short supply in this hell of a place. She felt as if she wanted to die – but enough of the old proud Benita survived for her to know that she wanted to live long enough to see Willum die first. And she hoped, fervently, that the manner of his death might be at least the equal to the living death he had inflicted upon her.

Corinna could not believe either her eyes or her ears, for was this not Willum now standing before her? The two guards had half carried her from her cell, lifted her up the stairs and then dragged her along the carpeted hallways, before thrusting her into the room in which they now were. Her first instinct had been that her father's brother had also been taken prisoner, but his first words had dispelled any such notion.

'It is so nice to see you here, my dearest Corinna,' he greeted her. 'And so much more attractively outfitted than the last time we met. This slave garb certainly does something for a wench. You shall have to wear it at all times from now on, I think, for I already feel my pole stirring at the very sight of you.'

'This is madness!' Corinna gasped. 'Willum, you are not making sense? Have you lost your mind?'

Willum smiled, but the smile did not reach his eyes. 'Not at all, my sweet Corinna. In fact, I feel I have only just begun to live properly. I have already dealt my treacherous wife a severe lesson and now I am free to concentrate on my real love... you.'

'Me?' Corinna's eyes were wide with astonishment. 'Whatever are you talking about, Willum? You are my father's brother—'

'Not by blood, as you well know.'

Corinna lost her train of thought for a few seconds. 'Well... as for Benita being treacherous, the only treachery I see here is yours – yours and that of whoever else is involved in this insidious scheme with you!'

'The real treachery goes far deeper than you could ever hope to realise, my sweet, and began many years ago. Your noble father and my dear wife began it. Now, however, the boot is on the other foot.' He looked her up and down.

'And on that same subject, how do you like *your* new boots, my dear?'

'I cannot believe this is the same man I have known since my first childhood memories,' Corinna gasped. 'Surely you are not well!'

'Never felt better, my innocent Corinna,' Willum swaggered. He reached out a hand and hefted her left breast. Corinna shrank back from him and the hobbling chains between her boots almost caused her to topple backwards. She regained her balance only with some difficulty. Willum seemed to find this amusing.

'So pretty in your new slave leathers,' he chuckled. 'So appetising. That fool of a husband of yours has no idea of how a real man should behave. Had you been my wife, the world would not have seen either of us for months on end, as the world shall now see nothing of you again, ever!'

'Please!' Corinna begged Willum. 'Please desist from this depravity. I am your niece!'

'You have *never* been my niece,' Willum corrected her. 'But now you *shall* be my love slave, Corinna. I had thought to woo you by degrees, but I have today learned that there are far swifter and more satisfying ways. Not that I think I shall be so hard with you as I was with that bitch who called herself my wife.'

'Benita – what have you done with her?' Corinna shrieked. She had visions of her lying with her throat slit, or worse. She had never particularly liked Willam's haughty wife, but the thought of her dead was too much to contemplate. Willum laughed at her apprehension.

'Oh, she still lives and she will continue to live for many years yet, though I fear she may wish she did not. I've taken what I was owed from her and repaid her for her infidelity, and now I will give her to any man who wants her and exact a small fee into the bargain. It is a fitting end for her, a whore for hire, for I swear that she would once have traded her favours for a country.'

'As you are now trading your country to appease your perverted appetite!' Corinna countered. 'You are a traitor, Willum, and your soul will roam the hells for eternity.'

'Perhaps,' William said. 'But that will be a long time in the future. Until then I have you.' He stepped forward, seized Corinna's shoulders, and kissed her harshly on the mouth, his tongue probing between her lips. For an instant Corinna fought to resist, but then she relaxed her grimace and his tongue slid into her mouth, searching for her own. Instead it found her teeth as Corinna bit down hard.

With a howl of anguish Willum leapt back, his right hand lashing out in a vicious arc. It caught Corinna on the side of the head, though she managed to ride some of the force. However, there was still enough power in the slap to knock her sprawling into the centre of the room. She lay on her back, glaring defiantly up at him. His chin now dripped with his own blood.

'Bitch!' he snarled, though his blood-filled mouth made the word sound like 'Vitch!'. Corinna tried to crawl backwards, seeing the murderous gleam that had appeared in his eyes.

'Do your worst, you bastard!' she hissed, with more bravado than she felt. Willum wiped his mouth on his sleeve and looked down at her as she lay there.

'I most certainly will, you vicious little cow!' he glowered. 'An hour from now you will be begging me to fill that near virgin slot of yours. I will soon have you wriggling on my hook and no mistake!'

Corinna tried to struggle back to her feet, but found that with her arms held so closely to her sides and her legs chained so closely together, the task was beyond her. Willum savoured her struggles.

'On your back, where you so obviously belong,' he sneered. 'And just look at the newly shaven mound. It begs for attention, does it not? And now it will receive the courtesy of a real man, at last, not the lungings of a scrawny youth.'

'Is that what you believe?' Corinna cried. 'Well, I have some bad news for you. That which you so desperately crave has taken some serious servicing these past two days, and by an engineer who is an expert in his field. Your piddling cock is no match for his, for I doubt you could stretch me as a true man has!' Corinna suddenly stopped, realising what she had said and unable to believe the crudity of the language she had used, but the effect on Willum was as though he had been struck over the head with a smith's hammer.

'What?' he choked. 'What is this I am hearing? You lie, girl. You lie!'

Corinna laughed uncontrollably, the sight of his purpling features just too much for her to bear. 'Oh, so I lie, do I? Well, here I am. I cannot spread my legs as I needed for Master Savatch, but then your piss-pole will not require such spacious accommodation as his did. Come on Willum, what keeps you from the task. Yes, look, I lay here like a slave, helpless and waiting. Put it in me, Willum, and let's see if your spunk is as vigorous as another's!

'Come,' she continued goading, her eyes narrowing. 'Come fuck your new whore and see if she is impressed by it.'

'Whore!' Willum roared and leapt forward, kicking out at her hip. His boot made a glancing contact but Corinna ignored the flash of pain. She wriggled her body enticingly, causing her full breasts to ripple. Willum stopped, his breath coming in short gasps.

'You will pay for this,' he rasped. 'By the gods, you will pay for this and beg me as did the other whore. And I'll stretch you. If my tackle isn't up to it, I'll find something that ensures that even the largest man would find space to spare within you. But first I'll have my enjoyment from you. I have spent a lot of time in order to ensure your safe arrival here and still I find I have been betrayed.'

Willum suddenly realised there was blood still dripping from his chin. He wiped himself with his sleeve again and stared down at the dark stain. He pointed an accusatory finger at his helpless captive.

'I shall go now to find the house physician, if the house indeed has one. But when I have stanched this annoying flow I shall be back to create another!'

Chapter Thirteen

Fulgrim paced back and forth across the thick carpet that covered the floor of Dorothea's private sitting room. His hawkish features were dark and even more brooding than usual.

'You have heard most of it, I think?' he said, turning to the lady of the house. Dorothea, lounging in her favourite deep chair, nodded.

'Of course,' she said. 'Almost as much as you did yourself.'

'The man is losing control,' Fulgrim snapped. Dorothea waved an elegantly manicured hand in the air.

'He is not losing control,' she said calmly, 'he has already lost it. He has been dangerously near the edge for some weeks now. This whole enterprise is too deep for him and he carries scars that are years beyond ever healing. We both saw what he did to his wife.'

'Nothing more than she undoubtedly brought upon herself,' Fulgrim said. 'The beating he gave her was severe, I'll admit, but she'll recover. And the rest of it was largely instigated by your woman, Agana. A nice touch that, I thought.'

'Agana is an expert,' Dorothea agreed, 'but Willum has not grasped the essential principle involved here. A calm detachment is needed in these matters. The slave must also receive something from the arrangement, as young Corinna evidently did at the hands of Master Savatch, judging from what we heard.'

'A surprising young woman, that,' Fulgrim said. 'I find myself curiously intrigued by her.'

'Which means, I take it, that you will shortly be sampling her delights yourself?' Fulgrim gave Dorothea a mirthless smile.

'I see I can have few secrets from you, my lady,' he said. 'However, first we must deal with the problem of Willum. It would be an easy enough matter to slit the fool's throat, but there are still several of his followers in this house.'

'They can be dealt with,' Dorothea assured him. 'And without yet more bloodshed,' she added, her face solemn. 'There has been enough of that already, I fear.' Fulgrim looked at her in surprise.

'I did not have you marked as squeamish, my lady,' he said. Dorothea shook her auburn mane.

'We must agree that we are different, my lord,' she replied. 'I seek my diversities at a different level from you. Pain for its own sake is gratuitous, in my opinion. Take my little Moxie, for example. A simple little country virgin with breasts you could farm on. No doubt she has grown up with ambitions no greater than to marry one of the local farm lads, dam his offspring and grow fat and rosy with grandchildren at her knee ere she reaches her fortieth summer.

'A sound application of the rod, an afternoon in Midnight's special saddle, followed by an evening under my own peculiar tuition and she hardly spares a glance for a male now. In fairness, most of my male staff would be of little use to the wench, but I vouchsafe that even Master Savatch would be hard pressed to bring her back from my camp now.

'I still keep the rod handy, I'll grant you, but that quick little tongue is as willing as a woman could wish.'

'That's as maybe,' Fulgrim said, 'but that still does not solve the problem of Willum.'

'As I said,' Dorothea emphasised, 'I have a solution. Let the madman have his fill of Corinna, and then leave things to me. My Moxie will prove most useful in this matter, but I will not bore you with the details of my scheme. I merely ask you to trust me, though I know your nature finds such a concept totally alien.

'I will attend to Willum and in a manner which will arouse no suspicion from his men here. All I ask, in return, is one small boon.'

'Which is?' Fulgrim prompted. Dorothea smiled and the smile became even wider.

'The girl, Corinna,' she said. 'She is to be mine for seven days, once the deed is done.'

Fulgrim met her steady gaze and he, in turn, smiled, this time his humour reflecting in his eyes. 'Agreed,' he said, 'but with one small caveat. I have the girl at my disposal for one evening first. I can assure you, my lady, that what I have in mind for her will make her far more agreeable to what you doubtless have planned for her.'

Dorothea rose gracefully to her feet and extended her right hand.

'We have a bargain, Lord Fulgrim,' she said, 'and you may have my hand on it.'

Chapter Fourteen

Left alone in the room there was little that Corinna could do, save to totter across to the nearest chair and perch herself on the edge of it. Whether such presumption would bring further punishment down on her she neither knew, nor cared. There was little worse that could be inflicted on her that had not already been done, she thought. However, she was soon to be proved wrong.

After nearly half an hour the door reopened, but it was not the expected return of Willum. Instead, the towering figure of Agana strode into the cell. She carried a cloth covered tray in one hand and a short crop in the other. Placing the tray on the central table, she crooked a finger at Corinna.

'Come over here, girl,' she said. Corinna rose and waddled across to her, the chained boots forcing her to take humiliating little steps. Agana smiled at her.

'It would appear those pretty little teeth of yours have bitten deep, my pretty one,' she said. 'The blood flow will not be stemmed easily and the physician is even now stitching the wound.'

'I wish I had bitten his tongue clean in two,' Corinna snorted. 'The man is nothing more than a raving beast.'

'That's as may be,' Agana conceded, 'but he is a beast who has you in his power, and not the sort of beast to cross readily. I had not thought you would fall to my services so soon, but Lord Willum has decided that, as you have consigned him to the needle, so shall he do likewise for you. I have come to ring you as I did to Benita, but I think you will make a prettier picture when I am done.'

'Ring me?' Corinna said, perplexed. 'What manner of torture is that to be, for I already have these heavy things at my ears?'

'The ears are not the only parts of a body that may be improved by the addition of rings,' Agana told her. She drew the cloth from the tray and Corinna gasped as she saw its contents. Her eyes filled with tears.

'Oh please,' she wailed, 'say this thing is not to be.'

Agana looked down at her with a contemptuous smile. 'Ah, but it is to be done and well done at that,' she said. She reached out and grasped Corinna's shoulder. 'However, I will give you a choice. You may stand erect and give proof of your noble courage, else I can strap you over the table here. There are cords in the cupboard, for I checked them myself this very morning.' Corinna choked back a sob and blinked her eyes clear.

'I will stand,' she affirmed. She thrust her shoulders back and stared straight into Agana's eyes. 'But I wonder, lady, whether you would do so if it were you in these boots!' Agana regarded her for several seconds and there was something akin to admiration in her eyes now, though it came there grudgingly.

'Very well,' she said. 'In which case I will go easier on your youthful flesh than I was with the other. Hold still now.' She took up the glass stoppered bottle from the tray, together with the cotton swab that lay neatly folded next to it. The liquid was ice cold as she wiped it over each of Corinna's nipples in turn and Corinna gasped slightly at each first touch.

'This will numb your flesh for several minutes,' Agana explained. 'When it wears off, there will be soreness, especially below, but they soon heal, for this preparation also contains a herbal ingredient to speed that process. You should thank me, for I do not usually show my charges such consideration.

'When I ring a girl's tits I like to hear her yelp, for I find that serves to remind her later that a nice juicy nipple, such as these, can be made to carry more than one ring.' True to Agana's word, Corinna felt almost nothing as the needle went through her flesh. Though she was not to know it, the instrument was considerably thicker than that which had been used on Benita, as were the rings that were slipped through the holes.

They were cunningly made, Corinna saw, with one end of the open circle sliding smoothly inside the hollowed other, locking into place with a soft click. Peering down, she tried to discern whether there was a release mechanism, but could see none. She concluded, therefore, that the four inch diameter rings were intended to be permanent.

Her labia and inner thighs were treated in the same fashion as Benita's and very soon her slit had been opened. Corinna swallowed hard, fighting back the tears. The operation may have been relatively painless, but the humiliation she now felt was a greater hurt than any whip could inflict.

Agana was still not through with her ministrations, however. Now she inserted the swab inside Corinna, who whimpered and jerked as the icy liquid touched her clitoris. She let out a low moan as she realised that the needle was about to be introduced to this most intimate of her flesh.

This time, however, it was not a ring that was introduced, rather a short little cylinder of gold, with a hole through each side of it. Deftly, Agana manipulated the little nubbin which, even in its frozen state, began to respond and engorge. After a minute or so, satisfied that the elongated flesh had reached its limit, she slipped the cylinder over it and worked it down so that it formed a collar. Turning it so that one of the holes was outermost, she now used the needle and pierced through it, through the clitoris itself and straight through the second hole in the metal.

When she withdrew the needle, it was replaced by a slender golden stud, which ended in a small ball at one end and which was then fastened by means of a screw-on ball at the other.

'There,' Agana said, standing up again. 'Your collar prevents you seeing the effect properly, but there is a mirror against the far wall and you shall admire yourself when I have fixed your ear rings.' She then removed the heavy pendants from Corinna's ears and replaced them with little bells. Now, whenever Corinna moved her head at all, she set off a merry tinkling sound which made her cringe from the shame that had been heaped upon her.

'One last adornment,' Agana said, and when she finally led her victim to the mirror, Corinna's navel glittered with the gold mounted stone that she set there. Coming up to the glass, Corinna cried out at the brazen picture she now made, for apart from her gaping sex, her collared clitoris now stood out in plain view, the gold cylinder preventing it from retreating beneath the sanctuary of the little hood of flesh that usually hid it.

'I think Lord Willum should be satisfied,' Agana said. 'But I suggest you say nothing of the deadening potion I used. Let him think you have already suffered agonies to be thus adorned.'

'The agonies I now suffer are far worse than any physical pain,' Corinna wailed. 'Look at what you have done to me! I am become a pretty plaything, without even the slightest pretence at modesty. What devilish minds could conjure up such misery for a woman?'

When Willum finally did return the expression on his face was dark and menacing. But when his eyes fell upon Corinna and he saw Agana's handiwork, it lightened considerably.

'Hah!' he cried. 'I see you have been well put to the needle, too.' His speech sounded a little indistinct and, when his mouth opened, Corinna could just make out the dark outline of the physician's thread. Despite herself, she winced and wondered if Willum had been offered the numbing solution Agana had used on herself. She fervently hoped he had not.

'I assume,' she said, returning his gaze with more confidence than she felt, 'that you are well pleased with what you see?'

Willum took a pace closer to her.

'Many years ago as a young man, I travelled far to the east,' he said, 'and saw many similarly ringed and belled females in the whorehouses there. You make as fine a whore as anything I saw. Perhaps, if I tire of you in time, you should be sent east and sold to a brothel, eh?'

'I could scarce be treated more abominably, no matter where you chose to send me,' Corinna retorted. Willum snorted.

'I shall find new diversions for you yet,' he threatened. 'This is just the beginning. Now, turn and face the table.'

Realising that resistance or rebellion was useless and would doubtless cause this madman to inflict yet more abominations upon her, Corinna did as she was told, jingling with every tiny step. Willum ordered her to move close up to the heavy wooden structure and she shuffled forward until the nearer edge pressed lightly against her lower abdomen.

'Now bend forward and get your head on the table top,' Willum instructed. Stiffly, Corinna obeyed, pressing her left cheek against the polished wood, her bells jingling noisily as she bent over. She felt Willum grasp her thighs, forcing them as far apart as her bondage would permit and then, after a few seconds delay and a rustling of fabric, she felt the warm nub of his erection pressing between them, searching for her beringed opening. Corinna closed her eyes and tried to pretend it was Savatch about to penetrate her, for she knew she was bone dry down there and his entry would be a painful one if she could not lubricate herself.

To her relief, the deception worked instantly and she felt herself becoming hot and wet. Just in time, for now the first inch of his pole was within her and she could feel the throbbing of the distended flesh against the walls of her slick tunnel. She heard him grunt and felt the warm breath between her shoulderblades as his hands squeezed between her and the table top to seek out her breasts.

'We'll play many a pretty tune with these,' he rasped, pushing further inside her. His fingers found the large nipple rings and pulled on them. Corinna let out a cry of anguish and Willum, hearing this, plunged full length within her in a single stroke.

'Now I'll show you how a filly should be ridden,' he said. 'And the bitch who is my wife has a prime view of the race, for yonder mirror is also a mirror from its far side and she stands there, neatly trussed, watching everything.' He began to pump steadily in and out of Corinna, who was still fighting hard to pretend he was Savatch.

'And well wet you are!' Willum roared. 'Not like that dried up harridan. D'ye hear that, Benita? This is real woman flesh here, by the gods!'

Corinna groaned, but not from any pain. Her dream image was working too well she realised, and at any second she was about to explode into what would probably be the first of many climaxes.

And then she came back to the reality and the fire within her belly died instantly. Instead, the tears dripped onto the smooth table top as she bent and was ravished by a man she had once loved and admired, but who now, without doubt, was no more than a drooling madman.

Moxie sat on the edge of her bed and stared up at her mistress, wide-eyed, as she listened to what Dorothea had to tell her. When the older woman had finished speaking, the young maid looked very subdued. Dorothea reached down and cupped the girl's chin in her hand, raising her face to meet her own.

'It will be all right, Moxie,' she said, reassuring her in a soft voice. 'He won't actually get to put his dirty prick inside you – no man will ever do that, my busty little angel.' She opened her other hand and passed the small packet to Moxie. She saw it was wrapped in some sort of oily cloth, and she took it from Dorothea gingerly.

'Before you open it,' Dorothea cautioned, 'you will need to swallow these.' From a pocket concealed in the folds of her skirt she withdrew two small pills. 'Take them now, for it is necessary to allow an hour for them to work. If you do not, the drug in the pad will affect you in the way it is intended to affect him.'

'But must it be me that does this thing, mistress?' Moxie whined. 'What if he realises something is up?'

Dorothea's lips formed into a grimacing smile. 'He won't, Moxie, believe me. I shall share a bottle of wine with him which will arouse both our passions to feverpoint. I think he knows my tastes do not extend to men, so he will become quite agitated and probably decide to return for another spell with Corinna

'However, I shall arrange for Corinna to be moved to another part of the building and I shall also ask Willum's senior officer here to place you in her cell, under the pretence that you are being punished for some minor misdemeanour. He will be told to strip you and chain you to the wall and bring all the keys to me.

Mistress Agana, however, has a key that opens all the cell doors below and, as soon as he has left you, she will come in with that package, which you will give back to my safekeeping for the present. It will be glued into the palm of your hand. As soon as he comes close enough, you will open your hand and press the patch against his naked flesh. Anywhere on his body will do.

'The poison works within seconds and he will appear to have died from a heart stoppage. Agana will then return and retrieve the poison patch. I am afraid you will have to remain chained for a while afterwards, but I will take steps to ensure his guard comes back down to check upon you. He will discover the body and naturally assume his master has indulged in one excess too many.

'You, of course, will confirm that he was overly excited and passed away in the very act of inflicting himself upon your naked and helpless body. Do this thing well, Moxie, for it is of extreme importance.' She touched the girl lightly upon her shoulder and smiled again. 'Do it for me, little one, and I shall reward you highly.'

But for the table to support her, Corinna would by now have fallen to the floor, for Willum's treatment of her had been rough and exhausting. She was amazed at his stamina, also, for he was scarcely in the first flush of his youth and not anything like the athlete that Savatch undoubtedly was.

Twice already she had felt his hot seed spurting into her belly and yet his shaft remained as hard as when he had started. Clearly his lust for her was driving him to plateaux he would not normally scale. And now he sought a change.

He drew his slippery pole from her and pressed the knob between her fullsome buttocks, seeking the small puckered opening of her bottom. It was too much for Corinna.

'No! No-ooo!' she wailed. 'Not there!' She clenched her muscles and his attack was easily rebuffed. With a roar of anger, Willum stepped back slightly and slapped her hard across her bottom, bringing a scarlet patch to her right cheek. 'Don't resist me, or I'll have you strung up by your tit rings, so help me.'

But Corinna was not to be so easily persuaded, no matter how dire the threat. Still she gritted her teeth and held her muscles firm and again Willum was rebuffed.

'I'll teach you, you stubborn whore!' he raged. Corinna heard him walking across the room behind her, but scarcely had enough strength left to waste any of it on raising and turning her head. She soon discovered his errand though.

She heard the whistle of the thin cane a split second before it cut into her upraised cheeks and she shrieked with a mixture of surprise and agony as it bit home. A second whistle and another bolt of fire shot through Corinna. Again she screamed, for the pain was as bad as any whip could inflict.

Unlike Savatch, who had used the small breast whip methodically and rhythmically, Willum thrashed her with neither control, nor precision. The cane cut across the tops of her thighs, across her shoulders and across her back, wherever the leather harnesses left any flesh exposed.

Corinna's wailing rose to a crescendo, until finally she could take no more.

'Stop, for mercy's sake!' she implored, her eyes blinded by the tears there. 'Spare me any more and have of me as you will, you foul creature. See, I resist no more, but I beg you release my legs from such close confinement, or you will surely tear me asunder.'

She heard the cane clatter to the table beside her head and then the only sound, for several seconds, was of Willum's laboured breathing. It seemed he needed to regain his breath before the next stage of his assault on her, or else he was considering what Corinna had said. She felt his fingers tugging at the lower of the two chains that kept her boots adjacent to each other and, a moment later, he was unhooking the second.

'Spread yourself,' He hissed, thrusting his knee between her thighs. 'Spread yourself good and wide. I want a nice tight ride, fair enough, but first I have to get properly sheathed.'

Corinna bit into her lip, but she slowly moved her feet wider apart. Willum stepped forward and once again pressed his weapon against the dark rosebud entrance. This time Corinna did not try to resist, but even so, the pain was worse than that of her wedding night.

'There!' Willum gasped as his stomach finally slapped against her womanly bottom. 'Full home I reckon, and now it's your turn to do the work. Come now girl, work yourself on me.'

Corinna was now totally past caring what was done to her, or what she in turn had to do, so long as she was spared the agonies of rod and whip. She slowly eased her torso forward along the table top, though there was little room left to her.

Seeing this, Willum himself drew back a little until only the first inch or so of his manhood still remained within the tight orifice. He growled like an animal; a dog or a bear.

'Push back now,' he croaked. 'Skewer yourself on my beast, you horny beauty.' Obediently, Corinna pressed herself back, though it was a difficult feat without the use of hands or arms, until she was once again fully impaled. Once again her own pleasures stirred. 'Forward again!' She moved forward until the edge of the table dug into her.

'That's the way!' Willum cackled. 'Faster now. I want to fill this lovely hole as I did the other!'

Alanna sat up in the darkness and looked up at the clear night sky above, frowning as she tried to concentrate her thoughts, carefully piecing back together the fragments of the images that had woken her. Alongside her, wrapped in her heavy sleeping cloak, Jekka snored slightly and slept on, undisturbed.

Vala Valkyr Kirislanna Friggisdottir. She had been named for her mother, Vala Friggis Minischdottir, who had been a truly powerful seeress, and some of Friggis' peculiar talents had been passed on to her, Alanna knew. This was not her first vision by any means, but never had there been one of such awful clarity. She rubbed her nose, a mannerism which she had had since a girl and one which, to anyone who really knew Alanna, told them that she was either worried, undecided, or as was the case now, both.

She continued to sit for several minutes, staring upwards, but not really seeing the myriad stars against their carpet of black. Finally she made a decision. Leaning over her companion, she grasped Jekka's shoulder and began gently shaking her awake.

Chapter Fifteen

Akol Frinim held the nominal rank of captain in Willum's guard, but in reality he was nothing more than a mercenary, quietly hired in by the Protector's brother, together with the thirty men he commanded, for one purpose only.

It was he who had led the murderous ambush on Lady Benita's escort and the promise of yet more gold to come ensured his loyalty and total silence, which was something, he knew, that Willum could not count on from the men who made up his regular guard. Most of those fools, Akol knew, would put their loyalty to the state above their loyalty to their paymaster. Akol knew exactly where his own loyalties lay.

And, these past few hours, it was not merely the money that was making his position so attractive. Since arriving at this house Akol had seen more naked, or semi-naked women in one place than he would ever have thought possible. It was a curious establishment without a doubt, and its owner, the tall, flame-haired Lady Dorothea, was even more curious herself.

She did not even seem to have any proper guard detachment for the place, for all Akol had seen so far were a collection of rather effeminate youths, a host of females who were certainly never intended for fighting, and one rather imposing looking brunette who strode about the place like a man, but who was undeniably female in every other way.

The original plan, from what Akol had heard, was for

Fulgrim and Willum to provide the guard for the house whilst the prisoners were incarcerated there, supplying a roughly equal number of their own cutthroats. But something had gone badly wrong during the hand-over of the younger girl. Sixteen of Fulgrim's men had failed to return from that mission and there had been talk, among the two who had been with Fulgrim himself, of a small band of Yslandic warrior women being involved in the matter.

Still, Akol reasoned, there were still more than forty of them here and nobody knew that the Lady Dorothea's chateau was being put to the purpose which it was. As for the two prisoners, from what he had seen of them, they were being kept under such rigorous bondage that a child could have handled them.

The same could also have been said of the delicious parcel of feminine flesh that was walking ahead of him now, naked as the day she was born and with her hands chained helplessly behind her. The chain leash leading to the collar about her throat hung loosely in Akol's hand and, in truth, he had nothing to do but follow the wench, for she was not only docile, but seemed to know exactly where he was supposed to be taking her.

He had been a little surprised when he had been summoned to the Lady Dorothea's private suite, but she had explained that the powerful Agana, who generally handled such matters, was engaged elsewhere and she could not trust any of the young pages to carry out the task of locking up this Moxie creature for the night. Apparently, the big-breasted teenager had offended her mistress and her punishment was to spend a night chained to the wall of one of the cold and cheerless cells.

As he studied Moxie's firmly rounded buttocks, which

rotated delightfully with every step she took, Akol began to consider adding a few extra punishments of his own to her overnight ordeal.

When they reached the cell, the door stood open. Inside, on the wall beneath the high narrow window opening, two sets of manacles dangled from heavy iron bolts, perfectly positioned to hold a prisoner's arms outstretched a little above shoulder height. There were two more manacles fixed at floor level, which would hold the legs nicely apart, Akol saw.

The girl moved across to the wall without a murmur and stood passively whilst Akol unlocked her wrists. She turned obediently at his instruction and lifted her right arm towards the first fetter. Akol laughed at such continued docility. It appeared, he thought, that the girl had had the spirit driven out of her in some way. He finished securing her limbs and stood back, admiring her superb young body.

He stepped forward again and cupped her right breast in one hand. Moxie tried to shrink back, but the stone wall behind her and the heavy chains left her no room to retreat. Akol laughed again.

'I can't believe you ain't had these beautiful bubbies manhandled before,' he taunted her, 'not in this rum place, anyway.' His hand moved down her stomach and probed the cleft between her splayed thighs. Moxie let out a little whimper. 'And I'll wager this little cunt has had some serious servicing,' he sneered. His finger probed between the puffy lips and forced a way inside the dry tunnel. Akol probed for a few seconds.

'As I thought, missy,' he chuckled, 'no virginal maidenhead this. He stepped back again and began unbuckling his belt. 'Shame to let such a soft little slot go empty, just because its mistress is under punishment,' he said. Moxie's eyes grew wider still.

'Please, no!' she squeaked. 'You cannot, sir, please. My lady would be most displeased.'

'Your lady can swivel on this,' Akol said, crudely raising his hand with the middle finger extended straight up. 'She may have title to this house, but my master controls it at present. The proud Lady Dorothea is beholden to Lord Willum and even that Fulgrim bastard has scarcely enough men left to carry him to his carriage. No, wench, you're for a good fuck and me too,' he continued, dragging his breeches down to his ankles. Tears trickled down Moxie's cheeks.

'Sir, there are plenty of other maids here who would be more than willing to share the bed of so sturdy a warrior,' she said, clutching at straws. 'I can give you the names of at least six who are off duty at present, and tell you which rooms in which they are to be found. Sala and Minika share the end room at the very top of the building and they would be happy to share not only their bed, but you too. Think of it sir,' she babbled as she saw the massive erection forming in Akol's right fist, 'you could have yourself two wenches in place of the one.'

'I thank you for the information, little Moxie, or whatever your name is,' Akol laughed. 'Maybe I'll have three instead of the one, but for now, the one bird is in the hand and she has a set of the finest titties a man could ever wish to lay eyes upon.' He moved forward again and Moxie screamed, but if anyone heard her, it was unlikely they would have paid the sound much heed, so many similar screams having echoed through these corridors these past few hours.

Akol leaned forward and nuzzled the side of her neck. Moxie simply sobbed, feeling the pressure of his rigid stem already thrusting against her lower lips. It began to force an entrance, but it was a painful process for her and an uncomfortable one for Akol, for her vagina remained as dry as dust. Realising that something was wrong, Akol stepped back.

'Aha, I think I see,' he rasped. 'A lady's girl, are we? And what did we do to irk our mistress this day? Close our legs over her tongue, or catch her clitty with those pretty white teeth? No matter, my little sweetmeat. What your mistress can do, I can do, though the final result might be better than you think.

'Tell me, girl, has any man been up there yet?' Miserably, Moxie shook her head. Akol nodded, knowingly. 'Well, maybe before this is over you'll not be so turned against the idea.' He dropped to his knees before her, drew back her labia with his thumbs and plunged his face into her soft warmth. Moxie felt the familiar tug of lips about her bud and gasped, a shiver going through her from head to toe.

And, a few minutes later, when Akol sheathed his thick shaft in her now juicy slot, it was not too long before she realised that a man could not only give her everything a woman could, the throbbing heat of real flesh reaming her tunnel was going to bring her to a climax far quicker than the cold leather phalluses that had been her womb's only visitors thus far in her experience.

'Damn the fellow,' Dorothea fumed. She looked across the back of the long sofa at Agana, whose expression mirrored her own. 'But then, I suppose it's my own fault. What man could resist the temptation of that succulent little body?' She walked around the furniture and stood in front of the fireplace. 'You did well to restrain yourself though, Agana,' she said. 'Brainless and cockled as he is, this Akol is central to my plan.

'There are too many of Willum's men here for us to chance anything foolish, but if this works as I calculate it will, even sacrificing poor Moxie's twot to some heavy handed man will be justified.' She paused and her mouth twisted into an ironic smile. 'So long as the bastard doesn't give her a real penchant for genuine cock,' she laughed.

Agana gave an expansive shrug. 'If so, ma'am,' she said, 'there are plenty more Moxies to be had.'

Dorothea raised her eyes to the heavens. 'I know, Agana,' she said, 'but that's not the point, is it? My little tavern virgin just happens to be very special to me and the thought of some hairy, sweaty mercenary pumping his cockstem in and out of my personal territory is more than I care to contemplate. When this affair is concluded to everyone's satisfaction, I swear I'll let you cut his balls off and cook them.'

Chapter Sixteen

Corinna could barely stand unaided, but she was determined she would not let Fulgrim see how near to breaking point she was. The hawk-nosed nobleman paced slowly around her.

'Very pretty, Lady Corinna,' he said appreciatively. 'This Agana woman is a true artist and no mistaking. However, her work is somewhat offset by the crudity of these slave leathers.' He prodded at the leather sleeve which held Corinna's left arm against her body. 'Such base devices may be practical in many ways, but I prefer my females far more delicately adorned.'

'My lord,' Corinna said, struggling to keep her voice steady, 'I know it is useless to protest at the treatment I have received, for this place seems full of men who are less than human, Willum high among them. However, sir, I must still appeal to you to consider this situation. My father is Lord protector of Illeum and I understand what I represent to you Vorsans, but this,' she continued, looking down at her bondage and piercings, 'is less than I should have expected from savages, much less a man of breeding, which is what I had been led to believe you are.

'Willum has apparently become unhinged, possibly through some imagined wrong from far in the past, and I can see that what he has done to Benita and myself might appear well justified in his tortured mind. But you, Lord Fulgrim, are surely involved in this enterprise for political reasons. Is there not some code which governs these matters?'

Fulgrim stopped his pacing before Corinna and looked down at her with a grudging admiration. He was a harsh and generally cruel man, but he recognised dignity and bravery when he met it, and he knew he had met it now.

'Lady Corinna,' he said, 'politicking and diplomacy are held up as noble pursuits, but in truth, they bring out the charlatan in the best of us. We must, at times, push aside certain standards. Willum became a part of this "enterprise", as you call it, for many reasons, most of which are founded, as you so rightly have concluded, on a variety of misconceptions, unless I am a very bad judge of these things.

'However, in a very short time, this slight imbalance of judgement has swollen into something far more serious and I do regret some of the things he has done. I promise you that I have already taken the steps necessary to avoid a repetition.'

'So you will release me from this base bondage – and Benita also?'

'Base bondage is right,' Fulgrim laughed, 'for such treasures deserve a better framing indeed. As for Benita, I confess I had not given her circumstances that much consideration. The woman certainly plotted to ensnare your father and also to kill Willum, which, as matters have turned out, you would be forgiven for thinking was maybe not such a bad idea.

'Speaking from my personal point of view, such behaviour is intolerable. When a woman seeks to inveigle herself in matters that should concern men alone, she has forgotten her main purpose. And that is something which, I am determined, shall never happen in your case, Corinna.

'You must surely have realised that there is no way in

which we could ever return you to your father. Willum was intending that he make you his personal love slave, truly believing you would eventually come to regard him with as much devotion as he started out feeling towards you. However, as you are only too painfully aware, something has given out inside his skull.'

'He is most definitely mad,' Corinna agreed.

Fulgrim waved a hand in the air. 'That much we agree on, my dear,' he said. 'Which means that the original plan, that you be removed to my own country and kept incarcerated as his plaything, as and when he was able to slip away and rejoin you there, is no longer acceptable – not by me and certainly neither would it be where my own master is concerned.

'Therefore, I have decided to make you my concubine. No, wait, milady!' Fulgrim raised a finger to his lips in a gesture that indicated Corinna should not interrupt. 'I warrant I may not be your ideal choice, but I warrant also, that you will fare better at my hands than would have been the case with your insane kinsman.'

'I know little enough of polite society among the Vorsan States,' Corinna retorted, 'save what I learned from my tutors and my study books, but if you, sir, believe that I should willingly consent to what you are proposing, you are as mad as he. I am a married woman, for one thing.'

'Aye, and married to a youth who struggles to get his mind above, or below, his stomach,' Fulgrim laughed. 'He'd have eaten the other half of Haafland if his father hadn't sent him to Illeum, by all accounts.'

'My husband's appetites have no bearing on this situation,' Corinna said stiffly. 'The fact remains that I have been abducted and brought here against my will and have had things visited upon me that should not be visited on even the commonest peasant woman. I demand that you take steps to rectify the situation, and do so immediately.'

Fulgrim resumed pacing around her, stroking his chin as if deep in thought, and there was considerable amusement in his expression.

'Your noble blood shows through, Corinna, and no mistaking,' he said. 'However, I think I prefer you as you are, to how you would be, though with perhaps a few refinements. I remember meeting your mother many years ago now, and thinking what a fine looking bedroom companion she must be. And now here is the daughter in all her naked splendour, and even slave leathers cannot disguise true breeding.

'No lass, you shall be mine, and like that addled Willum, I don't mind what methods I employ to ensure I have my way.'

'You will beat me also?' Corinna asked, in a small voice. Her flesh still burned from Willum's thrashing of her.

'Of course,' Fulgrim replied, stopping in front of her once more. 'However, not with the same frenzy that maniac employed. There is an art to the whip and cane. Both may be wielded in such a fashion that they induce passion as well as pain, preferably in equal proportions.'

Corinna could not shut out the memory of Savatch's multi-thonged whip and, though she would have had her tongue torn from her head before admitting as much to Fulgrim, she could not hide the truth from herself. Yes, Savatch had raised a passion within her, a passion that was beyond mortal means to control, she thought. But there was no way that this man could do likewise with her, surely?

'I see I appear to have touched upon some nerve, wench,' Fulgrim said. 'I noticed faint marks upon you when I first saw you. Doubtless the villainous Savatch has already demonstrated something of what I mean, but I think you will also find that he is but a novice in these matters.

'You wear your stripes as proudly as you wear your leathers and your slave rings, and yet I know you must hate them as fervently as you doubtless hate me now, but I will have you crawl to me and beg me for satisfaction, mark my words as clearly as Willum has marked your body.'

Corinna shook her head and stared down at the floor between them.

'Never,' she whispered, but as she spoke she remembered that she had made such an assertion before.

Moxie was still sobbing when Willum entered her cell, but she sniffled defiantly at his approach, her right fist clenched about the poisoned patch in the palm of her hand. Agana had adjusted her manacle chains, so that now her hands were by her sides, but her legs were still held wide apart by the original ankle fetters.

Willum halted just inside the doorway, studying his quarry with an expression of delight. He had been annoyed to learn that Corinna would not be available again for a few hours, but when Dorothea had explained that Agana was adding a few surprises to her appearance, for his benefit, and offered him the services of her maid as a temporary replacement, he had reluctantly agreed.

Now, seeing her naked for the first time, he understood that he had hardly taken any notice of her before, due, he supposed, to his preoccupation concerning Corinna. Well, this was no Corinna, at least not in overall looks, but she was a handsome wench and magnificently endowed, for one so young.

'By the gods!' he breathed. 'These titties are even bigger than hers!' He could feel his shaft starting to harden at the sight of them and he couldn't wait to get his lips around those swollen nipples. The gods had favoured this one all right, he thought.

Willum came right into the room and stopped before the helpless girl. He reached out and touched her left orb, his thumb tracing a line around the darker protuberance at its centre, and grinned as he saw the soft flesh hardening.

'Ye'll make a satisfying diversion,' he said, and reached out with his other hand for her right nipple, bringing the bare flesh of his forearm within reach of her manacled right hand...

Fulgrim, unlike Willum, preferred not to employ others to prepare his female flesh as he enjoyed it best, preferring to savour the ritual personally. He also, Corinna realised quickly, had a much more fertile imagination.

He stripped the leather harness from her and quickly recuffed her wrists behind her back, though she doubted whether it would have been worthwhile, or wise, trying to resist him had he not bothered. Having removed the temptation from her mind anyway, he slipped a gold coloured metal collar about her throat, locked it and clipped a chain to it.

'I have everything necessary ready laid out in my own quarters,' he told Corinna, 'and it is easier for you to walk there than it is for me to carry it all here. Come, my lovely, let's waste no further time. Willum will be well out of the way by now.' He gave a sharp tug on her leash and Corinna had no option but to follow him, padding along the long corridors barefoot now, bells jingling at every step.

Dorothea had quartered Willum and Fulgrim at opposite

ends of the chateau and they passed several of her staff during the journey from one to the other. However, none of the maids or pages seemed to find anything at all strange in the sight of a man leading a naked female through the house.

Fulgrim started with a gold coloured corset. It appeared to be made of satin, but it incorporated a layer of thin leather and was heavily boned for extra control. It was also extremely tight and, by the time Fulgrim had finished lacing it at the back, Corinna's face was as red as his and her breathing was coming in short, laboured gasps. Every time she moved, she winced, for the unyielding fabric of the garment pressed harshly against her ravaged skin.

The corset went from her hips to a point just beneath her bosom, leaving her breasts unhindered and her shaven mound still clearly on display, with access to her ringed sex totally unimpaired. Fulgrim stooped and buckled matching gold booties onto her feet, slipping tiny locks onto them, to which, he informed her, he had the only keys. The heels of this footwear were raised considerably, so that Corinna now stood perched upon two golden wedges.

Satisfied that his victim was presently in no mood to rebel, Fulgrim unlocked her wrists and drew long gloves up her arms, though they could better have been described as mittens, for they terminated in tapered sheaths that held her fingers tightly together, with her thumb folded into the palm of her hand. The gloves laced tightly to a point just below her shoulder, so that her arms were now golden like the rest of her ensemble.

Fulgrim now took up a thin metal band shaped into a circle, and Corinna saw it was designed so that it could be tightened using a delicate ratchet mechanism and the circle made smaller. Even before he put it on her she had guessed its purpose. Carefully, he slipped it over her left breast and began making the adjustments, closing it tighter and tighter against the base of her globe and causing the flesh to stretch as it was forced outwards. A few minutes later the other breast had been similarly treated and Corinna stood there with her melons thrust outwards even further than they had been by the leather slave harness.

A third metal band was placed about her forehead and tightened in its turn, though not to any degree of real discomfort. From its centre a fine golden chain descended, separating into two separate chains at the bridge of her nose and coming down over her cheeks at either side of her mouth, beneath her jaw and on to the collar, to which they were designed to be clipped. Level with each corner of Corinna's mouth was a slightly larger link.

'Nearly ready, my proud beauty,' Fulgrim said. He held up a golden rod, about four inches in length. It had a small clip at either end and at its centre a short, flanged metal plate jutted out about two inches. 'Willum has no true appreciation of beauty,' he sighed, lifting the bit to her mouth. 'Leather bridles are all very well for workhorses, but a thoroughbred requires something with a lot more finesse.'

He pressed the plate between Corinna's unresisting teeth, pushing the rod back into the corners of her mouth, and clipped it to the two vertical chains, using the strategically positioned larger link for the purpose. The plate pressed down firmly on her tongue and, although it was uncomfortable, rather than painful, she realised it made as effective a gag as had the earlier foul-tasting leather balls.

'There now,' Fulgrim said, stepping back and admiring her. 'I think that is just perfect. And when I finally get you back to my own castle, I have a smart little buggy to which you shall be harnessed. My estates are quite extensive, I assure you, so you will get all the fresh air and exercise a pretty young filly needs.' Corinna stared at him in her enforced silence, but her eyes conveyed all the sentiment she wanted to express.

Akol stopped in the doorway of the cell and took in the scene before him. The unmistakable figure of his master lay crumpled on the stone floor, whilst the girl, Moxie, was still chained as Akol had last seen her. Her cheeks were stained from crying and her lip trembled as she looked up at him.

Akol stepped forward and bent over Willum. He took hold of the noble's shoulder and hauled him over onto his back, though he already sensed it was too late. One look at Willum's ashen features and the bluish tinge about his swollen lips was enough to confirm his worst fears. Willum was dead all right, and to judge from the temperature of the corpse, had been dead for some time. The mercenary stood up again and confronted Moxie.

'What happened here?' he demanded. The girl was shaking all over now, her big breasts wobbling violently.

'He – he just fell, sir,' she sobbed. 'He was – you know... the same as you did to me and then... oh, it was horrid, sir. He let out a great cry, clutched his chest and fell back.' Her words were coming faster now, so fast that Akol could barely understand what she said. 'He laid there all twitching and moaning, his legs kicking in the air and still grabbing at his chest and then he sort of sat up and looked at me and his eyes went all funny and rolled up into his head and then they were all white and he started drooling and then he shouted once more and fell back again and he didn't move no more at all sir. Oh sir, it was awful to see!' She broke off into another bout of wailing and Akol sadly shook his head.

In his time he had seen many forms of death, generally death inflicted by one human upon another, but he had also seen this type of death, too. It was generally self-inflicted, brought about by too much dissipate living, so that even if the outer shell of a man retained some vestiges of his younger days, the inner flesh became weaker than that of an octogenarian.

Willum, he knew, had been under a great deal of mental strain these past few weeks, as the great plan drew closer to fruition, and just this same day he had indulged in more excesses of violence and lust than many a man would see in a year. The busty servant wench had simply been the final straw, Akol concluded. Willum, his body awash with wine and liquor, had been on the point of adding her to his catalogue of ravishment when his heart had simply given out on him.

He reached out and picked up the key which lay at Moxie's feet.

'C'mon,' he said, but in a surprisingly gentle voice. 'Better get you out of here and let 'em know upstairs what's happened here.'

Chapter Seventeen

Savatch came awake with a start and instantly his entire body was alert, but he made no immediate move to rise. Instead, his right hand crept beneath the roll of sacking that formed his improvised pillow and his fingers closed about the grip of the ebony handled dirk he had placed there before falling asleep.

His ears quartered darkness of the room and, when the soft scraping of leather upon packed soil came again, he had it placed to the inch. His arm shot out and up and the knife arrowed through the air with deadly precision, but instead of the scream or groan he had expected, there was just a soft thud as the blade embedded itself into the rotten timber of the door post. Savatch was already moving, hand reaching for the short close quarters sword that lay close to his right, when the familiar musical laugh stopped him dead.

'Alanna?' he said into the black void. She laughed again. 'You stupid bitch!' Savatch exclaimed angrily, searching now for the lantern and tinder box. 'I could have killed you!'

'I don't think so, my precious villain,' the Yslandian beauty countered. 'You are far too predictable for that and I am far too quick, I think.' The lantern flared into life and, by its soft glow, Savatch saw that Alanna was sitting calmly against the far wall, several feet from where the knife remained stuck in the door frame. He shook his head in undisguised admiration, for there were few people alive capable of tricking him in such a manner.

Beside him the slumbering form of Helda gave a small sigh, but the peasant girl did not show any sign of waking. Unsurprising, Savatch thought, considering the earlier evening diversions.

'So, I feel a fool,' Savatch grinned, setting the lantern down between himself and Alanna. 'But what are you doing here and how in the hells did you find me?'

'One question at a time, my headstrong lover,' Alanna said. 'How I found you does not really matter, what I am doing here does.'

'It must be of some importance for you to abandon our original arrangements.' Had it been anyone else Savatch would have suspected a motive not far removed from the fact that his saddlebags contained a small fortune in gold, but Alanna was one of just a few people he truly trusted.

'It is, my friend,' she confirmed. 'I come to bring you this.' She tossed something towards Savatch and it landed with a clinking sound a few inches short of where he sat. He peered down and saw it was the smaller leather sack in which Alanna had taken away her share of the gold coin. He looked up at her in puzzlement.

'What is this?' he demanded. 'That is yours and well earned it was too.'

'*Well earned*?' Alanna said. She shook her head and the light glittered on her ghostly tresses. 'I think not,' she said grimly. 'I contracted to help you deliver a hostage to a power that would use her as a bargaining tool. I did not think I was conspiring to deliver a member of my own sex into a hell-hole such as Corinna now endures. You will find Jekka's share of the coin is in the bag with my own. The other women are gone their separate ways, but I doubt they'll want to touch such tainted booty when they learn of its true worth.'

'I don't understand,' Savatch protested. 'What are you talking about? The agreement was that the Vorsans would have Corinna as their pawn and that Willum, who it appears is favourable to their cause, would have charge of her confinement. I'll own that I diverted myself with the lovely lady, but then I can also assure you that she contrived her own satisfaction from the encounter. Ultimately, at least,' he added, trying not to smile at the memory.

'Is that so?' Alanna challenged. 'Well, you have been seriously misled, of that I am certain. Corinna may well be a powerful bargaining ploy, but Willum's interest in the matter is not purely political, believe me.'

'How do you know this?'

Quietly, Alanna related the visions she had seen in her dream, but Savatch remained sceptical.

'Too much cheese before sleeping,' he suggested, but Alanna was adamant.

'I have the sight, you know that,' she insisted. 'That was no bad dream, nor do I have any great fondness for cheese anyway. What I saw was too clear, too awful. That poor creature was suffering agonies that no woman should have to endure. No man, either, for that matter.'

'And so you return the gold to me to salve your female conscience? I suppose you will also suggest that I ought to return mine? Even if I felt the same way as you, I have no idea where that bastard Fulgrim and his poxy crew are to be found.'

A slow smile spread across Alanna's face.

'I do,' she said quietly. 'I do.'

Chapter Eighteen

If Willum's assault upon Corinna's body had been frenzied, Fulgrim's ministrations were restrained and calculated, but were perhaps even worse for that fact. He worked slowly, pausing to sip small mouthfuls of wine from the tall glass that sat alongside the bottle in the centre of the small table.

Corinna perched helplessly in the middle of the room atop a special pedestal which, Fulgrim explained to her, was an invention of Agana's and which that forbidding amazon employed in the correction of certain miscreant maidservants. It was a devilish device indeed, though its construction, on first inspection, looked deceptively simple.

It comprised a raised plinth, about four feet square, from the centre of which rose a cylindrical pole, atop which was affixed a slightly curved bar. From the centre of this bar rose another, much shorter, but still at least eight inches in length and a good two inches in diameter. The height of the "saddle" could be increased by means of a foot operated lever at one side of the plinth and there were locking bands which slid up and down the main pole, by which the victim's ankles could be secured.

In this way and because the whole had been raised to lift Corinna's feet just clear of the dais, she now found herself immovably impaled on the metal phallus and, even though her mitted and sleeved arms had not been secured, there was nothing she could do to alter her situation. What was even worse, there was some sort of clockwork mechanism in the base section which, when Fulgrim pressed another lever, caused the shaft within her to vibrate erratically.

The entire apparatus had been brought in by a retinue of six pages, who had assembled it with an ease clealry born of much practise, and these now stood in a silent line, at Fulgrims order, to witness Corinna's further degradation.

Where Willum had used a cane of supple wood to whip her, Fulgrim employed a rod of slender whalebone. It was so thin it scarcely seemed to touch her flesh, but its every kiss sent darts of white hot fire surging to every nerve in Corinna's defenceless body. She writhed and waved her useless hands about in an effort to protect herself, but it was a hopeless situation.

Once again, as with Willum, she closed her eyes, ground her teeth against the bit, and forced herself back to that rustic forest shack...

'It's Dorothea's chateau,' Savatch said, when Alanna had finished describing the house she had seen in her vision. 'I'm certain of it.'

'If so, it will save us much time in searching. My original idea was that we should ask around, for there is only a certain distance they could have taken Corinna in the short time available to them. You are certain it is the place?'

Savatch nodded. 'As certain as I can be, and it would make perfect sense. Dorothea is acting as an agent in this business, much as she has done for so many others before, and the place is easily within the area you speak of. I have been there myself on several occasions and the description tallies exactly.'

'I saw turrets and a sort of battlement,' Alanna continued. 'The place is well defended?'

'Surprisingly, no,' Savatch said. 'Leastways, not under normal circumstances, for I never saw armed guards during my times there. However, these circumstances are scarcely normal. We know that Fulgrim has men other than the ones your warriors dealt with, and Willum will hardly travel without a personal escort. We could be talking thirty, forty, fifty men, maybe even more. It will be a difficult undertaking.'

Alanna smiled, her eyes mocking him. 'What?' she cried. 'Am I hearing talk of difficulties from the man who walked into Illeum City and calmly walked out again with the daughter of the most powerful lord on the continent?'

Fulgrim kept Corinna helpless on her perch until well into the small hours of the morning. Long before he finally released her, she had been reduced to blubbering pleas, promising him anything he wanted in exchange for some relief from such unbearable torture. Fulgrim, however, seemed intent on taking her sufferings to an extent where she would do more than just anything.

He strolled about her helpless form in leisurely fashion, wine in left hand, the whalebone rod in his right, delivering precise cuts with the vicious switch at well-spaced intervals and speaking to Corinna throughout. He explained, in intimate detail, everything she would do for him and everything he still had planned for her, but in truth, his words scarcely penetrated the haze which engulfed her mind.

At last, he pointed to two of the pages, who had remained stiffly at attention throughout Corinna's ordeal. They stepped forward, lowered the saddle, released Corinna's ankles and lifted her down. Fulgrim flicked her lightly on her already welted breasts.

'Kneel,' he commanded. Without hesitation she dropped to her knees. Fulgrim turned to the nearest youth. 'You fellows still able to get your rods stiff?' he demanded. The startled page nodded.

'Yes, sire,' he said.

Fulgrim's mouth twisted evilly. 'Well, shuck out of that hose and give the wench your cock to suck upon. If she's not as broken as I reckon she is, I don't want those teeth sinking themselves into my flesh.'

But Corinna had no resistance left in her, it seemed. When Fulgrim removed the bit from her she willingly parted her lips and sucked the lad's flaccid penis into her mouth, licking and sucking with a steady rhythm until his manhood was standing stiffly to attention.

'Now you get on your knees,' Fulgrim told the page, 'and she can do you on all fours. I'll take the other end and I don't want you firing off in her throat before I tell you.' The page suddenly looked very guilty and Fulgrim, understanding the reason, laughed heartily.

'So you can't shoot a load, is that it?' Miserably, the youth nodded, which contributed to Fulgrim's amusement even further. 'Ne'er mind lad. You just give her something to keep her quiet and I'll do the man's work. I might even take your place before I'm done.'

He quickly removed his breeches and turned to the second of the two pages who had released Corinna.

'Now, there's a thought,' Fulgrim said to him. 'One mouth is as good as another, at a pinch. Get your mouth around this, same as she's doing to your friend here, and see if you can do as good a job on my tackle as she's done on his. I want it nice and hard, mind, for the hole I'm after is probably still a tight fit.'

Benita had greeted the news of her husband's demise without any emotion, for it was already certain that whether he lived or died, her situation was going to remain unchanged. The only good thing about it, apart from the fact that she was glad the bastard was dead, was that at least she would be spared his madly frenzied assaults upon her.

The various guards who had used her since Willum had given her over to them did indeed slap her to urge her on, but compared to the flogging she had received at Willum's hands, it was nothing. However, the sudden appearance of Agana in her cell wrought a subtle change.

'I have decided to make you my personal servant for the time being,' she told the hapless woman. 'I take to the idea of having a member of the nobility at my beck and call quite handsomely. Therefore, you shall be my maid and I have offered the guards two younger wenches in your stead, an arrangement they seem to find quite satisfactory.

'However, I think you need to start learning about your new station without delay.' She paced up and down in front of Benita, her heels clacking on the stone flags. 'To begin with, despite your whipping, I sense you are still haughty, an attitude which is not permitted in a humble slave woman.

'I have a very interesting piece of equipment which will help in your training, but I have very generously loaned it to Lord Fulgrim and your sweet Corinna is at this moment discovering its peculiar character altering qualities. Therefore, I shall have to start with something else.'

She bent over Benita and took hold of a handful of her dark locks. 'We shall begin with your hair,' Agana announced and, despite Benita's wails of protest, produced a large pair of shears and began clipping off the luxuriant hair, until all that remained was a patchy stubble. Still not satisfied she sent for water, soap, brush and razor and returned to the attack. Ten minutes later Benita knelt before her, chained and humbled, her pate as smooth and shiny as a pig's bladder.

'Excellent,' Agana murmured approvingly. 'I think I shall keep you like that, at least for the present.' She peered down at Benita's lowered face and lifted her chin. Tears filled Benita's eyes, but she knew that any protestations or pleadings would be a complete waste of breath.

Chapter Nineteen

When Corinna was finally returned to her cell she was chained against the wall from her collar, in such a manner to prevent her from laying down, but she was so exhausted she fell into a deep, dreamless sleep sitting upright, oblivious even to the rough stones rubbing against her tender back.

Fulgrim himself was nearly as tired from his own exertions and slept late next morning, knowing that there was no urgent business to occupy his morning. His task now was to wait, keep Corinna secure and, when the first hiatus had subsided, get her safely out of the country by a circuitous route that the Illeum authorities would not be expecting.

Meantime, the Vorsan government would openly share in the rest of the world's concern over the disappearance of the girl and approaches would only be made to Lundt when they had his daughter safely tucked away in Fulgrim's own castle. Until then, a succession of hoax notes had been prepared, carefully worded to throw the searchers far off the trail.

Corinna, of course, knew nothing of these plans, but when she awoke and saw once again the stupid golden sleeves and the excruciatingly tight golden corset, affairs of state were furthermost from her mind. All she cared about was that she remained a helpless prisoner, as far from home as if she had been whisked away to the far side of the world, and with nothing more to look forward to than a continued existence of servitude, humiliation, and yet more pain.

The spyglass was something Savatch had acquired during an expedition to the distant eastern lands some few years since, and he had yet to meet its like in the west. He extended it and passed it to Alanna. Behind them, Jekka sat easily astride her bay and Helda sat on the driver's bench of the wagon.

'It all seems peaceful enough,' Alanna said, scanning the valley. 'A few peasants tilling the fields and a wagon on its way up to the chateau. A simple wagon, not a carriage.'

'Provisions,' Savatch grunted. 'With all those extra mouths to feed Dorothea's larder will be running low, I warrant. Besides, if they do have Corinna up there, I somehow think they will be in no hurry to move her again. The countryside is crawling with patrols and they will know that.

'Lady Dorothea is something to do with Lundt's family, I believe, so there is little chance of anyone suspecting her involvement in all this.' He leaned forward in the saddle and accepted the glass back from Alanna. 'No, they'll stay tucked up in their little castle for some while yet, I reckon, and they'll only bring her out when the heat has died down considerably.'

He raised the glass to his eye and swept it across the walls of the chateau, pausing at each turret for closer scrutiny. As Alanna had said, the place seemed quiet and there was no abnormal activity. There was a single figure atop two of the turrets, but that was only to be expected in any large house. Lookouts would be posted to scan the surrounding countryside, even in less turbulent times.

'They'll keep their troopers well out of sight,' Savatch

murmured. 'If any patrols do come this way, which they most likely will if only as a matter of routine, they won't want to tip their hands. It is well known that the Lady Dorothea employs no guard of her own, relying on the influence she has with surrounding nobles, as well as one or two bandit chieftains, for her protection.'

'Perhaps we should just find one of Lundt's patrols and tell them that we believe Corinna is a prisoner in Dorothea's chateau,' Alanna suggested.

Savatch shook his head. 'Lundt would send a rescue force, to be sure,' he said, 'but forty or fifty men could hold that place against a thousand, at least for a few days, and before the chateau fell I should imagine Fulgrim would slit the girl's throat, if he didn't use her to bargain his way out in the first place.

'No, if she is to be saved, then it must be done by stealth and cunning.'

'You have a plan?' Alanna asked, for where stealth and cunning were concerned, she knew Savatch to be a past master. Savatch turned in the saddle, lowering the glass, and grinned across at her.

'Not yet,' he admitted, 'but I'll think of something.'

Alanna returned his smile. 'I'm sure you will, you blackguard,' she said.

Fulgrim placed the bag on the table between himself and Akol. The mercenary raised his eyebrows in an unspoken question, though he was pretty sure he knew what this meeting was all about. The nobleman nodded at the bag.

'That is to pay your men, captain,' he said. 'Call it a gesture of good faith. Your master is dead and I would suggest that it would not be in the interests of any of us for you to take him back and let the world know of his decease.

Far better that they continue to believe what they may already believe, that he has gone to keep a rendezvous with the kidnappers of his wife and Corinna.

'I fear it would look most suspicious if you and your men returned the body now, even though Lord Willum's death was from natural causes.'

'I agree, my lord,' Akol replied evenly. 'Besides, with him gone and the lady here, there is no one left for us to serve. There were no children of the marriage, which means the estate will revert to Lord Lundt and the middle brother.'

'And Lundt will have no need of your services,' Fulgrim said. 'So, we appear to be thinking along similar lines, captain.' He sat down and entwined his fingers together, leaning his elbows on the table top. 'Therefore, I am prepared to make you a generous offer, Captain Akol.'

'I'm listening, my lord,' Akol replied, seeing that Fulgrim had deliberately paused for his reaction. Fulgrim continued.

'You transfer your allegiance and your men to my command and I will see to it that you all receive a generous bonus payment when this business is concluded. In the meantime, I will pay you whatever Lord Willum offered as your weekly retainers.

'Then, when we are safely back in Jerod, I will grant you a commission in my personal guard. In fact, I will give it to you in writing here and now and your new rank will take effect immediately. What do you say to that, *Colonel* Akol?'

Akol continued to regard Fulgrim passively for a few more seconds. Then, a slow smile spreading across his features, he leaned over and scooped up the bag of coins. His eyes met Fulgrim's without blinking.

'What can I say, my lord?' he replied. 'Your offer is a very acceptable one.'

Moxie was in a less agreeable frame of mind, for not only was she still genuinely distressed after having witnessed Willum's death agonies, it now seemed that her mistress, for whom she had willingly performed the dreadful deed, had abandoned her, albeit temporarily, in favour of the golden haired princess girl, or whatever she was.

Her mistress simply referred to Corinna as the golden girl, and had even made up her face to complete the image started by her coiffure and stringent garments. But Moxie would not have wanted to trade places with her at this moment, for Dorothea was introducing Corinna to the pleasures of Midnight's special saddle. Moxie was given the task of leading the powerful horse round and round the paddock at the back of the chateau, having been given strict orders to get both horse and rider back out of sight into the stables at the first shout from the sentries high above.

With her gold sheathed arms strapped neatly behind her, Corinna made an incredible sight now, for her lips and eyelids sparkled in the sun and her hair had been gathered atop her head to form a gorgeous plume as she bounced up and down, little gasps coming from her re-bitted mouth. Moxie looked back at the helpless girl and had no trouble remembering her experience in that saddle.

She just hoped her mistress did not afterwards take to Corinna the way she seemingly had taken to Moxie herself. Hers was a strange position in the household, it was true, but if she was ever demoted to becoming a mere maid, she would then fall under the auspices of the dreadful Agana, a prospect far too terrible to contemplate. She would run away if that ever happened, she swore to herself.

'There, see!' Alanna pointed a long finger and Savatch took the glass from her and swung it around to where she was indicating. Even with the magnifying properties of the unique device, the figures in the field behind the chateau were very small, but there could be no mistaking that golden plumage.

'What the hells are they doing?' Savatch muttered, twisting the focusing collar on the nearer end of the cylinder. 'They cannot be giving her riding lessons, surely, for I doubt there's a noble lady in the country that doesn't sit a fine saddle already.'

'They're too far away to be sure,' Alanna replied, 'but my guess is that that is a saddle like no other your young princess will have sat.'

Savatch lowered the glass and turned questioningly to her. Alanna held up a middle finger on her right hand and made a small circle with the thumb and forefinger of her left hand. She slid the circle over the finger and deliberately worked it up and down. For a few seconds Savatch continued to stare at her blankly, but then the coin dropped and his eyebrows shot up.

'By the gods!' he exclaimed. 'That's something even I wouldn't have thought of!'

Corinna could not believe the effect the gentle trotting of the black stallion was having on her. With her thighs strapped to the saddle and no stirrups for her feet, there was no way she could ease her weight off the dildo, but the up and down motion ensured that the thick shaft kept working in and out of her now well-lubricated slot.

There were tiny protrusions all up the front of the thing and, with the little golden collar forcing her clitoris into prominence, the friction they induced was driving her crazy.

Again and again she climaxed, shrieking from behind the bit like a madwoman, wishing she could plead with the girl to stop the horse, but also, in part, glad she had been prevented from so doing.

Whatever was happening to her? she thought, through the delirium of passion that had seized her very soul. Whatever had they turned her into? Images of the dark haired Savatch flashed across her consciousness and she came again.

Beneath her, Midnight trotted on, immune to such animal sounds, whilst in front, holding his lead rein, Moxie jogged steadily onwards, her eyes fixed pointedly straight ahead of her...

'The provision cart comes from a village about three miles east of here,' Jakka said. She picked up a twig and began scratching a crude diagram in the dust.

'There are two men, or should I say a man and a boy, for the lad can be little more than sixteen. They use a ford to cross the river about here.' She scratched another mark. 'They then stop at the mill I think, and collect flour, for I watched them stop on the return journey and the man paid some coins over to the miller.

'My guess is that the storekeeper buys most of his produce from the local peasant farmers, but that the corn for the flour is likely the property of Dorothea's estate. It is sent to the mill to be ground and the wagon driver collects and delivers it to the house and is charged with making the payment on the return journey.

'He probably buys some of the flower for his own store, I should imagine.' The tall red haired Yslander made a few more marks in her drawing. 'We can take the wagon either here, or here,' she suggested. 'We cannot do anything until they leave the mill and beyond this point the wagon will be visible from those towers up there.' She jabbed her stick in the direction of the chateau.

'This boy and the driver,' Savatch asked, 'are they father and son?'

'There is a strong resemblance,' Jekka said. 'They are certainly close kin, whatever the actual relationship.'

'Good,' Savatch murmured. 'That should help. However, we still need to find a way of making sure that at least two of us get inside the place. It all depends on where they unload the wagon.'

'And on how often they deliver,' Alanna pointed out. 'Even forty or fifty men couldn't eat a wagonload that quickly.'

'Maybe not forty or fifty men,' Savatch agreed, 'but there are other mouths, besides. Dorothea keeps a good two score pages and the same number of young maids. There are probably well over a hundred people in that chateau right now, if we have guessed correctly. It's going to be a tricky task and no mistake.' He sat back on his haunches and rubbed his chin thoughtfully.

'We need to establish a few more facts,' he said, 'beginning with that wagon's schedules. It oughtn't be that difficult.' He looked across at Helda, who sat cross-legged in the lusher grass nearby, watching and listening.

'We know you're very good at seducing young village lads,' he said, winking at her. 'How are you with storekeepers?'

Dorothea was furious and Moxie, the target of her anger, winced, cringed, and wished the ground would open up and swallow her.

'I told you no longer than two hours!' Dorothea raged.

'Two hours!' She held up two fingers to emphasise the point. 'You kept her out there on Midnight for more than three.' She looked down at the quivering mass of lovely female flesh, still clad in all its golden glory, but unable now to rise, even under the threat of the whip.

'The wretched girl will be useless for hours, now,' Dorothea said. Moxie wrung her hands and chewed on her knuckles.

'I'm sorry, mistress,' she whined, 'but I had no way of telling the time and I did not want to anger you by shortening her ride unnecessarily.'

'There are timepieces – small ones at that – all about the house,' Dorothea snapped. 'Why didn't you have the sense to take one out with you?' Moxie looked up at her, eyes rounded and innocent.

'It would have done me no good, even had I thought,' Moxie pleaded. 'I cannot tell time, mistress, for I never learned how. I was just an ignorant bar girl and now I am an equally ignorant maid. Please forgive an unlearned wench, for it was not intended.' Dorothea's expression softened just a little, but she was determined not to let the busty little creature off the hook so easily.

'Could you not tell from her condition that you had kept her out there too long?' she demanded. Moxie thought for a moment and then shook her head.

'I know little of these things, mistress,' she said. "Side from my own time in that saddle, and I recall little enough of that in any detail.'

At last, Dorothea smiled.

'I suppose not,' she admitted. She looked down at Corinna again. The girl's eyes were glazed and spittle drooled from the corner of her mouth, which was still held firmly open by the golden bit.

'Is she hurt, mistress?' Moxie enquired anxiously. In truth she had deliberately prolonged Corinna's ride, determined to reduce her usefulness to Dorothea by any means, but she had not intended the older girl any permanent harm.

Dorothea shook her head. 'Your efforts have done her less harm than those fools of men inflicted with their whips,' she replied, 'but she'll be a good while recovering from this afternoon, of that I can assure you. Summon two pages and two maids and have them put her on a litter.'

'Should they return her to her cell, mistress?'

'I think not. We'll leave her fettered and bitted, but we'll give the creature a comfortable cot in which to recover. Have a bed made up in your room and find a length of chain with which to secure her collar to its frame. Then ask the cook for some garlic broth and take it to her. You will have to unclip her bit to feed her, but replace it afterwards.

'Then, my mischievous miss, you may come to my bedroom and try to make some sort of amends for your stupidity.'

Chapter Twenty

Brod Mordis could hardly believe his luck. The dark haired little wench had drawn her wagon up in front of his store just as darkness was closing in and he was considering locking his premises for the night. She had sidled in the front door and spent some minutes looking around, until he had approached her and asked if she wanted anything.

The girl had looked embarrassed. 'Sir,' she had said, 'there are many things I need, for my journey has been prolonged beyond anything I allowed for. One of my horses went lame and then another threw a shoe, so I am both behind time and without funds.'

'No money, eh?' Brod said. 'Well, much as I sympathise with you, I allow no credit here, even for the locals. Where are you from?'

'Oh, a small village, several days north of here,' she replied. 'You wouldn't know the place, even if I told you.' She looked wistfully around again. 'My father and brother own a store not unlike this,' she said. 'I used to work in it, when I was young.'

Brod looked her up and down and chuckled. 'You're scarcely an old lady now,' he joked. 'How old are you?'

'Twenty,' she said and looked defiantly up at him. 'Old enough to have been married these past three years and now widowed, because my drunken oaf of a husband fell under a brewery dray. That is why I am returning to my home village, to be with my family. After Slad's death, I discovered that he owed money to the value of our small cottage and I was left homeless.'

'A pitiful story, to be sure,' Brod agreed, 'but I have heard worse and generally from those who don't have the cash to pay for their needs. If what you say is true, girl, then truly I feel for you and there are two loaves left over there. I always bake a few for wayfarers, but the road has been quiet today. You may take those and welcome, for by morning they will be too stale for selling, but for the rest, I have this meagre roof and a young son to pay for.'

'Where is your wife?' The girl's eyes seemed unnaturally large and bright to Brod, and he could not tear his own from the deep cleavage that her badly buttoned blouse revealed.

'Gone to the same place as your wastrel husband,' he said gruffly, 'though through no fault of her own. A high wind blew some slates from our roof about four years ago and one struck her across the temple. She died before she hit the ground without ever knowing what hit her. My only consolation is that she did not suffer.'

'Perhaps I could offer you another form of consolation,' the girl suggested. Brod stared at her, open-mouthed. She winked provocatively. 'Sir,' she continued, 'if I have offended you, then tell me so and I will go, though I should still like to take up your kind offer of bread. I need something to sustain me and perhaps I can find another place along my journey where I can trade what little I have to offer.'

'And exactly what do you have to offer?' Brod asked, suspiciously. He thought he knew exactly what she meant, but he could not be certain. By way of an answer, she quickly opened two more buttons, drawing her peasant blouse aside to reveal one firm breast, complete with its very prominent nipple. Brod swallowed and licked his lips, for his mouth had suddenly become very dry.

'I will spend a few hours in your bed,' she purred. 'The whole night, if you wish, for I hate to travel at night. Do you have somewhere I can stable my horses until daybreak?'

Dumbly, Brod nodded. 'I do,' he said, 'but there's my son.'

'Is he a young child?'

Brod shook his head. 'No, he is seventeen, though small for his age, like his mother before him.'

'I will share his bed also, if you wish,' the girl offered blandly. She stared up at Brod, her expression defiant. 'In truth,' she continued, 'I am no whore, but I was treated as if I was by my husband, and I have little shame when it comes to survival.'

'It will not be necessary for you to – er, well, with my son,' Brod said. 'My sister lives at the other end of the village and I can send him to stay with her. I will explain that you have offered a small sum in exchange for overnight accommodation and that I have offered you his bed. But what do you seek in exchange for this curious offer?'

She closed the front of her blouse and re-buttoned it, turning towards the door with a theatrical twirl of her skirt. Looking back at Brod over her shoulder, she smiled.

'Whatever you think I'm worth, come morning,' she said brightly.

Savatch grinned to himself in the darkness as he listened to the animal noises coming from the back of the building. This was one night the storekeeper would not forget in a hurry, much as he would not forget either the next day, or the day following, whenever it was he was scheduled to make his next delivery at the chateau. It would be some compensation for the traumatic hours yet to come.

Satisfied that the shop's owner was being well and truly distracted, Savatch slipped along the passageway and into the store area itself. It was quite likely that Helda would find a way to wheedle the necessary information out of the man directly, but in case she did not, Savatch was not going to waste the opportunity of exploring another avenue.

Somewhere in this place there had to be paperwork, for even in the remotest of outposts, the storekeepers could be counted upon for at least a basic literacy and numeracy, for they frequently supplemented their trading incomes by filling in the tax returns of the local peasants who could neither read, nor write.

Savatch gently closed the door that separated the store from the living quarters and peered into the darkness, trying to locate a lamp. He could read and write himself, but in order to do so he would need at least *some* light.

Chapter Twenty-One

Corinna opened her eyes and the red haired figure of Lady Dorothea swam into her vision. The older woman smiled down at her, but there was something about her that Corinna found odd. It was not just that the woman had ordered her to be impaled upon that dreadful saddle, that was since Corinna had first seen her and the feeling had been with her even then.

Now, as she struggled into a half sitting position, the chain at her collar preventing her from fully rising, Corinna recognised the redhead in a blinding flash of recall. She had been at the wedding, but then so had so many hundreds of others, Savatch included. But it was more than that.

'You!' she said accusingly, pointing a mitted hand at the older woman. 'You are an Oleanna, or close enough that it should not matter.'

'You are correct, Corinna,' Dorothea said gently, 'but if you are counting upon family loyalties, then you are wasting your hopes. Hasn't the behaviour of Willum been enough to teach you that there are loyalties and desires above duty?'

'That mad pig!' Corinna spat. 'Once he used to sit me upon his knee and then, as I grew older, he would take me fishing. He called me his own sweet princess and yet his was the hand responsible for most of these terrible marks I now bear.' Her gloved hand brushed against the heavy ring at her right nipple. 'These, I suspect, were your doing, even if the fitting of them was carried out by your cohort.'

'The rings suit you well, little princess,' Dorothea said.

'Even in your bondage you look every inch the princess you should be. Did you know, Corinna, that once the Oleanna's were called such, but that our great great grandfather abolished royal titles? Had he not, we should both have been called Princess and not simply Lady.

'So, a princess you are, but there is nothing more delectable than a princess in bondage. Corinna, my innocent sweet thing, were I to choose so now, I could dispose of you for a fortune greater than either of us could conceive. Not here, not in our so-called civilised world, but far in the east. There are sultans, viziers, rajahs – all would give five times your weight in gold and precious stones to have one such as you.' She paused and turned away, shaking her head.

'But they are men,' she continued softly, 'and no man truly appreciates the real depth of a woman's beauty.' She turned again and ripped open the bodice of her dress. 'They simply see these!' she stormed. 'They see a pair of titties, a fair face and a warm nest for their rampant little vipers. They know nothing, nothing at all.'

Mutely, Corinna stared up at Dorothea. There was something about the gleam in her eyes that was more than just disturbing, for it was plain to see that the woman was a zealot in her cause. She hated men – all men, but Corinna, despite her ordeals, remembered – could not possibly forget – one particular man. Finally, she found her voice.

'Some men,' she began slowly, 'may know more about us than we might like.'

Dorothea smiled indulgently. 'That may well be true, my golden girl,' she said, 'but no man knows as much as do we ourselves.' She turned and picked up something from the table behind her. With slow deliberation she held it up for Corinna to see, the straps dangling from her wrist.

'Do you know what this is, angel?' she asked. Corinna nodded and swallowed nervously.

'I think so,' she answered, in a small voice. 'They are two replications of a man's organ. I have seen enough of the real thing to know, these past days. But why are they fixed together thus?'

'That, angel, I shall demonstrate to you,' Dorothea said. She reached out with her free hand and stroked Corinna's cheek. 'And then, my precious child, we must consider how to stop the foul Fulgrim, for I fear his plans for you would be more than you could bear.'

'And what about Willum's plans for me?' Corinna said. 'The monster has already tupped and buggered me, and those are words no princess should ever know, let alone use, I grant you.'

Dorothea straightened up and ran a hand through her thick hair. 'But of course!' she exclaimed, in genuine surprise. 'There is no way you could have known, is there?'

Corinna's eyes narrowed. 'Known what?' she demanded.

'About Willum,' Dorothea replied coolly.

'What about him?'

And Dorothea told her.

'Well, now we know everything we need to know,' Savatch said. They had retreated from their vantage point on the ridge facing down the valley and made a small encampment about a mile into the woods. There was a fire going and Helda was cooking a rabbit that Jekka had shot with her short bow. That was one woman, Savatch thought, who would never go hungry.

He turned and looked at Helda and made a mental correction. No, those were two women who would never go hungry, for the little peasant girl had returned from her reconnaissance mission with a well laden wagon, so great an impression had she apparently made on the storekeeper.

'So, we know what we need to do in order to get ourselves inside the place,' Alanna said, 'but what do we do once we're actually in there? You seem to be forgetting the small matter of thirty or forty armed guards.'

'I haven't forgotten them, ice lady,' Savatch said, 'but I fear we'll have to make this one up as we go. I am hoping we can find somewhere to hide ourselves until the house goes quiet, and then we take advantage of the situation as we find it. It's far from perfect, I'll grant you, but I don't see an alternative.'

'Neither do I,' Alanna admitted. She looked across at Jekka, but the redhead merely shrugged. 'So, we take our chances?'

'Or leave the little innocent Corinna to her fate?' Savatch suggested. Alanna grimaced.

'If I thought you really meant that,' she growled, 'I'd cut off your balls and pickle them.' Savatch fell back on the grass, laughing heartily.

'Now that might even be worth becoming a eunuch for,' he roared. 'Oh, the sight of you in a kitchen. Even the *thought* of you in a kitchen. Oh yes, that I should live to see!'

Corinna sat astride Dorothea, one half of the double dildo embedded deep within her and gently kneaded the redhead's breasts in her mittened hands. She looked down at the beautifully aristocratic face and sighed. Dorothea, a lopsided smile on her features, sighed too.

'I am lost forever,' Corinna groaned. 'Lost and better that I were never found again, for I am become shameless.'

'Shush, my golden girl,' Dorothea said, pressing her

finger against Corinna's lips. 'You are woman, as I am, and nothing is beyond us, if only we can free ourselves from the stupid strictures of men who would rut a stable girl as soon as blink.'

Corinna leaned forward and gently licked Dorothea's chin, moving her mouth up and nibbling her lower lip. 'I can never go back now,' she whispered. 'Never. Not even were you to take these bonds from me now and throw open every door in this place, for I am a prisoner of my own shame, and captive of a lust that has been fired within me. I am no princess, Dorothea, nor am I a lady, for I am surely just a raging fire, needing to be stoked and damn who is stoking it!' she cried, her voice rising shrilly as she finished. She raised herself and then thrust fiercely down, driving the leather covered shaft cruelly into herself. Her whole body shuddered, but she fought to regain control.

'You see what I am become?' she breathed. 'Look at me, bedecked with rings and bells like some slave whore, and do I protest now? No, I crave more and the transformation frightens me so.'

'Then learn to accept your destiny,' Dorothea whispered. 'Why fight what was meant to be? Princess or peasant, lady or whore, why should we care what others think?' She reached up and seized Corinna's nipple rings. Corinna flinched slightly, but a soporific smile spread across her face.

'And what do you think, proud Lady Dorothea?' she rasped, grinding her buttocks hard against Dorothea's hips. 'Do you see me simply as your golden girl, fresh young flesh with which to satisfy your own peculiar lusts? Is that how you see me? Am I any different from your little tavern girl? At least you paid good coin for her, whereas I have come cheaper than that, have I not? Oh yes, I am certainly cheap, for I can be bought with the whip and a few trinkets. Well, enjoy me whilst you can, proud Dorothea, for I fear I shall soon be past being useful to anyone anymore.' She clenched her mitted fists as she spoke and fell forward, her arms grabbing at Dorothea's breasts and surrendered herself to yet another orgasm, whilst images of Savatch filled what remaining consciousness was left to her.

Chapter Twenty-Two

Brod stared at the three figures, and especially at the wicked looking miniature crossbow affair strapped to the redheaded woman's forearm, the handle and trigger mechanism held lightly in her hand. Like her female companion, her features and eyes carried more than a suggestion that she was an Yslander, and although she did not have the same white hair, Brod assumed it was because she had dyed her natural colour for some reason.

The man spoke quietly, but with the sort of easy assurance that left Brod in no doubt that he meant every single word.

'We have no quarrel with you or your son,' the man said, 'but this is a vital business which leaves no room for sympathy or foolishness. Jekka here will remain in the wagon and return with you to your store, in case you start getting any foolish ideas about returning to the chateau to warn them.

'Any slips and she will kill the boy first. She will probably even have time to kill you also. I suggest you take the route of caution where she is concerned, shopkeeper. You can see what she is, despite the red hair, and you have doubtless heard the stories about the warrior women – I promise you they are not exaggerated.

'So, all you need do, both of you, is exactly what you would normally do, no more, no less. The two of us will take what opportunity comes for us to get inside the chateau and hide ourselves away. If no such chance arises, we will travel back with you and you may go on your way.

'Tell me, Brod, when you were there yesterday, how many armed men did you see?' Brod shook his head.

'None sir, I swear,' he said. 'Just the usual wenches and those strange page boys the lady favours. But they have added to their supplies order considerably. I presumed they maybe had a banquet coming up, though why anyone should be celebrating with the Protector's daughter still missing is beyond me.'

'Are you a loyal subject of Illeum, Brod?' the tall man said. The storekeeper nodded fervently.

'That I am, stranger,' he said. 'That I most certainly am.'

'And if you had the chance to restore the Lady Corinna to her husband and father?'

'I'd give my life to that cause, sir, and that's a fact.' His chin tipped defiantly and the man, smiling, turned to his two female companions.

'Maybe,' he said, 'we'll have less need of coercion when our friend here knows the reason for our visit up the valley.' He turned back to Brod. 'I'm not asking you to give your life,' he continued, 'but here is a chance for you to do a great service to your country.'

Dorothea stared at Fulgrim and at the four guards with him, and her eyes blazed with anger.

'What manner of foul infamy is this now?' she demanded, clenching her fists in an attempt to control her rage. 'Is this how Vorsans repay hospitality and treat their allies? I give you the run of my house, I have kept my side of our bargain and now this? Explain yourself, Lord Fulgrim!'

'Explain myself, or what, my dear Lady Dorothea? You seem to forget that I am in control here now, and that these are all *my* men, not just these, but also the rest of them, all those who once served Willum. I am now their master and they have sworn allegiance to me.

'All the time Willum lived things were different. But now he is dead the balance swings, and I would be a fool not to protect my back where such as you are concerned.' Dorothea looked past Fulgrim to where the guard captain, Akol, stood passive and silent.

'And did Lord Fulgrim tell you how and why your last master died?' she said. 'I presume he has told you some story of my involvement, but I'll wager he said nothing of his true part in the affair.' A small flicker of Akol's eyes told her that she had hit the mark square, but other than that the ruffian mercenary showed no reaction. Dorothea sighed, for it was clear that Fulgrim's gold had bought them over.

'And you think now, Lord Fulgrim, that you are free to take over my house completely and make me a prisoner in it?' she continued. 'As to my intentions, I can swear to you that I harboured none against you. Had you left things well alone, this business would have been completed as planned. You are a very suspicious man if you believe otherwise.'

'Am I indeed?' Fulgrim said, an amused expression on his dark features. 'I am not to suspect the motives and actions of a woman who not only betrays her country, but also plays a leading role in the assassination of a kinsman, albeit a distant one? I should be a fool to leave you on the loose, madam.' He turned to Akol.

'As I explained to you, captain, had the lady informed me of her plans concerning Lord Willum, I should have chosen a different route to a solution. There was no doubt in my mind that your former master was becoming rapidly deranged and was a danger to himself as well as to the overall enterprise, but there was no need of murder.

'I would have spoken to you and made an arrangement

whereby we could have kept the poor fool in custody until we were ready to leave, but the Lady Dorothea pre-empted such a move.'

'Liar!' Dorothea sprung forward and, before any of the men could move, her long nails raked Fulgrim's face, leaving four scarlet tracks down his left cheek from which blood immediately began to ooze. Fulgrim lashed out, his arm swinging in a vicious backhanded loop, the back of his fist catching her on the temple.

Dorothea opened her mouth, staggered back, and her eyes glazed over. Akol leapt forward and caught her as she fell, lowering her gently to the carpet, before turning to Fulgrim, who was now clutching at his wounded face.

'Shall I put her below before she wakes up, my lord?' Akol asked. He peered down at Dorothea and his fingers felt at her neck, finding a pulse that was rapid, but strong enough. 'She is but stunned and there is no permanent damage done to her, I think.'

'Aye, but there will be,' Fulgrim snarled. He stooped down, seized the hem of the unconscious woman's dress and tore a strip from it, which he immediately pressed against his injuries. 'Yes, take her below and strip her and chain her for good measure. She's no better than the other two and will be treated the same.

'And you'd better send men for the other one, the Agana woman. Go carefully mind, for that creature is a dangerous one, or I'm no judge. Strip her as well and we'll have ourselves a nice little menagerie for our amusement this evening. You can tell your men they'll have great entertainment, as well as a handsome meal tonight.'

The moment she was dragged into the underground chamber, Corinna knew her situation had gone from terrible to something even worse. The sight of Benita, chained against a pillar and dressed in harness, rings and bells, her mouth gagged with a thick leather bit, was bad enough, but to see both Dorothea and Agana standing naked, arms bound at their backs, was even worse. Clearly, Fulgrim now held sway here and Corinna dreaded to think what his twisted mind had planned for them all.

He greeted Corinna's arrival heartily.

'Welcome to our little party, princess!' he called out as she entered the place, sandwiched between two burly guards. 'Now we are all assembled I can begin. I thought you might like to watch and see how I think all scheming women should be treated.'

Bitted as she now once again was, Corinna could offer no reply, but she glared at Fulgrim, wishing that she was free, for she would have tried to put out his eyes had she been able. The man, in his own way, was as mad as Willum, certainly when it came to his treatment of the fairer sex, and now there was not even Dorothea to intercede and attempt to moderate his excesses. Her heart sank.

'I think we shall start by attiring you all the same, including Benita, for she still wears Willum's leathers and, fetching as common slave garb can be on common slaves, my four beauties here are anything but common.' He nodded to Corinna's escort.

'Chain her to the other pillar so that she gets a good view,' he instructed. 'Then I'll start with the widow, as she is already ringed and belled. After that the big brunette, I think, and we'll save the good Lady Dorothea for our finale.' He turned, regarding each of the captives in turn.

'Tonight you will entertain my men, for they are becoming bored by our necessary current inactivity. I have a few novel ideas on that score, but I am sure you will also find them interesting, if not exactly to your taste. However, as two of you have already learned – and painfully so – tastes can be made to change, with a little expert application of whip and rod.'

Moxie watched the events unfolding in the main underground chamber with growing horror. From the relative safety of the secret viewing room she had a clear view of everything, peering through the narrow aperture with its high vantage point. She could not believe what these men were doing to her mistress, and it was clear from her expression that Agana was in a terrible rage.

However, there were five men including Fulgrim, and even Agana was no match for such odds, especially as she was deprived of the use of her hands. She did aim a kick at one of the guards, but her only reward was several lashes from a thin cane. The big brunette took the punishment without a murmur, but when she was finally hauled to her feet again, she was much more subdued.

Moxie could not tear herself away from the scene, even though every cell in her brain screamed for her to run, to escape the chateau and flee to some sort of safety. If they could do this to the likes of Corinna, Benita and Dorothea, who were supposed to be ladies of the aristocracy, what might they do to her, a mere peasant girl from the country?

She thrust the prospect from her mind, for she knew she could never abandon her mistress in such a fashion. Quickly, she ran through all the possibilities in her head. There were plenty of places to hide in the huge building, places she had discovered during the times Dorothea had left her to roam free and explore. If she ran to cook and explained what was happening, the old lady would give her food and she could remain out of sight whilst she worked out what she could do to help.

Perhaps she could rally the maids and the pages. Yes, that was a possibility. The guards were all powerful men, but they were not, apparently, properly trained and disciplined troops. Fulgrim had mentioned some sort of banquet to be held later that night and there would doubtless be wine flowing like rivers. If the young staff members all struck at the same time there was a fair chance they could overwhelm Fulgrim's men, for they did outnumber them quite heavily.

As she turned over her strategy, Moxie saw that they had finished with Benita now and the woman was attired in similar fashion to Corinna, except that her corset and sleeves were in white, as were the high booties which were now locked onto her feet and the metal bands and chains were silver coloured and not gold. The guards returned her to the pillar, locking a chain to her new collar, and turned their attention to Agana.

The tall woman winced as the silver bands were tightened about her breasts, which were much smaller than those of her three fellow victims. Nevertheless, by the time Fulgrim had finished, she too had two jutting globes and the bit in her mouth silenced any further threats and protestations.

In Agana's case, Fulgrim had selected corset, sleeves and boots in black, which Moxie heard him tell his men would complement the woman's handsome stature.

'However, big as she is, we'll cut her down to size. It won't be long before we have her crawling like a bitch and her mouth full of cock.' He prodded one of her nipples. 'And we have yet to attend to these, among other things,' he said. 'Of course, you will have to forgive me if I do not possess your artistry with the needle, but I reckon I'll get practice with you first and then show off my new skills when it comes to your former mistress's turn.'

Moxie turned away from the viewing port, her eyes bright with tears. Quietly she turned the handle on the door, opened it a fraction and listened. Hearing nothing, she slipped out into the empty passageway and ran barefoot to find the cook.

The room was a small outhouse at the rear of the main chateau building. Brod had told them that it was used as cold storage area, for the chateau itself was south of it and kept it in shadow all day. There were several carcasses hanging from a beam, most of which Brod had brought with him in the wagon, but there were also several sacks of vegetables and flour and crates whose contents they could not tell, but behind which the three of them managed to contrive a hiding place, should anyone from the kitchen come out to fetch anything.

'Are you sure we can trust that fellow?' Jekka asked, crouching in the gloom. 'For all we know he might well be selling us out right now, and this place makes a fine trap.'

'We can trust him all right,' Savatch whispered. 'He is straight enough and Helda told me he seems a kindly fellow at heart. He didn't even want to take the gold, not until I told him where to find Helda and that I was charging him with the responsibility of taking care of her should anything go wrong here.'

Next to Savatch, Alanna laughed, though quietly. 'By the look on his face when you said that,' she said, 'I reckon the gold wasn't the main inducement. Friend Brod would dearly love the chance to renew his acquaintance with that little lady, I think.'

'Let's hope it doesn't come to that,' Savatch muttered, 'though I don't think Helda would be too sad if she ended up with the fellow. He's a passable enough figure and not that old as yet. He'd take good care of her, of that I'm sure.'

'Knowing your little Helda,' Alanna said, 'it wouldn't be too long before she was taking just as good care of the son as well.' Savatch raised a warning finger to his lips.

'Listen,' he said. 'Something's happening outside.' Sure enough, the sound of voices and the jingle of a horse's harness came filtering through the high ventilation opening. Savatch pointed to a crate almost beneath it.

'Give me a hand to shift that,' he said, 'and I'll take a look. Quietly now. They seem to be making enough noise out there, but we cannot take any chances. Jekka, notch your bow in readiness.'

'It's notched,' Jekka's reply came back through the gloom. 'And my sword is in my other hand also.'

Alanna and Savatch slid the crate the few feet needed and then both climbed up onto it and peered through the long narrow slit. The sight that greeted their eyes was a singular one indeed and it seemed that the black stallion was being put to good use again, except that this time the unfortunate occupant of the saddle was certainly not Corinna, for she was very fair and this woman was raven dark.

For several seconds the horse stood so they could see only the back view of the rider, but when the two guards had finished tightening the straps over her thighs, the one holding the lead rein wheeled the beast around, giving the two watchers a full view of her face. Despite himself, Savatch gasped and only the fact that the motley band were making so much din with their raucous jibes at their victim prevented the sound from betraying their presence.

The horse was wheeled again and this time its handler

set off at a loping run, the horse trotting obediently beside him. The other men followed behind, laughing and jeering. Savatch waited until they had gone a fair distance before breaking his silence once more.

'Things have taken an unexpected turn here,' he growled. 'Something unexpected is afoot. This is either Willum or Fulgrim's work, and my money goes on Fulgrim. I know little of Willum, save that he is too stupid for his own good, but Fulgrim's reputation is well known.'

Alanna peered at his face, noting the concern she saw there. 'What is the problem?' she asked quietly. 'Who is that woman? Do you know her?'

Savatch nodded.

'Aye, I know her,' he confirmed. 'That's the woman Agana, and she's the last female I'd expect to see in that sort of situation.' He turned slightly towards Alanna and his mouth twitched. 'Well, the last female save perhaps one, but that's the point. It's usually she who metes out such disciplinary treatment, and I'll wager she's not so happy now she's on the receiving end.

'Dorothea would never agree to Agana being treated thus, that much I am certain of. This is Fulgrim without doubt, and that means that he and Willum have turned against Dorothea. Remember, she has no guard of her own, so they would have little trouble taking over control of the place.'

'But that need not concern us,' Alanna insisted. 'In fact, when thieves fall out it sometimes weakens their position. Whilst they squabble among themselves they leave us free to exploit any weaknesses.'

'Except that we are dealing with Fulgrim here, and he is not known for weakness,' Savatch grunted. 'Quite the opposite, in fact. And this latest turn I do not like. I like it less than even that poor bitch out there does, I think.'

Who was the least happy between Savatch and Agana was the last question on Dorothea's mind. She stood now, banded, booted, corsetted, ringed and belled, her tongue stilled by a bright red bit, held in place by red chains that matched the colour of the rest of her rig.

Fulgim had added an extra refinement to her bondage, wary of her temper and still feeling the pain from his torn cheek. Even though her fingernails had been neutralised by the mittens, he was not about to take any unnecessary chances.

About each of her thighs was now locked a red painted metal band, from which projected a short metal rod of no more than four inches in length. To this in turn was welded another fetter, which locked about Dorothea's wrist. Now, not only could she not raise her hands, but she was forced to walk with a curiously humbling gait.

'Your new accessories suit you,' Fulgrim sneered. He fingered the lines of congealed blood on his cheek gingerly. The wounds still stung harshly, but he was not about to rush his retaliation, for he savoured his triumphs as a connoisseur. 'The leg and wrist cuffs are an excellent addition,' he said. 'Unfortunately, only the red ones are here, for I had to restrict my baggage somewhat for this journey.

'No matter. When I finally get you back to Jerod, the four of you shall be identically attired and I have some delightful boots, complete with hooves, that you shall all wear for my pony races. Oh yes, as I have told the innocent Corinna, I have a special stable for my special fillies.

'However, for the present, let's see what we should do with you first.'

His hand went down and he fingered her yawning slit.

Dorothea flinched and a look of horror crossed her face. Fulgrim guffawed.

'Of course!' he exclaimed. 'In all the excitement I had nearly forgotten your peculiar tastes. I doubt there's been a cock up that delightful tunnel, has there? Ah well, we must right that oversight, but do we whip you first, or last?' He appeared to consider this conundrum, but there was little doubt in Dorothea's tortured mind that he had already decided this in advance.

'Perhaps a light whipping, to begin with,' he announced at last. 'Just something to limber you up and get your flesh warm.' He turned to the bench and selected a long, whippy cane, flexing it between his hands experimentally and then swishing it through the air between them. He prodded Dorothea into the centre of the chamber and walked slowly around her.

'Where shall we start?' he murmured, as though talking to himself. 'Where *shall* we start? Ah yes!' The cane swished again, but this time its target was not thin air, but Dorothea's buttocks. It cut a red line across them both and she squawked through the bit gag as the pain jolted through her. She staggered forward, barely able to keep her balance in the cruelly restrictive bondage.

Again the cane swished, landing at the top of her thighs, right in the crease where her soft legs met the lower curve of her rounded bottom cheeks. This time the pain was much more severe and, despite her resolve to bear his assaults in silence, Dorothea let out a long, wailing gasp. Fulgrim was delighted, for he saw her resolve would be easier to crack than he had suspected might be the case.

'There is one kiss that humbles all women,' he sneered, 'peasant and princess alike, as Corinna has already learned. However, I will not wait for you to beg in the way she did, for I think you would rather die than let any man take your honour. Unfortunately for you, you will not die, nor I think, will you have any honour worth speaking of, not when I am through with you.'

He slashed with the cane again and this time the blow fell across her newly pierced nipples. It was not delivered with as much force as the first two, but it did not have to be. Mouth agape, Dorothea howled in agony and tottered backwards in a fashion that would have been comic, had the circumstances not been so deadly.

'I'll have you as a cock-sucking, prick-riding, men's plaything before I'm through with you,' Fulgrim hissed. 'You may not believe me, even yet, but you'll get more cock these next days than most women would want in a lifetime. Corinna I will keep for my exclusive pleasures, though her mouth can be put to good use at times, but you, when I've had your maidenhead, you and the others will service my soldiers.

'By the time I get you back to Jerod you'll be well broken in, and then you'll have a whole new army to entertain. Between the three of you I reckon you can satisfy at least one brigade a week, don't you?!' He raised the cane to strike again, but stopped in mid-stroke, apparently changing his mind. He lowered his arm and tossed the implement carelessly aside, fumbling with his belt as he came towards her.

'Time to stripe you later, sure enough,' he growled. 'But first I'm going to enjoy rutting you, proud lady.'

Corinna, having watched Fulgrim take his pleasure with Dorothea, was then taken upstairs and out into the open ground at the rear of the chateau. She shuddered at the sight of Agana bouncing up and down in that dreadful saddle, for her own memories of its powers were all too fresh in her mind.

Agana, to judge from the look of fierce concentration on her bridled face, was making a more determined effort to resist the saddle's effects, but even she was fighting a losing battle and, every few minutes, low groans would escape past the bit and her pupils would roll up under her eyelids.

'She's made of strong stuff,' Fulgrim growled, and there was a note of admiration in his voice. 'However, she's yet to feel the whalebone kiss, and there's near on forty men to have her still. We'll see how strong she is come midnight.' He turned to Corinna and tugged on the short rein he had clipped to her bit.

'You, on the other hand, my innocent Corinna, are not for any rough soldiers. You are mine alone now, though you too can use that sweet mouth at the banquet this evening. Come, we'll leave these to their sport, for I feel a need for your soft cleft. We'll have Benita watch and Dorothea too, for I know that will stick in her craw. She was harbouring designs on you that extended well beyond our original bargain, if I know that conniving bitch.'

He took two steps and then halted again, as if an idea had suddenly occurred to him. When he spoke, his words confirmed that he indeed had.

'Of course,' he said, a smile creasing his face and causing him to wince slightly from the movement it caused to his scabbed cheek. 'You are possibly her main weak spot. With you I can tame her in half the time, maybe less. Come, my pretty little golden filly, let's see if we can make the mare prance to our tune.'

Savatch climbed carefully down from his vantage point atop the crate and related to the two women what he had just seen and heard. Fulgrim and Corinna had been standing close enough to the outhouse for Fulgrim's words to carry clearly, so close in fact, that Savatch had almost been tempted to call up Jekka and get her to use her crossbow to put a bolt through his neck.

Almost tempted, but not quite, for there was still the matter of Willum. This was a two headed snake with which they were dealing, and cutting off the one would only serve to anger the other and attract its venom before they were prepared for it.

'At least we know it definitely is Corinna,' he said. 'She's had a rough time, judging from those welts on her body, but then you already knew that, Alanna.' The blonde Yslander nodded and Savatch continued. 'It seems they've got some sort of celebration planned for tonight and the four women are to provide the entertainment. That may be our chance.

'If we wait until they're all drunk they may be too sluggish to realise what's happening until it's too late. What we'll need to do is get into the house when darkness comes, which will be simple enough, for the place is old. Then we must take care of whoever is left to stand sentry. I don't reckon there will be many, for they will all be wanting to see the sport in the main hall.

'As for Dorothea's own staff, we shall just have to bluff our way if we encounter any of them. With their mistress hostage they'll be frightened and confused, for many of them are scarce more than children anyway. We'll just tell them we are about Fulgrim's business, and my gold says they'll leave us well be.

'If any of the maids or pages become suspicious, we shall have to deal with them as circumstances deem expedient, but I should prefer to avoid shedding any of their blood if possible. We have no quarrel with them, but we must also look to our own hides first. It may be that we can move up to the top floor, which is where they all live and sleep when not on duty.

'It should be a simple enough matter to subdue any we find there. Agana has a punishment room which is full of harnesses, gags, bits and chains. We can make our move as the meal begins, for it will take some while for the wine to have its effect, by which time we can have removed as many others from the equation as possible.

'All four women will be in the main hall, that much I have just heard, and Corinna is likely to be close to Fulgrim himself, although it would appear he intends to let her be sport for his men, at least for a little while. I will try to get myself into a position from which I can spring upon him. With my knife at his throat his men'll not be so eager to rush in, I think.'

'And what about Lord Willum?' Alanna said. Savatch nodded to Jekka.

'Your companion's aim is good, I take it?' he said. Alanna and Jekka nodded together.

'She can hit the eye of a jackal at a hundred paces,' Alanna affirmed.

'Well, if she can hit this particular jackal's eye at fifty, it will do well enough for me. The man is some kind of monster, I think, for I knew the plan involved the abduction of the Lady Benita as well as that of Corinna, but it would appear he has had them all treated abominably.'

'His life is already numbered in minutes,' Jekka promised. Savatch grinned at the redhead. She said very little, but when she did speak it was with all the purpose and assurance of the skilled hunter.

'There will probably be one officer amongst this rabble

who is senior to the others,' Savatch continued. 'You, Alanna, will have to take him and do as I shall do with Fulgrim. If your man struggles however, slit his throat and grab the one next nearest. But let us pray it does not come to that, for once a fracas begins, Willum's death and my knife at the other bastard's throat will offer us no guarantees.'

Savatch stood up and paced the room, but succeeded only in banging his knee against one of the crates in the darkness. He cursed quietly and turned back to the two Yslanders.

'I have just thought of something,' he announced. 'Dorothea keeps no guard here, but the house was not always undefended thus. There remains, from her father's time I believe, a small armoury to which she alone holds the key. It is probable that Fulgrim knows nothing of this place and would have no need of it even if he did. The key is probably still in Dorothea's rooms, but we need waste no time in finding it. I have seen the lock and it is as ancient as the hills. I have the tool necessary and it will take but a minute to have the place open.

'Inside, there will be crossbows. Not such pretty little engines as Jekka's deadly friend, but useful all the same. If we take and load one each, we can drop at least three of the drunken wretches as we make our first assault. The sight of blood awash among their tankards will make them think twice.'

'I have one final suggestion, my cunning villain,' Alanna said. Savatch looked at her and nodded. 'I have attended many feasts in my time,' she continued, 'and some have been not unlike what this seems likely to be, a celebration among rough fighting men, with beer and wine aplenty.

'All men like to think they can drink till dawn and still remain on their feet,' she said, 'but I have yet to see the person, man or woman, no matter how tough they be, who can go that long on one bladder. Thus, if we delay our assault for as long as possible, it should be possible for us to thin their numbers singly.

'In all the noise and merriment, I doubt they'd miss ten or so of their fellows.'

'You're right, I think,' Savatch agreed. 'They'd probably assume their friends had passed out in the night air and tell each other how much better they all were for standing the pace so much longer.' He walked over and sat down on the edge of one of the cases, placing his hands upon his knees.

'Well, my sweet viper ladies, there we have it all,' he said, his tone becoming more sombre. 'Our chances are not good, in my opinion, but we have little enough in the way of other options available to us. Do we still want to go ahead with this little enterprise?'

There was a brief pause and then two heads, one white, one red, nodded in unison.

Chapter Twenty-Three

Fulgrim's preparations were quite simple and made more simple by the fact that one of the guards had discovered the trap to an ancient oubliette in the floor of the main dungeon chamber. They dragged the iron cover away and placed a plank across the opening.

Corinna, her hands now bound behind her, was pushed out onto the plank. Fulgrim stationed a guard at one end of the plank and issued him clear instructions.

'At the first cry of pain from me,' he ordered, 'tip the plank and let her drop.' Benita, chained against her pillar still, watched with rounded eyes. But Fulgrim ignored her, turning instead to Dorothea, who stood with chin proudly high, despite her bonds.

'I've had your one hole,' he told her, 'and I'll have the other at dinner tonight, but now you're going to eat and I don't think I need tell you what meat forms the main course. I know your woman, Agana, has some devilish clever little clamps for these exercises, but that takes away the sport, in my opinion.

'So you, my proud lady, will get down on your knees and you will take me into your mouth and bob and suck till you feel my jism hit your throat. You may still be tempted to use those sharp teeth of yours, but if you do the golden girl drops into the pit. You have heard my orders and, if the fellow fails me, I will have his balls cut off and pickled. Do you understand me?'

Dorothea, whose bit had now been removed, stared at

Fulgrim in silence for several seconds. Her eyes flickered from him to Corinna and from Corinna to the guard stood with his foot on one end of the plank on which the bound girl perched. She turned back to Fulgrim and slowly nodded.

'You have me beaten for the present, but my turn will come,' she said softly. She lowered herself stiffly to her knees and licked her lips. 'Come on then,' she whispered. 'What are you waiting for? Stick your pizzle in my mouth and I'll suck the thing for you.'

Fulgrim dropped his breeches to his ankles and stepped out of them. He walked forward, his organ already beginning to swell, but stopped just short of the kneeling woman.

'Not until you beg me to,' he said, and looked back to the guard at the oubliette. 'I want you to count to ten, under your breath. Not too fast, but then again, not too slow. If this one has not begged me to ravage her mouth in that time, you can tip the plank anyway.' The guard nodded his understanding and Fulgrim turned back to Dorothea.

'Of course,' he said, 'I don't know for certain that he knows all the numbers 'tween one and ten. He may just miss out a few.' Realising that Fulgrim was not just joking, Dorothea's eyes flew wide with alarm.

'No!' she shrieked. 'Don't harm her. I'll do it, whatever you want. Yes, please my Lord Fulgrim, ravage my worthless mouth!'

Fulgrim threw back his head and roared with laughter. 'Hah! Splendid!' he crowed. 'Absolutely splendid. You will make a fine whore back in Jerod and no mistaking. Once more with feeling and then we'll stuff that mouth good and proper.'

Dorothea closed her eyes and Corinna saw her face was burning with shame. This time her words came less loud, but her voice was clear and steady, nonetheless.

'Please, my Lord Fulgrim,' she said, 'your slave begs you to ravage her worthless mouth.' She paused and opened her mouth wide. With a snicker of triumph Fulgrim placed his now rampant cock between her red lips and thrust himself into her.

True to his promise, Savatch had the lock to the armoury open in seconds. He turned to Alanna, who was holding an unlit lantern.

'Be ready with the tinder as soon as we are inside,' he hissed, 'for there will be no windows and it is all but dark outside by now anyway.' The heavy door creaked slowly open and Savatch stood aside to let the women pass inside first. He pulled the door to behind him and, as the lantern flared into life, used the curiously shaped pick to relock it. As he straightened up he heard a cry of surprise from Alanna and swung round to find the source of her alarm.

The girl sat huddled in one corner, knees drawn up to her chin, arms wrapped protectively around them, her eyes wide with fright.

'Well, what have we here?' he grinned, striding across the space between them. 'What have we here indeed?' The girl's eyes began to fill with tears and her whole body trembled.

'Please sir!' she wailed, in a childlike voice. 'Oh please sir, don't hurt me! I am only a humble maid and I mean no harm.' Savatch held up a hand and stopped before her.

'We'll not harm you, wench,' he said in a gentle voice. 'Stand up and let us see you. C'mon now, I promise you'll suffer nothing at our hands. What's your name?'

'Moxie, sir,' the girl said, scrabbling to her feet. Savatch whistled when he saw her properly. 'Well Moxie, it seems you're not such a child after all.' He put out a hand and took her shoulder gently, but she cringed back from him, nonetheless. 'By the gods, Alanna,' Savatch chuckled, 'I thought young Corinna well padded, but this little thing takes some beating.'

Moxie snivelled. 'Please sir, don't!' she protested. 'That's all men want me for, and that's all I ever hear from them.'

Savatch patted her cheek. 'I'm sorry, Moxie,' he said, 'but I can see why. What I don't know is what you are doing in here.'

'Hiding, sir,' Moxie said. The strength was returning to her voice as she began to realise that these strangers really did mean her no harm. 'Hiding from those brutes who have treated my mistress and Mistress Agana so terribly.'

'But why should you fear them if you are only a simple maid as you claim?' Savatch asked. Moxie wiped her eyes with the back of her hands.

'I was Lady Dorothea's personal maid,' she said, her bottom lip trembling. Savatch understood instantly.

'Aha, I see!' he exclaimed. '*Very* personal, I assume, for I hear tell that Lady Dorothea's tastes differ very little from those of most men.' Miserably, Moxie nodded. Savatch laughed again and took her hands in his. 'Cheer up wench,' he said, 'for I'm not here for your body, nor do these good ladies share your mistress's tastes – well, not exactly, anyway,' he added and Alanna shot him a look of pure poison. Savatch stepped back and regarded the girl.

'Do you love your mistress, Moxie?' he asked.

Moxie nodded again. 'Yes sir, I do,' she said. 'I should like to kill that awful Fulgrim man.'

'And Willum too, I suppose?' Moxie looked up at him, her face registering surprise and confusion.

'Lord Willum is already dead, sir,' she cried. 'Did you

not know?' Savatch could not conceal his surprise, nor his pleasure.

'By my old granny's eye teeth!' he exclaimed. 'Is that a fact?' Behind him, Alanna snorted in amusement.

'Your granny's been dead these ten years and she hadn't a tooth in her head, as I recall you once telling me,' she said. She stepped forward and looked down at Moxie. Moxie, realising she was but three feet away from one of the legendary Ysladian warrior women, paled before her.

'Is this true, girl?' Alanna demanded. 'Willum Oleanna is dead?'

'Yes madam,' Moxie mumbled. 'And it was not of my doing, only it was, but my mistress told me what to do and he had done such cruel things to that Lady Corinna and his mind was gone, madam, and that's the plain truth, I swear it.' Her words came out in a torrent and Alanna let her finish before she spoke again.

'Who killed the wretch and why, I care not, child,' she said. 'The important fact is that he is dead and you and your mistress have saved my companion a bolt shot, at least.' She turned to Savatch. 'This alters the balance considerably, I think,' she said.

Savatch nodded. 'You are right. Clearly Fulgrim has staged a coup here and rules the roost, so we have rid ourselves of one head and now have a serpent of a different nature on our hands. Tell me, Moxie, what of your fellow maids and the pages, too? Where are they all now, for the house was uncommon quiet when we came through?'

'All in their quarters, sir, saving for a handful who will wait table tonight. Lord Fulgrim has threatened dire things if they do not remain out of the way.'

'Are they locked in?' Savatch asked.

Moxie shook her tousled head. 'There is no need, sir, for

truly they are all terrified of that monster. I tried to get them to help me, for I thought there might be enough of us to spring upon Fulgrim's men and maybe cut their throats before they knew what was happening, but only five of the boys and four of the girls would even consider such a plan, and that was by no means enough.'

'By no means indeed,' Savatch agreed, and there was a note of admiration in his voice when he spoke. 'So you would risk death for your mistress?'

Moxie nodded and held her head defiantly. 'If needs be, sir, yes, for truly she is in a living death right now, and if Fulgrim finds me I may well join her, for he knows well my position and would use me to bait her, of that I am sure.'

'And these others, these few bravehearts, what of them now? Would they join us in trying to free their mistress?'

'I couldn't say, sir. Perhaps if you spoke to them, but we are none of us soldiers, not by a long way.'

'But you could shoot a crossbow if I showed you how,' Savatch murmured, his eye travelling along the neat row of weapons at the far side of the armoury. 'It is not difficult and there would be no range.'

'If you showed me, sir,' Moxie said, 'I should be willing to try.' Savatch leaned forward suddenly and kissed her on the forehead.

'Good girl,' he said. 'Brave girl. We may yet work a miracle this night.'

'We may,' Alanna agreed. She turned her remarks to Moxie. 'There is a cook here, presumably?' she said. Moxie nodded. 'And how does her loyalty lie?'

'She gave me food to bring here,' Moxie said, 'but she is truly terrified of these people and hates them for what they have done to Lady Dorothea, who she has known since she was a child, by all accounts.'

'Good. Then take her this,' Alanna said, pulling out a small vial from beneath her cloak. 'Tell her to add it to the gravy when she roasts the meat. It is a poison of sorts, though not a fatal one. It is a strong sleeping draught, but there is little enough of it to go around so many mouths. However, combined with the wine, it will induce a feeling of sluggishness and that may be enough for our purposes.

'If we can add seven or eight bowmen to our three selves and you, then we can perhaps drop half their number before they come to their senses.' Moxie took the bottle from her and nodded.

'I'll get you a dozen and a half bowmen,' she promised earnestly. 'But you will need convince some of them yourselves.'

Chapter Twenty-Four

Mennick Harsoff was in a foul temper. It was unfair, he thought, for he had already stood sentry duty atop one of the towers for half the day and now he had been chosen as one of the five guards who would miss out on the banquet. Akol had awarded each of the five an additional two crowns as compensation, but that hardly mattered. He savoured the thought of having his member in one of those aristocratic mouths and now there would be no chance of that happening.

At least, he thought, he had avoided the towers again, for he had been detailed to patrol the upper floors to ensure that the off duty servants remained in their quarters. He mounted the stairs with a heavy tread and, as he climbed, an idea came to him. It would not be the same as spurting down the throat of a princess, that was certain, but it was better than nothing and the maidservants were a comely enough bunch, from what he had seen thus far.

And not just comely, but docile also.

Mennick grinned as he remembered the little fair sylph who had served him breakfast. He couldn't remember her name, but that did not matter. It would be easy enough to find her and she would make a good little ride. If the celebrations below continued at any great length, there were plenty of others, too. He reached the landing and rounded the turn and, so engrossed was he in his thoughts and anticipation, that he had taken four or five steps before he registered the figure ahead of him.

She was tall and, despite her red hair, he just knew she was Yslandic. Mennick's hand went to the hilt of his sword, but the woman merely smiled at him.

'What are you doing here?' he challenged. Still she smiled and took a step nearer, her long cloak billowing about her legs.

'My name is Jekka, sir,' she replied, in that musical accent so peculiar to the warrior women. 'And, as for what I am doing here, I am afraid you will not live long enough for that to concern you.' Her right arm came up from beneath the cloak and there was a sharp click and a loud hiss.

Mennick's last thought as he fell back with the crossbow bolt through the dead centre of his Adam's apple, was why should an Yslandian woman want to dye her hair red?

Long trestles had been laid out around three sides of the hall and Fulgrim's guardsmen were so intent on the food and wine set before them that they barely spared a glance for the four figures bound to the timber frames set in the middle of the rectangular space before them.

Fulgrim, sitting in the centre of the main table, surveyed the scene all around him. Yes, it was going well, he thought. These scurvy ruffians needed no incentive to eat and drink and they would need even less than that when it came to the women later. He looked across at Corinna, who stood rigidly bound to her post, her eyes staring straight ahead of her.

In a way, Fulgrim thought, she was wasted on these roughnecks, but the experience would serve as a good lesson to her for the future. Perhaps she would become more pliant and willing, given the alternatives she would by then have experienced. The thought of the curvaceous, long legged blonde girl willingly coming to his bed was a pleasant one. Fulgrim took a perverse delight from the inflicting of pain, but there were circumstances and certain individual cases, he believed, when that pain was better confined to a minimum.

And Corinna was one of those individual cases, he had concluded. The vivid welts on her body did not really sit well and displeased his eye when he looked upon them. Such creamy fair skin should remain unblemished and he resolved that once these marks had healed, he would not add to them if possible. There were, after all, other methods, no less brutal in their own ways, perhaps, but unlikely to leave scars, at least of a physical nature.

He looked at Benita, equally marked on the outside, but obviously already scarred far worse within. The woman slumped in her bonds like a rag doll, already beyond comprehension and shocked into some twilight world of her own by the horrors she had endured and witnessed. Ah well, Fulgrim consoled himself, she would be useful for these brutes. After all, it was not every day of their lives that they got to ravish a member of the ruling classes.

The remaining two women, like Corinna herself, were made of stronger fibre, for both Dorothea and Agana remained alert to what was happening all about them and stood proud and straight, trying to hide their natural apprehension behind an outward display of bravado.

Good, Fulgrim thought. It would make what was to come all the more enjoyable. He entertained the thought of setting up a temporary gallows and repeating the trick of using Corinna as hostage and then having Dorothea crawl around the tables offering her mouth to each of these brutes in turn. The problem with that, he knew, was that the men were getting more drunk by the minute and an accident could all too easily occur with the golden one.

Despite his performance earlier, which had clearly convinced Dorothea, Fulgrim had no wish to waste such succulence by seeing it swinging at the end of a rope with its neck snapped. No, Dorothea would service them in many ways, but they would have to take their chances with her teeth. Fulgrim chuckled to himself and refilled his glass from the heavy carafe before him.

Taking a sip, he looked around and spied one of the young pageboys standing to attention against the wall. Fulgrim clicked his fingers and the youth instantly sprang forward.

'Were you one of the lads who brought Agana's little perch for me?' Fulgrim asked. For a second or so the page looked blank, but then realisation dawned and he nodded dutifully. 'Good,' Fulgrim said and belched. 'Now, go find some of your friends and bring it down here for me,' he continued, wiping his mouth with the back of his hand. 'I think it will get tonight's entertainment off to a fine start.'

As the youth scurried off to carry out his orders, Fulgrim regarded the four women again. His brow furrowed and his eyes narrowed as he considered the choices. Benita was a waste of time. Yes, she would thrash about atop the devilish mechanism, but she would scarcely know what was happening to her and it would show. Corinna was the hottest of the four, for certain. Fulgrim smiled.

The girl was incredible, he knew. Something had happened inside her head in the same way that something had snapped inside Benita's, but where Benita was just a compliant puppet, her mind shattered by her sufferings, Corinna had become quite the opposite. Fair enough, Fulgrim thought, she despised herself and him, among others no doubt, for what they had done to her, but there was no escaping the truth. The wench was on a hair trigger and almost anything now was enough to send her into a frenzy of sexual abandon.

Which was why she would be wasted on that perch, he concluded. There was then the question of Dorothea herself, but then Dorothea had doubtless had more artificial phalluses inside her than most men had had hot dinners. She needed real man meat inside her for her to suffer further.

Which left Agana.

Yes, that was just too perfect, he thought. Agana mounted on her own pedestal, hoist by her own petard. The picture of that impressive body writhing atop her pole swam before his eyes and Fulgrim liked what he saw. He stared at Agana, who still remained stiffly rigid in her bonds. He would soon change that, without a doubt. He tipped up his glass, drained it and looked around for a page to bring a fresh carafe.

Kallik Ensa rose unsteadily from his seat and swayed towards the door of the hall, cursing under his breath. It was not just the drink, he told himself, for he had been suffering from a mild ague these past few days and it seemed to have affected his bladder more than anything else. Not only that, but it burned every time he relieved himself. He cursed again, but consoled himself with the thought that he'd have no trouble pissing down the throat of one of those haughty bitches when his turn came.

The passageway beyond the hall was gloomy, the only illumination coming from single candles set in brackets at intervals of every ten feet or so, and several of those seemed to have been blown out by the draughts. Still, they had been here some days now and Kallik was beginning to know his way around.

He turned left, heading for the small door that led out to

the kitchen garden, grimacing as the pressure began to build to a painful level, and broke into a trot. He passed through the kitchen itself, ignoring the old cook woman and ran out into the fresh air. To his right stood a clump of bushes, their shadows creating a dark patch in the moonlight. He headed straight for them, his hands fumbling at the front of his breeches.

As the hot stream gushed forth and the stinging pain seared through him, Kallik gasped and blinked back the tears.

'By the gods!' he hissed, and those were the last words he ever spoke, as the razor sharp blade severed his windpipe and his blood spurted forth to join the pool he had already made on the hard baked earth.

Fulgrim could not believe how weary he felt, for he had slept in that morning and his day had not been a particularly arduous one. He yawned and stretched and tried to remember how much he had drunk. It had not been that much, especially by his standards. Perhaps, he concluded, it was just a reaction to all the tensions and activities of this past week.

He yawned again and blinked, watching as the two guards unchained Agana from her post and dragged her towards her waiting mount. Yes, this would be worth watching, he thought, and was suddenly wide awake again.

Pester the page regarded Moxie with an unblinking stare.

'Why should I risk a sword through my gut?' he demanded sulkily. 'What's that woman ever done for me, save have my balls removed before I ever knew what it was to be a real man?'

Moxie sighed. 'If you had known the outside world the

way I have,' she said sternly, 'then you'd realise that you've had an easy life here, balls or no balls. And whatever you think of the mistress, these men are devils. I hear they will be staying some time yet, and don't think they won't tire of the maids and those wretched women down in the hall. I've already heard some of them talking and it would appear that certain of their number prefer delicate male flesh to female. You'll dance on the end of a shaft or two before this adventure is finished,' she threatened.

Pester went even paler than his usual wan colour. 'You're trying to frighten me!' he accused Moxie.

Moxie shrugged. 'I shouldn't have to,' she said. 'If you aren't frightened already, then your brain's addled. I'm scared half to death and then some. Listen,' she added, patting the small bulge at the front of his tight hose. 'I know you can still get it up, balls or no. Do this for me and I'll make it worth your while later. You're one of the very few among us who's ever shot a bow before.'

'You'll make it worth my while?' Pester said. 'In what way?'

Moxie grinned. 'In lots of ways,' she promised, and turned away before Pester could see how her smile quickly disintegrated into a look of sheer distaste. He may have been scarcely a man anymore, she thought, but he was still a man, after all.

Savatch crawled forward between the pews in the minstrel gallery, his chest and stomach pressed close to the timber floor, until he finally reached the balustrade along its front. Peering between the pierced carvings of the screen, he looked down and surveyed the scene in the hall below.

As he had suspected, the proceedings were already becoming quite rowdy and several of the guards were more interested in arguing drunkenly among themselves than in watching the scene that was unfolding in the centre of the tabled area.

Two of the men had just finished lifting the mighty Agana onto a strange pedestal contraption, impaling her on the long shaft which jutted up from the narrow bar which now supported her weight. As they secured her ankles in the metal straps at either side of the main post, Fulgrim stepped forward and clapped his hands for some semblance of order.

As the noise descended to a low buzz of mutterings, Savatch listened, fascinated, as the nobleman explained the purpose of the curious apparatus. Savatch barely stopped himself from whistling in appreciation, for it truly was a cunning device. And the fact that it was Agana's own invention made it even more poignant.

Oh yes, Savatch thought, this Fulgrim is a true artist in his chosen field and that's beyond all argument. He continued to watch, fascinated, as Fulgrim depressed the lever that activated the mechanism. Agana, groaning through her bitted mouth, started to twitch and spasm almost immediately. Savatch grinned and had to force his mind back to the business at hand.

Alanna wiped the blade of her knife in the grass, slipped it back into its sheath and bent to drag the man's body deeper into the bushes, where it would join the neat row she had already assembled, six in total now. She looked up at the position of the moon and stars, calculating the time.

There was perhaps an hour to go before the earliest moment they had agreed would be practical for their assault. Time to double her tally, in all probability, but she knew she would have to exercise some restraint. Too many killed out here might arouse suspicion inside and ruin the element of surprise which would be their main ally.

Settling back into the shadows, Alanna smiled to herself. Whatever the time, six more would be her maximum and then she would go and find Jekka and make sure she had dealt with all the sentries satisfactorily. Knowing Jekka as she did, Alanna doubted there would be any problems.

Savatch peered upwards and out into the gloomy recesses of the vaulted ceiling. The nearest of the five main crossbeams was perhaps twenty feet away and he calculated it was almost directly above where Fulgrim sat. Almost, but not quite, for a straight drop from it would bring a man down about five feet behind the nobleman's seat, which, for Savatch's purpose was just about perfect.

His eyes travelled around the side walls, picking out the narrow ledge that ran around at the same height as the beams. It was wide enough for a man to ease his way along whilst standing upright with his back pressed against the wall, but not sufficiently wide to crawl along. Never mind, for with most of the hall lighting provided by candles just above head height and even the three suspended candelabra hanging well below the three centremost beams, the roof area was in deep shadow and it would be almost impossible for anyone looking up to make anything out.

Slithering along to his left and dragging the coiled line with him, Savatch began the last stages of his preparations. Soon it would be time to go down and round up Moxie and her band of less than enthusiastic volunteers. He peered down again and counted the number of empty seats around the tables. Alanna, it seemed, was working to her usual high standard of efficiency.

Using one of the crossbows from the armoury, which was heavier, but had a better range than her own weapon, which had been designed for different purposes, Jekka picked off the second tower sentry with little difficulty, for he made a perfect target, framed against the moon. He toppled over the low rampart and fell without a sound, the light wind carrying the noise of any impact with the ground away on its wings.

Jekka reckoned up the tally on her fingers. The two in the towers, the one up in the servants quarters, the one at the main door and the one patrolling the lower corridors. Five in all. She wondered if there might be any more, though she doubted it. With so much on offer in the hall, the duty guard would be kept to a minimum and five seemed the right sort of number.

She slung the heavy bow over her shoulder effortlessly and turned back towards the house. Time to find Alanna and see how she had fared. Jekka was willing to wager that the tall blonde had notched up a few more than she herself so far, but then she had the easier targets, when all was said and done.

They were using Benita as a prelude to the main event, Corinna knew, and she also knew that herself and Dorothea *were* that main event. Sorrowfully, Corinna watched as Benita crawled along the line of eagerly waiting guards, dutifully accepting their members into her mouth in turn and licking and sucking until they were fully erect, but being urged onto the next shaft before she could bring the first to a climax. Meanwhile, Agana continued to writhe and moan on her fiendish pedestal, now at last almost as far beyond caring as the pitiful one on her knees.

Fulgrim strolled over, glass in hand, and stood alongside

Corinna. He gestured towards the grovelling Benita.

'In many ways,' he drawled, 'it is a great shame Willum could not be here this evening. Such a sight would have gladdened his heart. Of course, the woman's mind is gone now, but he would have enjoyed the spectacle, nonetheless. Are you ready for your duties, my little golden whore?' he laughed.

'Count these blackguards, little golden princess. Every one will spurt into that sweet mouth of yours ere this night is done, and every one of them will have that conniving, murderous bitch Dorothea, front or back, it's all the same to me.' He laughed and took a generous mouthful of wine.

'And I dare say it'll be all the same to them, including Dorothea, eventually.'

Corinna closed her eyes, but she could not block out the sight from her mind. She felt like weeping, but she was determined not to give Fulgrim that victory. Grimly, she ground her teeth into the cruel bit and tried to think of Savatch.

This time, however, her fertile imagination seemed as though it was finally going to let her down.

Savatch held out his arms and Alanna came to him. They embraced and kissed, though it was not a passionate exchange, being more in the manner of two comrades exchanging a greeting. Or a farewell.

'The time is nearly come,' Savatch murmured.

Alanna bobbed her blonde mane. 'Yes, the time is nearly come,' she agreed. 'We have done all we can, and now we must take them head on.'

'You and Jekka have done well,' Savatch whispered. 'They number barely five and twenty now, and the fools are too drunk to realise that there numbers are so thinned.'

'They have plenty else to distract them,' Alanna said, 'but I am surprised at Fulgrim.'

'Don't be,' Savatch said. 'Your potion has doubtless helped dull his senses as it has the others, but his wits are concentrated below his stomach now. He has eyes only for Corinna. I have been watching him. He is not really even concerned with Dorothea.'

'Do I detect a note of jealousy?' Alanna asked and then gave a small, low laugh. 'Don't worry, my ignoble, savage Savatch, I know the signs. You fell in love with the wench the moment you set eyes on her, and then set about using your own spurious talents to deprave her to your touch.' She drew back from him, but she was still smiling. 'You and I, my devious, villainous lover, have been comrades and bed companions for some few years now, yet both knew it was a thing of convenience. Oh shush, speak not, for I will have my say. Yes, you do love me, as I love you too, but it is a companionable love, rather than a belly fire beast.

'And the golden princess has you by your belly and no mistake. I could tell that from the moment it was time to hand her over to Fulgrim. Your face was in your boots when we left them.'

'What use is it, however I might feel?' Savatch said bitterly. 'If we succeed, I cannot but send her back to her family, whatever my heart might say.'

"Tis true,' Alanna said, 'but then the fates have a strange way with us.' She kissed him lightly again. 'Now shake out of this mood, for we have work ahead of us and, win or lose, 'twill be a good fight.'

Corinna eyed the whalebone switch in Fulgrim's hands and could not suppress a shudder. He leered at her when he saw her reaction.

'This ain't for your hide, sweet one, not this night,' he said. His words were slightly slurred now, but he stood steadily enough. He jerked his head to where two of the guards were strapping Dorothea to a hastily erected whipping frame, spread-eagling her cruelly and allowing their rough hands to wander over her helpless flesh at will.

'No, my precious golden one,' Fulgrim continued, 'this is for her, the bitch who prefers other bitches. By the time I am done she will scream out for me to let her take a whole regiment of hairy brute men, and the other one will be there to witness her capitulation.'

He waved the switch to indicate Agana. The mechanism inside her had been stilled now, but her body still twitched uncontrollably. The pedestal had been turned so that the two women, Agana and Dorothea, faced each other, with but a few feet separating them. Fulgrim was taking great delight in explaining his stategy to Corinna, who could only stare at him in dumb horror.

'I shall reactivate the mechanism in due course,' he said. 'I want Dorothea to see her minion's final surrender at the moment of her own.' He reached out and stroked Corinna's distended breasts. 'And then it will be your turn, pretty one,' he said. 'You who have abandoned your innocence as easily as a snake sheds its old skin – you will go out there and prove to yourself that you are now nothing more than what I have made you.'

Corinna closed her eyes again and shook her head, the bells at her ears mocking her. Fulgrim was worse even than Willum, she knew now, for Willum's madness had come about through jealousy and mistrust, whereas this beast was corrupt to the core and there were, she now knew, no depths to which he was not capable of descending.

Savatch finished knotting the line about the heavy beam, laying full length to work and keeping as small a silhouette as possible. It was not easy with the heavy bow slung over his back, and he had even considered leaving it behind and relying on his short sword, but the chance to get off one shot before he abseiled down the rope was too tempting, for every man dropped in the first moments of confusion was one less to worry about later.

He peered across at the minstrel's gallery and at the shadowy figures who were moving down to the balustrade. Moxie had rounded up fourteen more volunteers, but they were a motley crew. Most of them had handled a crossbow before, for the majority of children learned to hunt rabbit or wild pig from an early age, but the crossbows from the armoury were a far different proposition to the light weapons they had used previously. None of the maids – and there were seven of them, plus Moxie – could reload for themselves, for all the bows had to be re-cocked by hand.

In any case, Savatch reasoned, had there been any with the more modern winching handle, they would have been too slow to have been of much practical use. He had come up with a partial solution, by distributing the three spare weapons among the girls, ready cocked and needing just a bolt slotted home, but he was still not that confident of their abilities to hit a target and had warned against aiming anywhere near the four prisoners below.

There were three exceptions to his doubts. Moxie herself claimed she could hit a rabbit at fifty paces, which was pretty good shooting, and two of the pages, Pester and Dollis, claimed similar skills. Alanna and Jekka each now carried two bows, but there were still nearly thirty men in the hall. Their one big chance was that none of them seemed to be armed with anything larger than a short sword like Savatch's own.

A lot still hung upon that first volley, though. Savatch peered down towards the door through which the two Yslanders would attack, their appearance being the signal for everyone else to act. He saw one more guard stumble unsteadily towards it and grinned in the gloom.

One more down, though this one would not even reach the bushes outside before he died.

Fulgrim's switch rose and fell at steady intervals and Dorothea, now un-bitted, whimpered as the vicious whalebone stung her soft flesh. Her back, buttocks and thighs were already criss-crossed with angry lines. Yet still she refused to submit to her torturer's demands, despite the fact that she had previously been violated several times.

Now Fulgrim decided to add another refinement to his act. He signalled for Corinna to be brought over to him and made her kneel, whilst he took up a position between Dorothea and the still moaning Agana. He removed his breeches, unclipped Corinna's bit and tossed it aside.

'Time to use your pretty mouth, golden one,' he sneered. 'Otherwise these bitches get some of this!' He slashed left and right, each stroke catching one of the helpless women across her breasts and drawing a cacophony of howls from them. Corinna blanched.

'No my lord!' she shrieked. 'I will do it!' She leaned forward and took his flaccid organ in her hands, stroking and coaxing it and licking the tip. Immediately it started to rise and she quickly drew it into her mouth. Dorothea wailed piteously.

'Don't do it!' she howled through her pain. Fulgrim grinned with a mixture of triumph and ecstasy. The sight of the flaxen haired Corinna kneeling humbly before him, her mouth full of his meat, was a greater torture for Dorothea, it seemed, than the kiss of the whalebone. Which was just as he had suspected it might be.

'Get to it, princess!' he roared, tapping Corinna's back above the golden corset with the tip of the switch. It was not a hard blow, but the touch against her already tender flesh made her jump and her teeth nipped him slightly. It was all the excuse Fulgrim needed, even though he realised it had been unintentionally done. He lashed out again at Dorothea and Agana, setting off another chorus of agonised screaming.

Corinna closed her eyes and redoubled her efforts, desperate to save the two women further suffering as far as she was able. She heard the hiss, louder than ever this time and flinched, expecting to feel the deadly crop biting into her, but no blow fell. Instead, she heard several shrieks and screams that came from no female throat. She opened her eyes and the sight she saw made her forget all about Fulgrim.

All about her men staggered and fell, clutching at the shafts of arrows that had miraculously appeared in chests, shoulders, stomach's and throats. She threw herself backwards, not caring whether Fulgrim turned his whip on her again, but Fulgrim had other priorities. As the guard nearest to him made to rush forward, a small bolt pierced his skull precisely between his eyes. For a brief second those eyes registered a look of disbelief, and then they went completely blank and he fell forward without a sound.

Fulgrim jumped back in alarm and dropped into a crouch, grabbing at his discarded breeches and belt, hands fumbling in the folds of the cloth in an attempt to draw his short sword from its scabbard. However, before he could manage to disentangle the weapon, a dark figure seemed to drop from the heavens, landing squarely behind him. A powerful hand reached down, seizing the panicked noble by the hair and hauling him to his feet, whilst the other hand swept round, pressing a wickedly sharp looking blade against his throat.

For a few seconds Corinna thought she must have reverted to her trance dreams, but this was no fancied imagining. The screams of the dying men were real enough. Fulgrim, standing naked from the waist, his horn rapidly shrinking, was real enough. The blade was real enough and so was the figure holding it.

'You!' she gasped.

Savatch grinned. 'In person,' he said and wrenched Fulgrim's head further back. 'Tell your men to drop their weapons!' he shouted, but Fulgrim's order was almost superfluous. Seeing their master in such imminent danger of death, those that were left on their feet were already throwing down swords and raising their hands above their heads. Only Akol refused to surrender.

Raising his sword high, he lunged towards Savatch with a defiant scream, which died in a froth of blood as Jekka's final bolt flew straight into his open mouth. He staggered, grabbed at the bolt with his free hand and still tried to advance, even though he must have known he was doomed.

Savatch half turned, dragging Fulgrim to form a protective barrier, but it was not needed. There was one final, dreadful hiss, and another bolt pierced Akol's skull just behind his ear. His eyes rolled up and he fell back as though poleaxed.

High in the minstrel's gallery, Moxie let the heavy bow drop from her numbed hands and turned slowly away, a small smile on her lips, but there were tears in both eyes and she stumbled as she picked her way through the pews.

Chapter Twenty-Five

'I do not know how to thank you, Master Savatch,' Dorothea whispered weakly. She was laying on her bed now, propped up by the softest cushions the maids had been able to find. Alanna had found and administered pain killing draughts to all four victims, but they could only do so much and Fulgrim's switch had inflicted some severe wounds.

'I came to rescue the Lady Corinna, no one else,' Savatch said blandly. 'You and your woman brought this upon yourselves – she did not. Had I known what evil was planned for her, I should never have let myself be involved in this business and I should have done all within my power to prevent your scheme succeeding.'

Dorothea raised a limp hand. 'I swear to you, Master Savatch,' she croaked, 'that I knew nothing of what was to happen. Like yourself, I saw her only as a means to an end. You may question my loyalties, but I did not feel I owed loyalty to a branch of my family which usurped power from my grandfather so many years ago.

'Had not that blackguard of a great uncle not corrupted the court, I should now be Lady Protector of Illeum, and that title is still rightfully mine.'

'And would have come to you again with Vorsan help, no doubt?' Savatch said. 'Well, I know little of such things and care even less, but I will make sure that the lady is returned to her husband and father safely.'

'And what of myself and Fulgrim?'

Savatch shook his head. 'Why should I care about that?' he asked. 'I shall leave it to Corinna to decide if she tells of your part in all this. I cannot say what her decision will be. Fulgrim, meantime, is now chained and locked safely in your dungeons. I am no judge, nor am I executioner, but I assumed I could leave your Mistress Agana to take care of him. Fulgrim had not yet given her the dubious benefit of his full, foul talents. She will recover quickly and, when she does, I should not like to trade places with that devil below.' He turned and began walking to the door, but half way there he stopped and turned again.

'It may be that the thought of Fulgrim at Agana's mercy will persuade the Lady Corinna to remain silent about you, for he has treated her very badly and she may see the justice in this arrangement. If she gives me her confidence before we leave, I shall let you know.'

Savatch finally found Alanna in the stable, having searched the chateau for her fruitlessly for over an hour. His eye fell upon the saddlebags and upon the bridle she held in her hands. Behind her, in a spare stall, her horse shuffled its hooves impatiently.

'You are not yet going, surely?' Savatch asked. Alanna shrugged her shoulders.

'Why be so surprised?' she said lightly. 'My work here is done and Jekka and I will now be on our way, once she has finished exploring that armoury. I don't know what it is about that woman, but she has a deadly fascination for old weaponry.'

'Deadly is most certainly right,' Savatch said, 'but surely there is no need for such haste.' Alanna smiled, a rather pale smile, Savatch thought.

'There is nothing for me here, so I will be on my way,'

she said simply.

'But we shall still meet up as planned?'

The smile faded a little and her eyes looked mournful. 'Perhaps,' she said, 'but I shall understand if not.'

'Perhaps it is I who do not understand,' Savatch retorted, 'for you are surely talking in riddles that are beyond me.'

Alanna let out a sharp laugh. 'So like a man,' she sighed. She placed a hand upon his shoulders and fixed him with a steady stare. 'I've seen the way you look at her, my noble villain, and I also saw the way she looked at you.'

'But that is ridiculous!' Savatch retorted. 'She's a bloody princess, or as good as, and I was the man who kidnapped her, or are you forgetting?'

'No I am not, and neither, I think, is the Lady Corinna.' Alanna patted his cheek. 'It takes a woman to understand a woman,' she whispered, 'and love recognises no rank. And as for me, I understand both of you. I have always known that we two would not settle peacefully to our hearths together.

'What we had was good and still might be, but only for a while. Once the adventure is gone, so will everything else be. We would row and fight and spend days not speaking. Besides, I do not know if I want to share the rest of my life with a man. There is always Jekka to consider.'

Savatch studied Alanna's eyes and for the first time he thought he could see into her very soul. He leaned forward and kissed her on the forehead.

'You would let me go?'

Alanna suddenly laughed and the mood was broken. 'Let you go?' she echoed. 'Oh Savatch, I never had you, no more than you ever had me, for I know you and your ways and tastes only too well. Don't you think I know that every time you look at me you envision me hanging helpless and naked in your chains? Of course, that could never be.

'I know you would never harm me and that your whip would seek to induce emotions other than pain and fear, but it could still never be. I am a warrior princess. Oh yes, you never knew did you, for I never told you and you never asked. Of course in Yslandia our ranks and societies are different from here, but my mother is ranked as a queen, and this princess could never consent to being chained by a man.'

'Nor did that other,' Savatch replied. 'And I doubt she'll ever forget what I did to her, less likely forgive.'

Alanna's smile returned again. 'Is that what you think?' she challenged. 'Well, those eyes of hers were not cow-like for nothing, or I'm a blacksmith's bastard. Tell me now, did you use your whip on her?'

'Yes.'

'And to what ends?'

'To teach her a sharp lesson and make sure she stayed docile.'

'And nothing else?'

'Perhaps.'

'Did you seek to hurt her?'

'No, not to really hurt her.'

'Did you seek something else?'

'Perhaps.'

'And did you find it?'

'Again, perhaps.' Savatch's face began to betray his growing embarrassment.

'I think that you did,' Alanna said. 'And more to the point, so did she. As I said, no woman makes those eyes at a man she does not reckon herself in love with.'

'Nonsense. She was just frightened and relieved and maybe a little grateful.'

'Aye, but grateful for what?'

'I don't know what you mean,' Savatch protested.

Alanna shook her head and snorted. 'I know,' she said, 'but then you are a man.'

Agana, once again clad in her favourite black leather, regarded the spread-eagled figure before her. The lamplight reflected off the sweat that covered Fulgrim's naked body. Blood vessels stood out clearly on his newly shaven skull.

'Not so noble now, my lord,' Agana sneered. She began slowly to unlace the front of her breeches. Fulgrim's eyes were round and staring. As she eased the clinging fabric down her long legs, Agana smiled.

'Look well, Fulgrim,' she taunted him, 'for I want you good and hard for this. You will make a good page when I have finished with you, but I'll grant you what I grant them all, a good last fuck to empty their balls before I cut them off.'

She kicked the breeches away, picked up the razor-edged blade from the table and padded towards him. She touched his straining stomach lightly with the tip of the knife, pricking the skin and drawing a single bead of blood, and then held the knife up to his face.

'Don't worry,' she hissed. 'I'll tie the wounds off well when I'm done, my lord pageboy, for I don't want you to die. At least not for a long time yet!' With her free hand, she began to massage his limp shaft and, for the first time in his life, Lord Fulgrim of Jerod, High Adviser to the Vorsan federation, failed to respond to a woman's touch.

Corinna stood in Dorothea's private sitting room, a silk sheet wrapped about her body. She had removed the tinkling earrings and the tight bands from about her breasts, but the rings and the navel jewel still remained in place, for she could see no way of removing them without tools. She turned to receive Savatch.

He studied her features closely and nodded. She was a remarkable girl, he thought, for many women, having suffered as she had, would be taken to their beds for weeks afterwards. To his surprise, she smiled at the sight of him.

'Come in, Master Savatch,' she invited and pointed to the bottle of wine on the table. 'Will you take a drink with me?' For the first time in his life, Savatch found himself tongue-tied in the presence of a female. Corinna's smile widened. 'Come, sir,' she said, 'have you no words for me, my daring knight errant?'

'I am no knight, lady, and well we both know it,' Savatch replied. 'All I have done this night is to attempt to put right a grievous wrong that I did you. I do not ask for your thanks, nor for your forgiveness, merely that you understand I did not know to what fate I was delivering you.'

'I believe you,' Corinna said. 'Now, take a drink and sit, for your legs must be weary after your adventures.'

Savatch hesitated, but turned and picked up the bottle. he looked around, but could see no glasses. Seeing his indecision, Corinna stepped forward, extended one hand from beneath her makeshift robe and took it from him, lifting it to his lips.

'Drink, my lord,' she said softly. 'And no, it is not poisoned. Here, I shall show you.' She put the bottle to her own lips and swallowed a healthy draught, coughing slightly and spilling some down her chin. She passed the wine back and wiped her mouth prettily with a corner of the sheet.

'You see?' she said, as Savatch followed her example. 'The Lady Dorothea keeps a fine cellar and even those ruffians were not able to exhaust it. Now, sit and explain what is to happen, for I am still a prisoner, am I not?'

Savatch shook his head. 'Not a prisoner, lady, no. I will escort you back to safety, or at least to the gates of your city, for my life would be worth nothing were I to set foot inside again.'

'Perhaps,' Corinna said, 'but not so for the man who rescued the daughter of the Lord Protector, I think.'

Savatch laughed and placed the bottle back on the table. 'But that man also happens to be the man who abducted her in the first place,' he pointed out, 'or had you forgotten?'

Now it was Corinna's turn to laugh.

'No sir, I had certainly not forgotten, but I bear you no malice for what you did. As you say, you believed it to be a political affair and your motivation was money. In that you are no different from most other men, but I doubt most other men would have returned as you did, once they knew they had made such a terrible misjudgement.'

'Are you saying you would not betray my true part in this to your father?'

'I am,' Corinna said, her eyes serious now, 'for what gain would there be in it. You have righted your wrong and I am now safe. Illeum is freed from the extortion that would surely have soon followed and my husband will welcome me back into his bed with open arms – always assuming he can be persuaded to empty his hands of food, that is,' she added with a sudden, wicked grin.

'Of course, I shall undoubtedly need a period of convalescence, following my ordeal. I shall need to get away from the city to somewhere more conducive to a peaceful recovery. I thought Willum's palace would be ideal. I can arrange for nurses to attend Benita there, but I'm afraid her recovery – full recovery, at least – may be in some doubt, for the poor woman's mind is gone, I am sure.

'However, I can at least do my best for her. But there will have to be changes made at my new palace, for I do not know which of Willum's guards can still be trusted. I would need a new commander, a personal chamberlain, perhaps.' She stared at Savatch, straight faced. His features creased into a grin of disbelief.

'You're offering me the job?' he gasped. 'Ha! Now I have heard it all, my lady.'

'You find the proposition so amusing? Or is it that you have so much gold from this latest escapade that you do not need an income any more?'

'Well, there is that,' Savatch admitted, 'but that's not it.' he perched on the arm of the heavy settle and placed his hands on his knees. 'It's just that I'm the sort of man who has never had a home as such. I travel, I fight, I eat, I womanise.'

'And you doubtless belch and fart,' Corinna added with a wicked laugh. 'Yes, I know what sort of man you are, Master Savatch, or at least I know what sort of man you used to be. Somehow I think you have changed, much as I have changed these past few days. We have both had good cause.'

'Aye, that's the truth, certainly in your case,' Savatch agreed. 'But what you are proposing is ridiculous. It could never work, for I could not remain in the same place as you and not remember certain things and nor, I venture, could you.'

'You are assuming that there are not things I would like to remember,' Corinna replied, softly. Her other hand suddenly appeared from beneath the sheet and Savatch saw she was holding a small, multi-thonged whip. His eyes opened in surprise.

'Remember?' she said, her voice still soft.

'Where did you get that from?' Savatch demanded. 'I thought—'

'Oh, it's not yours,' Corinna replied, with a light laugh. 'It's Agana's I believe, but it is very similar to one I remember, is it not?'

'Remarkably so,' he admitted. 'But why do you offer it to me thus?'

By way of reply, Corinna shrugged and allowed the sheet to slide from her and form a rustling pool about her feet. Standing almost naked in her golden slave trappings, she tossed the whip to him and spread her arms wide.

'Not now, Master,' she whispered, 'for in truth my poor flesh is still far too tender, but look upon what you see and remember something else.'

'And what should I remember?'

Corinna's eyes twinkled mischievously. 'There are dungeons at my new palace, too,' she said. 'Master.'

Exciting titles available now from Chimera:

1-901388-20-4	The Instruction of Olivia	*Allen*
1-901388-05-0	Flame of Revenge	*Scott*
1-901388-10-7	The Switch	*Keir*
1-901388-15-8	Captivation	*Fisher*
1-901388-00-X	Sweet Punishment	*Jameson*
1-901388-25-5	Afghan Bound	*Morgan*
1-901388-01-8	Olivia and the Dulcinites	*Allen*
1-901388-02-6	Belinda: Cruel Passage West	*Caine*
1-901388-04-2	Thunder's Slaves	*Leather*
1-901388-06-9	Schooling Sylvia	*Beaufort*
1-901388-07-7	Under Orders	*Asquith*
1-901388-03-4	Twilight in Berlin	*Deutsch*
1-901388-09-3	Net Asset	*Pope*
1-901388-08-5	Willow Slave	*Velvet*
1-901388-12-3	Sold into Service	*Tanner*
1-901388-13-1	All for Her Master	*O'Connor*
1-901388-14-X	Stranger in Venice	*Beaufort*

Coming soon from Chimera:

1-901388-17-4	Out of Control	*Miller (Aug '98)*
1-901388-18-2	Hall of Infamy	*Virosa (Sept '98)*
1-901388-23-9	Latin Submission	*Barton (Sept '98)*

All the above are/will be available at your local bookshop or newsagent, or by post or telephone from: B.B.C.S., P.O. Box 941, Hull, HU1 3VQ. (**24 hour Telephone Credit Card Line: 01482 224626**).

To order, send: Title, author, ISBN number and price for each book ordered, your full name and address, cheque or postal order payable to B.B.C.S. for the total amount, and allow the following for postage and packing:

UK and BFPO: £1.00 for the first book, and 50p for each additional book to a maximum of £3.50.

Overseas and Eire: £2.00 for the first book, £1.00 for the second and 50p for each additional book.

All titles £4.99 (US$7.95)